T0019569

"These mesmerizing stories of disconnection and detritus unfurl with the surreal illogic of dreams—it's as impossible to resist their pull as it is to understand, in retrospect, how circumstance succeeded circumstance to finally deliver the reader into a moment as indelible as it is unexpected. Janet Hong's translation glitters like a blade."
—Susan Choi, author of *Trust Exercise*

"*Flowers of Mold* shows Ha Seong-nan to be a master of the strange story. Here, things almost happen, and the weight of their almost happening hangs over the narrative like a threat. Or they do happen, and then characters go on almost like they haven't, much to the reader's dismay. Or a story builds up and then, where most authors would pursue things to the last fraying thread of their narrative, Ha elegantly severs the rest of the story and delicately ties it off. And as you read more of these stories, they begin to chime within one another, creating a sense of deja-vu. In any case, one is left feeling unsettled, as if something is not right with the world—or, rather (and this latter option becomes increasingly convincing), as if something is not right with *you*."
—Brian Evenson, author of *Song for the Unraveling of the World*

"Brilliantly crafted with precision and compassion, Ha Seong-nan's heartbreaking collection dives into the depths of human vulnerability, where hopes and dreams are created and lost, where ordinary life gains mythological status. A truly gifted writer."
—Nazanine Hozar, author of *Aria*

"Ha Seong-nan's stories are familiar, domestic, and utterly terrifying. Like the best of A. M. Homes, Samantha Schweblin, or Brian Evenson, her elegantly terse style lures you in and never fails to shock. She writes the kind of stories I admire most. Ones you carry around with you long after reading."
—Brian Wood, author of *Joytime Killbox*

"Wrapped up in fantasy or dreams, these men, women, and children are often confused over what is and isn't real, the reader seeing before they do how their anxious yearning will go unfulfilled."

—Laura Adamczyk, *The A.V. Club*

"Be forewarned: it might make you reconsider your interest in your neighbors, because it could lead to obsession and madness—or something odder and less reassuring than a tidy end, of which there are few in this wonderfully unsettling book of 10 masterful short stories."

—John Yau, *Hyperallergic*

"Joining a growing cohort of notable Korean imports, Ha's dazzling, vaguely intertwined collection of 10 stories is poised for Western acclaim."

—*Booklist*, starred review

"This impressive collection reveals Ha's close attention to the eccentricities of life, and is sure to earn her a legion of new admirers."

—*Publishers Weekly*, starred review

"If you're looking for a book that will make you gasp out loud, you've found it."

—*Kirkus Reviews*

"Ha's ability to find startling traits in seemingly unremarkable characters makes each story a small treasure."

—Cindy Pauldine, *Shelf Awareness*

"Her characters are trying their best to get by, and I found them deeply sympathetic, but they often face obstacles they just do not know how to confront. The stories are beautiful, inventive, gorgeously-written, and often heart-wrenching."

—Rebecca Hussey, *Book Riot*

"Like *The Vegetarian*—another surreal and haunting text by a Korean woman—*Flowers of Mold* unsettles and unnerves, effortlessly. . . .

Flowers of Mold offers readers an alternative perspective on city life, relationships, and ambition; and while it may be dark and unrelenting, it is also hauntingly lyrical."

—Rachel Cordasco, *World Literature Today*

"As horror and art continue to steal and mix with each other, I'm sure we'll find more—on both sides of the aisle—that continue to push the envelope. *Flowers of Mold* pushes that envelope with its impressive style and stifling isolation, creating something that's as strange as it is incisive."

—Carson Winter, *Signal Horizon*

"In these stories, readers will find tales of alienation and unruly behavior that will likely jar them as much as any narrative of sinister creatures and haunted spaces."

—Tobias Carroll, Words Without Borders

"These aren't bedtime stories. Indeed, reading them before bed might not be a good idea at all."

—Peter Gordon, *Asian Review of Books*

"Here is, undoubtedly, one of the best translated short story collections of 2019."

—Will Harris, *Books and Bao*

"I'm raving about this book. . . . It is brilliant, modern, and surprising."

—Charles Montgomery

"In Ha Seong-nan's gripping and courageous *Flowers of Mold*, the author triple-underlines those distasteful aspects of our lives that we'd rather ignore: the putridity of leaky trash; the greasy, lingering smell of fried chicken; children's crackers crushed underfoot; the solid clunk of an alarm clock to the jaw. . . . Ha is a master of the short story and hooks the reader without revealing or resolving too much too cleanly."

—Samantha Kirby, *Arkansas International*

BLUEBEARD'S FIRST WIFE

HA SEONG-NAN

TRANSLATED FROM THE KOREAN BY JANET HONG

OPEN LETTER
LITERARY TRANSLATIONS FROM THE UNIVERSITY OF ROCHESTER

Copyright © 2002 Ha Seong-nan
Originally published in Korea by Changbi Publishers, Inc.
All rights reserved
English translation copyright © 2020 by Janet Hong
English edition is published by arrangement with Changi Publishers, Inc.

First edition, 2020
All rights reserved

Library of Congress Cataloging-in-Publication Data: Available.
ISBN-13: 978-1-948830-17-1 / ISBN-10: 1-948830-17-5

The translation was undertaken with the support of the Daesan Foundation.

*This project is supported in part by an award from the National Endowment for the Arts
and the New York State Council on the Arts with the support of Governor
Andrew M. Cuomo and the New York State Legislature.*

Printed on acid-free paper in the United States of America.

Text set in Caslon, a family of serif typefaces based on the designs
of William Caslon (1692–1766).

Design: Anthony Blake
Cover image: Anthony Totah © 123RF.com

Open Letter is the University of Rochester's nonprofit, literary translation press:
Dewey Hall 1-219, Box 278968, Rochester, NY 14627

www.openletterbooks.org

Contents

BLUEBEARD'S FIRST WIFE

The Star-Shaped Stain

It must have been tough for the photographer to squeeze over sixty children into one picture. Not only that, but he'd also needed to include the sign above their heads that said Myeongjeong Hall. He managed to fit everyone in, but the children's faces came out so small they were difficult to make out. The woman had trouble picking out her own child among the tiny faces. To make matters worse, they were dressed in the same yellow uniform, marked with the name of the kindergarten. She moved the tip of her finger over each face until she came to a girl standing at the end of the last row. Only her eyes and nose were showing, the bottom half of her face hidden by the children in front.

With photos spread out over the living room floor where she sat, the woman was in the middle of choosing the clearest one of her daughter. They were all taken at the kindergarten and sent home for parents to buy. It took studying a few photos intently before she could spot her child at once. The girl was always off to the side with her face cut off, or in the last row, the top half of her face barely showing above the shoulders of the children in front, like a sun peeking over the horizon. In all of them, it seemed everyone had been gathered for a picture and the stragglers, their absence noted only then, had been dragged over and placed anywhere.

The woman had already examined dozens of photos, but there wasn't a single one properly focused on her child. Even in the pictures where the children were eating lunch with their mouths full of kimbap, or proudly holding sweet potatoes and radishes they'd just pulled out from the red soil, her daughter was caught in mid-motion as she turned toward the camera, or her face wasn't raised at all and her forehead and the part in her hair were the only things captured. Once her husband had complained, as he looked through the pictures their daughter had brought home.

Go and meet her teacher for once. Don't act like there isn't anything you can do.

She knew instantly what he meant. *Do you even understand how things work these days? Teachers aren't allowed to accept gifts, even soft drinks.*

Her husband tossed the pictures on the floor near her feet. They scattered around her. *It's not me who doesn't understand. It's you.*

If she had listened to him and met with the kindergarten teacher then, would they have gotten at least one good picture of their daughter?

Their daughter was much too ordinary. There wasn't a single special thing about her looks, personality, or even her eating habits. If she had gone on to elementary school, that ordinariness could have worked to her advantage. After all, the woman had seen many cases where teachers singled out children with unique personalities; attention sometimes invited trouble.

There was a friend she'd been meeting for the past ten years. Once every two years, sometimes even twice a week, they would meet for lunch or dinner, ask after one another, and joke and laugh together. But once she said goodbye and returned home, she wouldn't be able to visualize the friend's face. It was the same with her daughter. Now a year later, it was difficult for her to recall the child's face. Sure, she could pick her out among the many faces in group pictures, but the moment she shut the album, all that remained in her mind would be her daughter's round face and the hazy outline of her features.

She looked all morning, but couldn't find one decent picture. In the end, she pulled out the same photo she'd used the previous year. It was of her daughter in profile, cropped and blown up from a group photo, taken when the class had gone on a field trip to the historic Seodaemun Prison. Her daughter's face—already hazy to begin with—became even fuzzier when enlarged to portrait size.

•

Three charter buses were parked in single file in front of the Deoksu Palace entrance. The narrow sidewalk swarmed with people heading to work or out of town on vacation. Those passing by accidentally kicked coolers, crates of beer bottles, and plastic bags filled with fruit and beverages.

A driver smoked out on the road, in front of an idling bus with a paper sign in the window that said Morning Star Kindergarten. He watched the electronic news board on top of a building across the boulevard. Headlines from the morning papers raced across the display in large letters. Hun's mom who had notified her about the time and location hadn't arrived yet. The woman placed her bag on the ground and leaned against the stone wall of the palace. On the subway, the corner of the frame that held her daughter's picture had kept stabbing her in the thigh.

A large woman lurched up to the bus, checked the paper sign in the window, and wiped the sweat from her face. It was Hun's mother. She'd put on even more weight in the two months, and age spots had settled on her right cheek, like grains of sand. Hun's mother recognized her and clutched her hand. A sour tang escaped from the big plastic bag hanging on her shoulder. She laughed, blinking her thick eyelids.

"I couldn't find a place that does sweet-and-sour fried chicken this early," she said. "I had to go to ten different places. I finally found one where the owners live right next door, so I convinced her. I just had to get it. It was his favorite after all . . ."

Tears like discharge oozed along the corners of her eyes that were crusted with sleep.

One by one, familiar faces appeared. In the past year, they'd met many times in the parents' committee meetings. They nodded to each other and some men shook hands. The driver opened the luggage compartment on the side of the bus, but closed it shortly after. All they had were purses and shoulder bags.

The bus reeked of gasoline. She plugged her nose. The blue vinyl seat covers made her dizzy. Since it was the middle of summer, it was probably the bus company's peak season; there were still mop streaks on the floor, as if the bus had come straight after cleaning. The mesh pocket in front of her knees contained an empty beverage bottle that hadn't been collected. Miseon's father counted heads, moving from the back of the bus to the front, and stood next to the driver. As the chairman of the parents' committee, he looked after everything from renting the bus to other trivial matters.

Her husband emerged from the subway exit. He strode faster upon seeing the bus, his suit jacket in one hand and a bouquet of white chrysanthemums in the other. He held the bouquet up in the air out of people's way; the crowds seemed to be slowing him down.

Once, she'd walked past a flower shop with her daughter when the florist was standing outside, arranging the white chrysanthemums to be used for funerals. The florist discarded the leaves and stems, and poked the blossoms into a round floral foam. Petals and leaves drifted even to the middle of the road. *Look Mommy,* her daughter had said, pointing at the blossoms. *They look like steamed buns.* She could still hear the girl's voice in her head, but her face was blurry, just like in the class picture taken in front of Myeongjeong Hall.

Her husband rushed onto the bus, nodding at those sitting in front, and sank into the seat next to her. Her body tilted over to his side. He breathed heavily for a long time, as if he'd hurried to make it on time. His shirt was wrinkled and the collar, grimy. The flowers reeked. He was late, because he'd stopped to buy the flowers.

After passing the Singal Interchange, the bus pulled into the bus lane and sped up. The other lanes were clogged with cars from all the people going away on vacation. Every time the bus braked, her stomach turned. The smell of the sweet-and-sour chicken wafting from the back made things worse. Goose bumps rose on her arms from the air conditioning, but the bus trapped the smells inside.

Installed beside the driver's seat was a karaoke machine, along with a microphone. The driver, who'd probably been expecting a group of tourists, seemed to gauge the situation only after Miseon's father told him the destination. He'd turned off the radio after and been chewing gum ever since. Once in a while, buses packed with vacationers passed by. People danced ridiculously in the narrow aisle, moving only their upper bodies.

Around noon, the bus pulled off the expressway. Scenes of tranquil farms passed outside the window. Women in visors with towels wrapped around their heads pulled weeds in the paddy fields, crouch-ing, as if waiting in ambush. Under a bridge, children frolicked knee-deep in the stream.

Once the bus entered the first town, it was forced to slow down, because of the motorcycles and tractors that dashed out unexpected-ly. The rice mill, post office, clothing store, and fire station lined the street. They passed an empty school playground equipped with wall bars, a jungle gym, seesaw, and swing set, and then passed more fields and rice paddies. In the distance, houses stood in clusters. When they had passed several more towns that looked the same, the road narrowed and the paved road came to an end. It was just gravel after that. The bus rattled along the gravel road, sending her bouncing on the seat.

Both sides of the road were thick with pine trees. The shade they cast made the road appear wet. After traveling on the gravel for about twenty minutes, the view opened up and she could finally see the ocean. It was low tide; the water was out almost as far as the horizon.

It was past two o'clock in the afternoon when they finally arrived at their destination. They walked down the trail to the beach, since the bus couldn't go any farther than the parking lot. There was hardly a trail left, for it was overgrown with weeds that came up to her knees. They scratched her legs as she pushed her way through.

The wreckage had long been cleared away, and where the building once stood was now thick with weeds. The swimming pool had never been filled up. A dead pigeon floated in the fetid rainwater that had collected at the deep end.

As the tide went out, it left behind a small boat stuck in the middle of the mud flat. The day before their daughter had left for summer camp, the woman had cut off the mouth of a plastic bottle and punched holes in its side, then threaded a cord through them and tied the ends together. If everything had gone according to plan, the children would have taken their plastic bottles and gone digging in the silt for clams and crabs. With the bottle hanging from her neck, her daughter had hopped up and down in excitement, saying she was going to fill it with crabs.

It was not easy to find where Room 204 of Building B had been. Several parents moved from spot to spot, guessing and arguing over the correct location. A mat was rolled out on the ground and a simple memorial table was set up. They lined up the frames in a row. Favorite toys like stuffed dolls and toy cars were placed before the children's pictures.

Hun's mother placed the sweet-and-sour chicken, now cold from the air-conditioned bus, in front of her son's picture and sank to the ground. Before their daughter's blurry photo, the woman's husband placed a bouquet of white chrysanthemums—the ones that had reminded the girl of steamed buns—and glared up at the sun blazing above his head. The sky contained not even a speck of cloud. Tears left salt streaks on the woman's cheeks. Her cracked lips stung from the salt.

The fire started in Room 204 of Building B, the middle structure of three, and it swallowed up the entire place in seconds. Inside Room 204, children exhausted from the day's travel and activities lay fast asleep. Because the campsite was in a mountainous area, there were many mosquitoes. The teacher had left after lighting a mosquito-repellant coil in the middle of the room. Rumors spread. The room was locked from the outside to prevent the children from wandering out. The teachers had left the kids sleeping on their own and were drinking out on the beach.

By the time they smelled the smoke and came running, the fire had raged out of control. It was impossible for anyone to get near Room 204, located at the end of the hallway. Inside the room, twenty-two students from the Forsythia Class of Morning Star Kindergarten had been sleeping. The cause of the fire was the mosquito coil.

By the time the woman arrived at the scene, the fire was already put out. The building had collapsed in a heap of ashes and the walls had melted away, exposing the skeletal metal frames of the cargo containers. She stood in front of the black wreckage and howled her daughter's name until she fainted. Her child had been one of the twenty-two lost in the fire.

The woman gazed at the blurry photo of her smiling daughter. Her job had required an unusual amount of overtime. Whenever she had rushed to the kindergarten after work, she had found her daughter sleeping in a corner of the room and the rest of the children gone. As she urged the sleepy child home, she was so exhausted she felt as if her spine would snap. So when her daughter would lag behind to look at every little thing, she would smack her in the back with her purse. The girl would then sniffle quietly as she followed. Her daughter had wished that she worked at a bank instead. In her kindergarten class, there had been a classmate whose mother worked at a bank; she always got picked up early. Too busy catching up on sleep during the holidays and weekends, the woman never once took her daughter to an amusement park. When she'd wake around ten in the morning, her daughter would be sitting by her feet, eating a big bowl of cereal.

Once the parents were able to accept that their children were gone, they wanted to claim the bodies as quickly as possible. But it was nearly impossible to identify the bodies, which were burned beyond recognition. The six-year-olds had been wearing identical outfits, and they had been more or less the same height. At the news that they would not be able to see their children's bodies intact again, the mothers beat their chests and swooned.

The woman wasn't able to write down a single distinguishing trait about her child on the form that the police distributed. The girl didn't have a wart or even a birthmark on her fingers or toes. She didn't have any scars, either. Her hair had been kept short, since there was

never enough time to comb or style it in the morning; so of course
there would be no special accessories in her hair that would help tell
her apart from the other children. She never had cavities that would
have required her to get fillings, and she didn't have braces. There
wasn't a single clue the woman could think of that would distin-
guish her daughter from the rest of the children. The girl was truly
ordinary in every way. But this girl, who had never received much
attention, earned her greatest distinguishing trait that summer, when
she became one of the victims of the tragic fire that filled the front
page of the newspaper for days.

Hun's mother rolled about on the sand, clasping her son's picture
to her chest. Her face was crumpled with pain, but no tears came.
Saliva driveled from her parted lips, the way crabs foam at the mouth.
Her black pants became covered with sand. Several men tried to help
her up, but she swung her arms and legs so violently that she knocked
them down. The men didn't get up. They simply sat on the ground
and buried their faces between their knees or gazed out at the mud
flat with vacant eyes.

Two months after the fire, their daughter's remains were returned
to them, but the woman's husband would not allow her to see the
body. She tore at his chest, demanding to see their daughter one last
time. His shirt buttons flew off and a red scratch appeared on his
neck. A fistful of ashes was the last thing she saw of the girl.

The tide was coming in quickly. The parents who'd been sitting
along the beach got to their feet. They unpacked the food they'd
brought as an offering and scattered it along the sand. They then laid·
out the rest of the food, but no one really touched it. Hun's mother
stuck the box of cold chicken between her legs and stuffed a piece in
her mouth until her cheeks bulged out. Before she could even swallow, she crammed another piece in her mouth. She beat her chest as
if she couldn't get it down. Half-chewed chunks of chicken fell out
of her mouth and onto her shirt and pants. It was clear how she had

gained so much weight in just a few months. The woman's husband pitched the flower bouquet as far as he could into the water and lit a cigarette.

They gathered up the pictures and boarded the bus. The bus bounced along the gravel road. The woman kept glancing back. She could see the ocean spread out below as the bus climbed to the top of the cliff. The bouquet of chrysanthemums was rolling on the rising waves. The last time she looked back, the bundle had separated and the flowers were floating toward the deep.

Hun's mother sat next to her, sweat beginning to bead on her forehead. Her round face turned white and she hurriedly covered her mouth. Stringy fluid leaked out from between her fingers. Instantly, the pungent smell of the sweet-and-sour chicken hit the woman. The driver had to make a sudden stop. Hun's mother raced frantically toward the pine trees with her hand over her mouth. Hun's father hadn't come. The woman followed Hun's mother off the bus and pounded her back. Every time she heaved, vomit splattered between the weeds. Hun's mother looked up at her with watery, bloodshot eyes.

"It's sick, right? I know I shouldn't do this to myself, but if I don't eat, I keep thinking about what happened. I eat, then throw up, eat, then throw up. I don't know if it's because of all the weight, but my back and my knees hurt. And my husband, he doesn't even come home anymore. I don't blame him . . . I know I look hideous. I disgust myself."

When they came to the first town a bit later, the bus driver stopped in front of a small store. The woman's knees buckled as she stepped off the bus, but her husband reached out to steady her. The store had been converted from a traditional house. A middle-aged man woke up from the noise, sluggishly put on his slippers, and came out from the back room where he'd been sleeping.

Connected to the store was a courtyard with a water pump in the corner. While the men sat on benches, drinking cold drinks and beer, the women went to the pump and washed their faces and splashed water on their feet. The water was ice cold. The woman brought her mouth to the spout and drank greedily. Some water went up her nose and she choked and spluttered. Coughing, she remembered how she'd been the year before. When her daughter had died, she had wanted to die as well. But now, she felt guilty that she couldn't even tolerate the heat or thirst.

A thick layer of dust had collected on the snack bags, balloons, and a plastic toy bugle on the store shelves. The storeowner seemed to have thrown back a few drinks earlier. Every time he opened his mouth, the stench of alcohol assaulted the woman's nose.

"So, where you all coming from?" he said, accepting the change and putting it in the pocket of his coveralls. "Been a while since we've seen a tour bus round here."

He took in the dusty bus windows and the people sitting on the bench or standing around listlessly.

"Ah, I see you went down there. Business was good for about three years until the accident, but it's nothing but flies now."

When no one answered, he put his grimy fingers in his tangled nest of hair and scratched.

"It sure was a sight to see. Could see the flames from all the way up here." He licked his lips. "But you know, just before the fire, around eleven or so, a wee little thing in yellow passed by, crying all by itself."

"Did you say yellow?" cried several of the women in unison.

"That's right. The kid wasn't from around here, that's for sure. Stuck out like a sore thumb if you ask me, dressed all in yellow, top to bottom. Was headed for the new road right over there."

The people who had been standing around the store gathered around the owner. The students of Morning Star Kindergarten had also been wearing yellow. The fire had started around eleven o'clock that night and it sounded like one of the children had passed the store right before eleven. One woman moaned and sank to the ground.

"Do you remember what the child looked like?" asked a trembling voice.

"Not too sure. Couldn't really see 'cause of the dark. I think it was a girl . . . I called out to ask where she was headed, but she just kept walking, crying for her mama. Then shortly after, I saw the flames shoot up. I had no time to worry about her after that."

When he mentioned that it had been a girl, the women who'd lost their sons in the fire burst into tears and clung to those standing next to them. The mothers of girls pressed in around the owner and begged for every detail. The woman started to feel dizzy and leaned against the cooler. She saw her daughter crying out for her while walking toward the new road. The image then vanished, as quickly as it had come. If the storeowner was right, one of the twenty-two children could still be alive. If it really was a girl he saw, one out of thirteen girls could still be alive. Whose girl could it be?

"Well now, can't be too certain. It's a little foggy, but I think she had short hair—"

"That's her!" shouted several women to their husbands. "Our daughter had short hair!"

"But if the child had short hair, couldn't it easily have been a boy?" yelled Hun's mother, who had been sitting in front of the store.

At her words, the parents who had lost their sons grew excited.

"Well, I'm pretty certain it was a girl. Sure seemed like it, from the way she walked. And she wasn't wearing her shoes properly. She was just scuffing along."

"That's our girl!" another woman shouted. "She always wore her shoes that way!"

The women's eyes shone. Then an older woman pushed her way in through the crowd, slapping a towel against her dusty trousers. As soon as she saw the storeowner, she began to rail at him.

"You been drinking again, in the middle of the day? That's it, I've had it! What's the point of working myself to the bone when you go drink every penny away?"

The storeowner coughed and cleared his throat. But the people pressed him for more details. "Please! Do you remember anything else?"

"Well, I don't know. Only saw her for a second. And it was dark, too."

"Damn it, what kind of nonsense is this?" the older woman cried, raising her voice. "Now folks, don't pay any attention to this good-for-nothing. He lives with a bottle all year round. Says he even saw a ghost once—in broad daylight, too!"

"You think I was the only one who saw it?" he barked. "Mr. Choi from the electronic shop saw the ghost, too!" He turned to the mothers again. "Let's see, she was wearing a yellow T-shirt with yellow shorts, isn't that right?"

"That's right!" cried the women.

"So it's this nonsense again?" said the owner's wife. "Buses full of kindergarten students passed by all summer last year. Every day this store was packed with kids buying ice cream and drinks. You must be mixed up. You think it makes sense for a kindergartener to walk three kilometers from the camp at that hour? Alone and in the pitch black? So keep your mouth shut and leave these good people alone. They've already been through hell, so don't go turning their whole world upside down again."

There wasn't a single streetlamp on the gravel road leading to the campground. Occasional signs that announced the camp were all there was. If the child had passed by the store around eleven that night, she would have had to leave the campground at nine. There would have been no cars passing at that hour. It was a little farfetched to think that a six-year-old would walk so far in the dark by herself. Deflated by the older woman's words, people began to climb aboard the bus. The woman's husband pulled her along. The ground seemed to sink below her feet. The new road sparkled in the sun and disappeared into the mountain. She felt dizzy and put her hand on the dusty store window to steady herself.

"You think I was seeing things?" the storeowner grumbled. "I even saw the pin on her chest. I saw it with these two eyes. It was a pin in the shape of a star!"

"Idiot," his wife jeered. "Why don't you just go back inside and sleep?"

He returned to the back room, dragging along his slippers. The woman found her seat on the bus, but the dizziness didn't go away. A pin? Her daughter didn't own anything like that. If she'd been wearing a pin, it could have helped identify her after the fire. Even if a child had walked past the store at that hour, it couldn't have been her daughter.

When they arrived in front of Deoksu Palace past midnight, the area was completely deserted. But it was a different story across the boulevard, with its flashing neon signs. The bus sped away as soon as it had unloaded its passengers. The men shook hands. Because Jonghyeon and Mihyeon's families were planning to move out of the country soon after, the goodbyes took a long time. Under a different sky, they probably thought they could be free from the thoughts of their children. The parents' committee had refused to accept that a mosquito coil had started the fire. The parents had demanded that the government carry out a detailed enquiry into the true cause of the blaze. Couldn't an electrical short-circuit have started it, for example? But their request was never fulfilled. Jonghyeon's mother said she couldn't bear to live in this country any longer. She clasped the women's hands.

"I just can't shake off that man's words. We identified our son's body, so we gave up hope a long time ago, but that doesn't mean you should give up. Please, you need to find out who that child was."

As soon as they came home, the woman went straight to her daughter's room. Everything in the room—her pillow, blanket, clothes, notebooks, and sketchbooks—had been left exactly as they had been from a year ago. She took out a notebook and flipped through the pages. The edges of the pages were worn, as though they had been thumbed through countless times. She gazed at the writing that was full of spelling mistakes. She had always been too busy to sit with her daughter and fix her spelling or read her a story. The letters were large and uneven, going outside the lines.

Im 6 yeers old and I dont hav a yonger sister or broter I can play with. I dont have a older sister ether. Daddy is waching tv and mommy is on the computr. I hav to be qwite. So I just sit heer qwitly.

The woman buried her nose in the pillow and inhaled deeply. It still smelled faintly of her daughter. She stroked the spot that had turned yellow from her daughter's drool. Her husband was washing up; through the thin wall she could hear splashing.

Even though a year had passed, her eyes still opened every morning at six. She would rush to the kitchen without washing her face, rummage through the fridge, toast some bread, and fry up an egg. Just when she was about to call her daughter, she would realize she no longer had a child to wake up.

She stopped working after the accident, since she and her husband no longer had need of a second income. Instead of going to work, she began to roam the streets aimlessly. When she came to her senses, she often found herself standing in a dead-end alley in an unfamiliar neighborhood. She had a difficult time finding her way back home, since she had no memory of how she'd ended up there. Sometimes she headed to Morning Star Kindergarten, located three blocks from her house. It had since closed down. There was always a *For Lease* sign next to the stairs that led up to the school. The colorful animal stickers on the windows were peeling off. The windows were shut tight, even though it was the middle of summer. After stumbling home, she would munch on the hardened toast and greasy fried egg that awaited her on the table.

The woman found a strand of hair fluttering on the edge of the pillow. It was fine, short, and a little wavy—it was definitely her daughter's. Her husband, who had come out of the bathroom, seemed to be standing just outside the door. The knob turned a little, but then his footsteps moved away. Before long, she heard the door to the small room by the front door open and close. After the accident, she and her husband had started sleeping in separate rooms. She took the strand that quivered between her thumb and forefinger and carefully stuck it to a long piece of Scotch tape. Already stuck to the tape was a collection of her daughter's fingernail clippings and strands of hair that she'd found in the room.

.

It was Kyeonghui's mother who called to say they had finally managed to track down Miss Kim. Miss Kim had been the Forsythia Class homeroom teacher. The woman hurried to the meeting place Kyeonghui's mother had mentioned, a basement coffee shop about an hour away by bus. The mothers, who had already arrived, were sitting in a corner.

For the past month now, Miss Kim had been working as an assistant in the apartment manager's office across the street. Kyeonghui's mother had to call Miss Kim several times before she finally came. The teacher perched on the edge of the sofa and stared at a spot on the floor. One of the mothers erupted, unable to wait any longer.

"You remember everything that happened that night, don't you? Well, there's a man with a store a little ways from the camp, and he's saying a little girl in a yellow uniform passed by right before the fire started. He said she was crying."

Miss Kim didn't raise her face. If the woman's memory was correct, the teacher was now twenty-four. The fire would have certainly scarred her as well. Miss Kim's lower lip quivered.

"I don't understand—"

"What we're saying is, right before the fire started, a little girl apparently left the camp and was seen somewhere else."

Miss Kim sat up in shock. "That's impossible. I made sure they were all there before they went to bed. They were all there in the room . . ." She couldn't go on. Her shoulders shook with sobs.

One of the mothers moved closer. "You might be able to cry still, but we ran out of tears a long time ago."

"The campfire ended around ten o'clock. Then they all went inside to sleep. The kids were all there. Please believe me."

As they all knew, it would take a kindergarten child a little over two hours to walk the gravel road to the store, and about thirty minutes by bus. If she had passed the store around 11 P.M. she would have had to leave the campground by nine at the very latest. The campfire was still in full swing at that time. Amid the noise of fireworks and the children's excited hollering, a child could have easily slipped away without anyone noticing.

The woman's throat was parched. "Are you positive my daughter was there? Can you swear?"

Miss Kim gave a deep nod. "She was sleeping next to Jinhye. She said her hair pin was bothering her, so I took it off for her."

The girl that Miss Kim was remembering was not the woman's.

"That's not her, you're thinking of someone else. My daughter's never worn anything in her hair before. Her hair wasn't long enough."

Miss Kim had stopped crying and was now biting her lower lip. Kyeonghui's mother, who was sitting across from the teacher, raised her voice.

"It's obvious you're not sure of anything! You wouldn't have noticed even if ten kids went missing."

Cornered, Miss Kim turned white. She started to stammer. "They were all there, I swear. Listen, I know how you feel. This past year wasn't easy for me either. But they were all there that night. I wish what you're saying is true. I wish at least one of them were still alive."

The woman's daughter had been ordinary. She was barely noticed, just like in all the pictures. If someone like her had slipped away during the campfire, no one would have noticed. All of a sudden, Miss Kim slapped her knee, as if she'd remembered something important.

"We recorded the campfire that night! I have the video."

A bonfire was set up on the beach. The children's laughter rang out. Even the sound of the waves hitting the shore could be heard. Children in yellow stood around the fire, giggling, yawning, playing with the friend next to them, or gawking around them, waiting for the wood to be lit. When a burning stick of kindling was brought near and the wood caught fire, the children whooped and hopped up and down. Cheerful music soon blared, and they moved closer to the fire and started to dance, shaking their bottoms.

One by one, the camera panned over the children, who wore party hats and had their faces painted like Native American chiefs. The mothers wailed and burst into tears when the camera captured their children, but the woman's daughter was nowhere to be seen. This time, too, the camera had passed over her too quickly, or else she was standing out of frame.

When the campfire died down, the children's candlelight time began. Lit candles filled the dark screen. The children sang quietly, holding their candles with care so that they wouldn't go out. The scene stopped abruptly at that moment. The next scene showed the children shoving one another as they filed into the dormitory. At that instant, the woman saw her daughter. She saw her for only a split second, but it was definitely her. This time, again, the camera caught only the side of her face. But the woman was more used to seeing her daughter's profile anyway. Her daughter's eyes looked sleepy. Then she disappeared outside the frame, pushed by the child behind her. As she fell forward, the stain on the chest of her yellow uniform caught the woman's attention. There was no need to rewind the video; it was her child. It was only then that she remembered the stain. She had completely forgotten it over the past year.

·

The waves crashed and retreated below. It sounded like the tide was coming in. Her husband found the shortcut to the campground easily enough, since they had been to the site many times. The store where the owner had claimed to have seen a little girl in yellow was now closed. The house connected to the store was also dark. It was past midnight and the small town was as quiet as the inside of a well. From time to time a young woman came out of the teahouse and sputtered away on her scooter to go on a delivery.

As the paved road came to an end, so did the occasional light by the side of the road. The car rocked from side to side as they drove along the pitch-black gravel road. The woman and her husband had not said a single word to each other after leaving Seoul. He turned on his high beams. Though they could see a little farther than before, they couldn't go any faster, because of the bends in the road. Beyond the lights' reach, the cliffs fell away into nothingness. A squirrel caught in the headlights huddled, motionless in the middle of the narrow road. Her husband honked the horn lightly and scared it away into the forest. A sign to the campground appeared in the headlights.

After traveling on the gravel road for nearly an hour, they finally reached the camp parking lot. Even with a flashlight, they couldn't find the trail that led down to the campground proper. After trying repeatedly to make his way through the bushes and overgrown grass, her husband gave up and got back in the car.

A year ago around this time, a child had come this way after slipping away from the campground. The light from the campfire would have made it easy enough for her to find her way up, and the lights in the parking lot had been working back then. The gravel road didn't split off or lead anywhere else, so she couldn't have wandered off.

"This is crazy," her husband said, speaking for the first time in a few hours. "I want to believe that old man just as much as you do. When I heard him, it felt like something inside me was coming alive again. But I saw her body with my own eyes."

She opened the door and stepped out of the car. The mosquitoes caught a whiff of her flesh and swarmed in. She moved forward slowly, trying to match her steps to those of a six-year-old. The gravel was slippery, as if dew had fallen. Her husband followed behind in the car. The road sprang to life in the white of the headlights. He yelled out the window.

"They found twenty-two bodies! They could have gotten them mixed up, but no one was missing. Listen to me, stop this nonsense and get in the car! Let's try to forget. Let's forget and move on."

The woman sometimes imagined what kind of girl her daughter would have become. She pictured the child getting her first period and washing out her stained underwear in secret. She pictured her heading to school in a new spring outfit and spotless white socks. The woman had planned to get off work early the day her daughter came back from camp. She'd planned to go to the kindergarten to wait for the bus to arrive, and when the bus came and her sunburned child trudged off, she'd planned to give her a big hug. On the way home, she would have peered into the plastic bottle to see how many crabs her daughter had caught. But instead, she was compensated for what she'd imagined, using the Hoffman tables to calculate future losses.

"He said it was a star-shaped pin!" the woman cried without looking back. "But it wasn't a pin, it was a stain!"

"What are you talking about?"

The morning their daughter left for camp, the woman had woken up at six o'clock as always. She'd made toast and fried an egg, while her daughter, who had gotten up earlier than usual, wandered around the living room in her underwear. It was only after she'd put the yellow uniform on her daughter that she realized she'd forgotten to wash it. On the chest was a chocolate syrup stain, the size of a large coin. Her daughter whined about the dirty shirt. The woman tried to wash out the stain, but instead of disappearing, the syrup spread into the shape of a star.

"The other kids are going to make fun of me. They'll say my shirt's dirty and I spill food like a baby."

She soothed the girl, while helping her arms through the sleeves. "You're bound to get dirty by the end of the day. Your friends' clothes will get dirty, too, so just hang tight."

She helped her daughter put on her backpack and hung the plastic bottle across her chest. Because of the stain, she was going to be late for work again. She grabbed her daughter's hand and half ran to the kindergarten. Her daughter had a hard time keeping up and stumbled a few times. After saying goodbye in front of the building, her daughter walked up to the front door, and then all of a sudden, she turned around. "So long, Mommy!" she called, waving her hand.

"What do you mean 'so long'?" she said, as she waved back. "You're supposed to say 'see you soon.'"

Stamped across the bottom of Miss Kim's footage, at the moment the woman's daughter was captured on camera, was the time of the recording: 9:50 P.M. A six-year-old could not have gone from the camp to the store in a little over an hour, even if she had run all the way. The star-shaped pin the owner claimed to have seen could have actually been a star-shaped stain. Children that age were always getting stains on their clothes. Or just as the owner's wife had said, he could have been spewing nonsense because of the alcohol.

Her husband honked lightly from behind, as if to scare away a squirrel, but she didn't scamper into the forest. Little by little, she walked forward. No matter what everyone else said, she wanted to believe the missing child was hers. She wanted to believe the reason her child hadn't come home in over a year was because she took such small steps. If she were to come home at that pace, they would have to wait much, much longer. No matter what everyone said, this is what she wanted to believe.

Bluebeard's First Wife

The wardrobe was so heavy the three movers struggled for a long time outside the front door, sweating and catching their breath. I hovered by the entrance, afraid they might dent the corners. All I could do was shout, "up!" "down!" "left!" and "right!" which pretty much summed up my English. But whenever the wardrobe tilted or came dangerously close to scraping the doorway, Korean sprang from my mouth: "Josim haseyo!"

After repeated maneuvers to get it in the house, my twelve-foot-wide princess tree wardrobe, which had made the long journey from Incheon's port to Wellington, New Zealand, finally occupied one side of our bedroom.

The move took half the day, since there were more things shipped from my parents' house than I'd thought. After the men brought in the last box, filled with knickknacks like my old journals and high-school graduation album, I sat hugging my knees on the corner of our bed and gazed at the wardrobe.

I could almost smell the morning air from back home. I could even hear the wind sweeping through the forest. Whenever I heard that sound, lines from a poem I'd read as a child would come to me.

Who has seen the wind?
Neither I nor you:
But when the leaves hang trembling,
The wind is passing through.

My heart swelled. I'd brought my princess tree, which had stood on the hill behind my childhood home, across thousands of miles to our bedroom in this foreign land.

My father, who'd been an elementary school teacher, had planted the sapling on the hill behind our house when I'd been born. The princess tree grows fast and is used to make furniture and musical instruments because the wood won't split or warp, but he wanted to turn it into a wardrobe for me when I got married. The forest behind our home was full of chestnut trees; in order to easily find the princess tree among the chestnuts, he even had a plaque made. Written on it was my name, as well as the date the sapling was planted.

The life of my tree was nearly cut short. If things had gone according to plan, I would have married at the early age of twenty-two, before I graduated from university. But as the wedding day approached, both my fiancé and I changed our minds. His short height, which had at first made him appear sweet, suddenly struck me as unsightly, and his field of study—astronomy—which seemed to guarantee he'd stay wholesome and romantic, felt all at once like an awfully impractical choice. The wedding gifts our families had exchanged were returned, and all ties were severed. I never heard from him again. And the tree, whose life should have ended when I was twenty-two, was allowed to grow for another ten years before it was chopped down to become a twelve-foot-wide wardrobe. Just as Mother said, a wardrobe was best at twelve feet. The wood grain flowing like a quiet stream in the pale, pumpkin-colored timber was lovely. Not a blemish was to be found anywhere.

I still remember the moment it was cut down. It resisted stubbornly as the chainsaw dug its teeth into the trunk. The saw spun in place, bending as though it would snap. Sawdust sprayed in all directions. The whine of the saw was deafening, and the air was heavy with the smell of sap. When my thirteen-meter tree, which had grown unhindered for thirty-one years, began to tip over, people laughed and cried: "Timber!"

Inside the wardrobe, three large drawers sat beneath the clothes rail. Because the drawers were brand-new, they kept sticking in the tracks. I put my journals and graduation album inside. To be honest, when I first arrived at the Wellington International Airport, I'd been both nervous and excited. Staring about like some country bumpkin, I'd hurried after Jason so that I wouldn't lose him. But soon enough, these drawers will slide in and out easily. By then, this foreign land will have become our children's home.

Jason, who had come home late, seemed stupefied by the wardrobe that took up an entire side of our bedroom. "*This* is what you've been waiting for?"

You couldn't exactly say the bulky, pumpkin-colored wardrobe complemented the white wooden house. As I picked up the clothes he tossed onto the bed, I launched into an explanation about the princess tree.

"The first tree you cut down is called a *modong*. When it re-sprouts from the stump, it's called a *jadong*. When it re-sprouts again, it's called a *sondong*. *Sondong* princess trees are the best, in terms of quality. I'm going to watch over that tree, and make a wardrobe for our daughter out of the *jadong* and one for our granddaughter out of the *sondong*."

Of course he didn't understand any of this. Jason had lived in New Zealand since tenth grade. When I explained everything again, slowly this time, Jason waved his hands in the air, drew his lips together in a small circle, and enunciated, "No thanks."

I wasn't sure if "no thanks" referred to children or the wardrobe, but either way, he didn't seem too fond of the latter.

·

I followed Jason into a restaurant, gazing at the back of his head. His hair was neatly combed, not a single strand out of place. From the back, he looked like a stranger. Did he not like children? All of a sudden, I realized I hardly knew him. But the same went for him. In fact, he probably knew far less about me.

We had married three months after meeting. My married friends warned that a couple needed to get to know each other before marriage, but I knew they'd failed to take their own advice. But from the very beginning, I could tell the kind of person Jason was.

We had met three thousand feet in the air. About 90 percent of the passengers en route to Jeju Island had been honeymooners. Those traveling to the island for different reasons occupied the few remaining seats in the back. Although it was a clear day, there was a lot of turbulence. Every time the airplane rattled, the brides in the front shrieked.

I was gazing out the window when someone said, "Aren't you even a little scared?"

Nothing felt real when I looked down at the flat roofs of houses below, or the mountain peaks that didn't seem much taller than the cars crawling around like ants. Without bothering to turn my head, I said, "There's no husband to impress."

He chuckled. Shortly after, he asked, "Did you drop something?"

I checked the floor under the seats, but there was nothing. Only then did I look at him. There was a greenish shadow on his face from shaving, like the end of a daikon radish. He laughed again.

"I meant outside. You've been staring out that window since takeoff."

Our families wished for us to marry as soon as possible. I was past the age where I could take all the time I wanted, but he was twenty-nine, three years younger than me, which wasn't a late age for a man to marry. Still, his parents hurried the proceedings along just the same as mine, if not more. Once our parents met, we held a lunch reception at a hotel where we exchanged engagement rings in the presence of family and close friends. Everything happened so quickly. And unlike ten years before, there was no time to change my mind.

My mother, who had just returned from selecting an auspicious date for the wedding, glanced toward the living room where my father sat and said a man's heart was impossible to understand, even after a lifetime together. After doling out some more advice, she said, "I wonder if a twelve-foot-wide wardrobe will fit in your New Zealand bedroom."

My friends teased me when they learned I was marrying a man who was not only younger, but also from New Zealand.

"Immigration is hard work. No matter what happens, make sure you sit tight for two years."

What they meant was that I could always get a divorce once I had my citizenship in hand. We clinked our beer glasses together and cheered: "To a brand-new life!"

He was different from the men I'd known, those who would slip their arms around my shoulders or take me to dark lounges with partitioned booths. He had escorted me home late one night when I'd had too much to drink. After coming into my apartment where I lived alone, he left promptly once he'd finished his coffee. I knew he was trying to be honorable, waiting until we were married. I found his old-fashioned behavior charming, and respected him for it.

Out of the three months I'd known Jason, we ended up spending only a month and half together, since he headed back to New Zealand once the wedding date was set. We talked on the phone for over an hour every day, and I discussed the wedding preparations with his parents. When Jason would be having dinner at the bottom of the world, I'd drive to the industrial complex on the outskirts of Seoul. The manager of the furniture factory took me on site to show me the princess tree wood that had gone through two cycles of the soaking bath and drying process to prevent warping. The lacquer fumes stung my eyes. As I was leaving, I reminded him once more that I needed the wardrobe on time.

Jason flew back to Seoul the day before our wedding. When he kept delaying his return date, his parents called the pharmacy more frequently. They made small talk, asking if I'd eaten lunch or if there were many customers that day, but I knew they were checking to see if the wedding preparations were going smoothly. They seemed a little uneasy. Because there wasn't enough time for a fitting, Jason's suit was a little big in the waist and had to be taken in with pins, which created wrinkles in the seat of his pants. My father's past colleagues came by shuttle bus. Those from my hometown came on the same bus, but they kept talking throughout the ceremony and the officiant had to stop four times to tell them to be quiet.

The officiant, whom Jason and I had never met before, spoke about the groom who was currently studying at the Victoria University of Wellington and the bride who, after having graduated from a regional pharmacy program, was now a fulltime staff member at a large pharmacy in Jongno. He exaggerated our credentials. I glanced at my father, but he nodded fervently at the end of every sentence, as though confirming what the officiant said. The speech went a little long.

Jason's Korean name was Hyogyeong, but he seemed more used to his English name. He would drive his yellow sports car to the university in the morning and return late at night. He didn't have to worry about making a living. His parents sent us more than enough to cover his tuition and our living expenses.

While Jason was gone, I would clean the house and take a nap, or flip through the Korean newspaper. Unlike Australia, there weren't many Korean immigrants in New Zealand, perhaps less than a thousand altogether. My in-laws would have given me a car of my own had I asked, but because the steering wheel was on the right side of the vehicle, I needed to learn to drive all over again. Once I had nearly rammed Jason's car into our fence.

The house was full of light because the living room ceiling was two stories high. I would lean back on the sofa and gaze out the window at the distant city skyline until sunset. When I used to sit behind the glass counter at the pharmacy, sunlight would stream into the store. Then the other pharmacists and I would nod off in the warmth as we waited for customers.

Jason's study was at the end of the hallway from the master bedroom. After returning home late, he would hurry through dinner and then shut himself up in his study. I fell asleep alone in the master bedroom, which contained only a bed and the wardrobe. The bed was large and cushiony. When my eyes snapped open in the middle of the night, I would hear the wind. Then I'd whisper to myself the lines from the poem whose ending I couldn't remember:

Who has seen the wind?
Neither I nor you:
But when the leaves hang trembling,
The wind is passing through.

Every morning, Jason shaved before breakfast. He used an old-fashioned straight razor, like one I had seen a long time ago when I'd followed my father to the barbershop. After lathering his face, Jason puffed his cheeks, angled the razor, and scraped it down to his chin.

"What?" He seemed annoyed that I was watching him shave.

"I was thinking about getting a dog . . ."

Instead of answering, he turned on the tap and rinsed the razor vigorously. I watched his face in the mirror. Was he going to say "no thanks" again? He jutted out his bluish chin, examining it in the mirror, and muttered, "Didn't I tell you? I can't stand dogs."

That was the end of the discussion. This time too, I didn't prod. I didn't ask why he didn't like dogs. As he changed out of his pajamas, he glanced over at me. "Just hang on until summer break. We'll go to Lake Wakatipu then."

It was Chang, Jason's friend from the university, who later told me that Jason disliked dogs because they shed and got hair on his clothes.

Chang was Chinese and four years younger than Jason. He had a slight build and a bright and cheerful personality, unlike Jason. I didn't know the details, but it seemed they were carrying out a research project together. Sometimes, over coffee, they talked about things I couldn't understand.

Soon there were more days where it was the three of us. Chang helped with the cooking, as well as the dishes. He talked slowly, so that I'd understand. He even knew how to speak a little Korean, though he frequently stumbled over words.

Thanks to Chang, our dinners became jovial and lighthearted. I began to look forward to the days Chang would be coming. After dinner, they would disappear into Jason's study at the end of the hall.

"Should I make coffee or cut some fruit?"

Whenever I would offer to bring in refreshments, Jason would purse his lips together and say, "No thanks." And as if he'd just remembered, he would add, "Don't bother waiting up. We've got a lot of work to do tonight."

A few days after I'd arrived in New Zealand, Jason had said I was free to do whatever I wanted, except disturb him when he was working. Just as he'd requested, I avoided the study, even when I got up for a drink of water in the middle of the night or went out onto the balcony to listen to the wind. Light outlined the door at the end of the hallway, and the sound of low laughter drifted out.

Slowly I adjusted to my new life. When Jason spent the night at the lab, I would have an early supper and go out for a stroll. I walked among subtropical trees that kept their leaves all year round. In the evenings, the temperature tended to drop rapidly. Even if I became ill with fever, I didn't make a fuss. The medicine cabinet was full of pills, with which I prepared a prescription for myself.

On my way back, I'd always see our house from a distance. Arched windows and linen, floral-patterned curtains I had put up myself, the wind chimes I had hung outside the window. Everything was picture perfect, exactly what I had dreamed of, but like the village I had seen from high up in the airplane, it all seemed unreal.

When I came back from my walks, I would write my friends and family back home. On one postcard a steamship cruised the waters of Lake Wakatipu, which I had yet to see in person. Another showed a panoramic view of the Auckland waterfront, crowded with hundreds of yachts. I wrote about our white, two-story wooden house. I wrote about the trees that didn't lose their leaves all year round. I wrote about July being a winter month in New Zealand, and how you could get over two thousand hours of sunshine a year. I wrote all sorts of information I'd copied from travel brochures.

I always ended with these words: "Make sure you come for a visit. This place is heaven on earth. And don't forget to bring your sunglasses and sunscreen—you'll need them!"

Even after I'd written everything I wanted to say, I found myself still gripping the pen. I didn't write that our white house felt artificial, like a dollhouse, even though it was spacious and full of light. If I did, all my friends would have no doubt said: "Count your blessings! Do you realize how many people can't find jobs here? My husband barely makes anything and the kids are always whining. You're lucky you get to live in a palace and don't have to work like the rest of us. You better tough it out no matter what!"

I got to know the streets around our house. Auckland was an hour away by plane. I bought a map and learned which bus to take to the airport. One day, as soon as Jason's car disappeared down the street, I stepped out of the house in jeans and a sweater.

Once in Auckland, I spread open my map and cut across Queen Elizabeth Square. Many of the streets were bumpy and steep. It was warm enough for short sleeves. I walked slowly between the towering trees. The sunlight couldn't penetrate the canopy of branches and leaves high above. The forest behind my parents' house couldn't compare to this forest. I could tell these trees were at least a hundred years old.

Around two in the afternoon, I walked to the Victorian-style restaurants and boutiques that lined the streets of Parnell Village. After a simple meal on a patio, I was about to spread open the map to plan my next stop when someone bumped into my arm, knocking my map to the ground.

It was Chang. Not having noticed me, he ran across the street. I was about to call out to him when he ran into a side street where a man stood waiting. It was Jason.

Jason came home late next morning. Scruffy and unshaven, he looked exhausted. I didn't mention Auckland; I didn't ask what he and Chang had been doing there. I didn't know everything about Jason, but I knew enough to know he'd never tell me.

When summer break came, I didn't mention the trip to Lake Wakatipu. I no longer waited up for Jason at night. In the end, he was the one who remembered the promised trip. But it was only when we arrived at the airport that I realized the trip wasn't meant for us alone, for there was Chang again. I handed my luggage over to him as if nothing were the matter.

Like old friends, we strolled around the Queenstown Mall together. To my surprise, Chang and I had similar tastes. Chang watched patiently as I tried on over ten outfits, and helped me pick one out, and we even bought matching visors. We boarded a steamship called the *Lady of the Lake* and cruised the waters of Lake Wakatipu, which I had only seen on postcards until then. Chang told me it was the third largest lake in New Zealand. I could see why the Maori would call it Greenstone Lake. We stepped out onto the deck and stood leaning against the railing, but Jason didn't emerge once from the cabin.

"Jason! Come join us!" I called to him. "Look at the color of this water!"

Chang poked me in the side. Speaking slowly, he explained that Jason had a fear of water. He had gotten swept up in the tide at the age of five and nearly drowned; after that he never went near water again. It was a big deal for him to set foot on the boat. In fact, Jason's courage was to be praised.

I looked Chang straight in the eye and muttered in Korean, "Do you even know Jason's real name? It's Hyogyeong. Choi Hyogyeong."

"Huigyeong?"

"No."

"Hyegyeong?"

Chang twisted his tongue this way and that way, and burst into laughter, flashing his full and even set of teeth.

I drew my face close to Chang's and grinned. "You idiot . . . you don't even know how to say Hyogyeong . . ."

Unable to understand, he shrugged and asked, "What? What?"

Even at the hotel, I fell asleep alone. Chang and Jason returned from the bar late.

When we got home, I was busy for over a week, writing my family and friends. Jason, Chang, and me—everything was fine. I didn't concern myself with them.

I bought a day pass and roamed about downtown Wellington on a trolleybus. I had lunch at a restaurant that caught my eye and went into a nursery to buy enough flower plants to nearly snap off my arms. At home, I planted them along the fence until the flood light came on at dusk.

I woke up to the sound of fighting. I opened the bedroom door and stepped into the hallway. I heard something bounce off the floor, and Chang's voice over Jason's whispers. It was the first time I'd heard them argue.

I ran down the hall and shoved open the door to the study. Jason was backed into a corner, blood trickling down one cheek. Empty beer bottles rolled on the floor. Drunk, Chang staggered back and forth, holding a fruit knife. Jason saw me and yelled, "Get out!"

Chang noticed me only then. He dropped the knife and sank down to the floor. "Get out!" Jason yelled again.

I went back to the bedroom and shut the door. I heard some more fighting and a series of thuds, but soon everything grew quiet. The sound of weeping echoed into the hall.

The next morning when I stepped into the kitchen, Chang was making toast and freshly squeezed juice. Jason was in the bathroom. Chang grinned. As if reciting lines from a book, he stammered in his faltering Korean, "I'm sorry. I'm very sorry."

The three of us sat at the table and chewed on scraps of toast. Every time he chewed, the gash on Jason's cheek opened to reveal the raw flesh underneath. I didn't ask why they had fought. Instead,

I announced I would be going on a three-day trip to Auckland. Jason suggested I book a tour, but I didn't respond.

I didn't need a map this time. Victoria Park, Albert Park, Auckland Art Gallery, Auckland Domain, and the streets of Parnell Village where I had seen Jason and Chang—I roamed through them all. From time to time, someone would bump into me, but I didn't mind. All this took three hours and twenty minutes. I walked east along the Hauraki Gulf from Waitemata Harbour, and saw hundreds of anchored yachts. The billowing wind-filled sails looked like fish bellies. When night fell, I dragged my swollen feet to the hotel and fell asleep in my clothes. I slept soundly for the first time in a long while.

When I came home from my trip, the flowers I had planted along the fence had withered. I turned on the sprinklers and watered the lawn for a long time. It was cold inside the house, as if no one had been home for the past few days.

I got the luggage I'd used on my honeymoon from the storage room and opened my wardrobe. The wood still smelled new and two of the drawers were empty. I recalled the moment the princess tree had been felled. I pictured the disappointed faces of my parents.

My eyes flew open in the middle of the night; I sensed someone was home. The hands on the clock pointed to 2:10 A.M. I headed to Jason's study to tell him I was planning to return to Korea the next day or the day after that. His light was still on. Rough, irregular breathing came from inside. I pushed open the door without knocking.

The first thing I saw was Chang bent over the desk and Jason standing directly behind him. Jason's pants were down around his thighs. He cursed as soon as he saw me. Perhaps he was more Korean after all, because in that moment, he swore in Korean.

Of course. It was no surprise. I closed the door softly, went back to the bedroom, and waited for Jason. He came to the room right away. I'd never seen him move so fast. I stared up at him, as if he were a stranger. He was short of breath and the flush hadn't left his face.

"Didn't I tell you never to come in?"

In that instant, I recalled how a gust of wind would shake the trees behind my parents' house. Whenever we heard that rustling noise, my mother would say, "Storm's coming."

"I want to go home."

Jason spotted my luggage in the corner of the room. He licked his lips. He strode toward the wardrobe and took out my purse. He turned it upside down and shook. Out spilled my passport and bankbook, my lipstick and compact I hadn't used for a long time, as well as several plane tickets to and from Auckland. He checked the dates and grimaced.

"Ah, I see. You've known all along. Guess I was the moron, right? It must have killed you to keep quiet this long."

I tried to grab my passport, but Jason was faster. He ripped it in half and tucked my bankbook in his back pocket. "Who says you can leave? Maybe it was your choice to come here, but it's up to me now. You expect me to just sit here and let you ruin everything?"

"I don't care. I want to go home."

I was so dizzy I had trouble standing. Jason shoved me. I must have hit my head on the corner of the bed, because the ceiling bleached out and grew distant. I heard the gust of wind and the shaking leaves—the storm was coming.

When I regained consciousness, I was inside the wardrobe. I heard Jason and Chang's footsteps. I pushed on the doors with all my strength, but it was no use. I peered through the keyhole and saw Chang pacing the hallway beyond the open bedroom door. He looked distraught. I knew they were talking about me. I strained to hear them.

"What are you going to do with her? You're not—you wouldn't dare—"

"Shut up!"

Chang put a hand over his mouth. "Oh my God, what are you going to do? What are you going to do?"

"We can't let her go back to Korea. Then everything's over."

Chang started to cry. "I love you . . ."

I was more hungry than scared. I hugged my knees to my chest. I remembered I hadn't eaten anything after coming back from Auckland. I thought long and hard about where my life had gone wrong. I couldn't die like this. I clenched my teeth. I got up and threw myself against the doors. But they wouldn't budge. After all, it was princess tree wood. I never thought my wardrobe would one day become my coffin.

"Help!"

I screamed as loudly as I could, but all I managed was a croak. There was no way my voice would reach the next house, which was over three hundred feet away. I scratched at the doors. My nails soon peeled back from the skin. I groped through the clothes hanging above me and found a belt. I tried to pick the lock with the buckle, but it was pointless.

Jason flung what sounded like a knife at the doors. I heard it quiver as it plunged into the wood. He prowled back and forth before the wardrobe.

"If you hadn't opened the door, nothing would have happened! You brought this on yourself, you know that? How about this—why don't we pretend none of this ever happened? Let's go back to how we were. Promise me. Then I'll let you out."

I wanted to swear at him, but my voice broke. I opened my mouth to try again, but I passed out instead.

When my eyes opened, my pajama pants were drenched. I had wet myself. My lips were cracked and peeling. I tried to call out to Jason, but my tongue felt as if it were coiled; it was impossible to form any words.

I lost all sense of time and place. I didn't know how long I was trapped inside that wardrobe. Was it hours or days? After a long time, the doors opened. Jason swore, perhaps because of the smell. Chang grabbed me under the arms, and Jason my legs, and together they pulled me out of the wardrobe. I sagged like a corpse.

"Oh my God, she's dead!" Chang stammered, terrified.

I had no energy to get up. I continued to lie there as if I were dead. Jason prodded my cheek and then put his ear up to my nose. "No, she's still alive. Let's move her to the car. Go open the trunk."

Chang hurried out. Jason went to the storage room, probably to look for a sack to put me in. I crawled to the bathroom. I saw Jason's razor on the shelf. I hid it in my pant pocket.

"Hurry!" Chang called urgently from the entrance. "I started the car!"

A sack big enough to fit a person isn't easy to find. Jason, who had been rummaging in the storage room for a while, came back empty-handed. He covered me with one of the coats from the wardrobe. He tried to hoist me on his back, but it wasn't easy. He grunted and dropped me onto the floor. This time, he grabbed me by the ankles and dragged me toward the living room. It hurt every time my spine went over a threshold, but I clenched my teeth and stayed quiet.

When Jason stopped for a moment to catch his breath, I mustered every last ounce of energy and sat up, swinging the razor. Jason clutched his chin and backed away. I got up and ran blindly out the front door. My legs moved on their own accord, independently, like a squirming octopus that had been chopped to pieces. The only thought in my head was to live. I swung the razor at Chang, who was sitting in the driver's seat. He scrambled out. I got behind the wheel and locked the doors. I gripped the steering wheel and slammed on the accelerator. Jason's car sprang forward and headed straight for the fence. It upset me to run over the flowers I had tended so carefully.

I rammed into the fence and burst onto the road. For about ten minutes, I zigzagged along at top speed. I wasn't used to driving with the steering wheel on the right side. Cars sounded their horns and kept their distance.

In the end, the yellow sports car leapt onto the sidewalk, hit a fire hydrant, and came to a stop. Water sprayed from the hydrant like a fountain. I heard the approaching sirens.

I was kept in the hospital for three days because of dehydration. Jason came to see me. He had a big scar on his chin. He said the whole thing had been a big misunderstanding, that they had been planning to take me to the hospital. I didn't divulge to the police what had actually happened. I had played my last hand. Jason knew it, too. I was able to return to Korea.

Shortly after my return, Jason's parents came to see me. They had known all along. Jason's mother wept. "So he hasn't changed . . ."

Jason's father, who seethed with anger, didn't say a single word. Until Jason would marry a woman once more, he would receive no financial support from his parents. He had never made a living on his own.

•

A year has passed since then.

Every morning at seven-thirty, I get on the subway in Seoul, famous for its crowds, and go to work. There aren't many pharmacies willing to take on new female pharmacists well past thirty. My friend owns the small pharmacy where I work now, but I'm just filling in for her while she's on maternity leave.

Whenever I find myself rocking back and forth on the packed subway car, I wonder: If I hadn't opened the door that night, would our marriage have carried on?

In the end, I couldn't tell my parents the truth. I couldn't tell my friends either. Our marriage had lasted nineteen months. They would have said, "You were so close—why didn't you just hang on for another five months?" Just as I had before marriage, I went back home once a month to visit my parents. On the hill behind their house, a new sapling was beginning to grow from the princess tree stump.

The divorce was finalized during that time, and I talked to Jason only once on the phone. He asked for my address in order to send me the wardrobe. He mentioned he'd grown a beard, that he'd needed to cover up the nasty scar on his chin. Eventually, Jason will marry another woman in order to receive his parents' help. His parents, too, will refuse to give up. These things will repeat themselves.

Exactly a month and a half later, the wardrobe arrived. The five movers struggled in the narrow entrance and steep staircase, and demanded that I pay extra. An older mover was eager to share his expertise. "There's no way princess tree wood is this heavy. I don't know where you got this made, but I guarantee they pulled a switcheroo on you."

I had no energy to go to the factory to confirm whether what the mover said was true.

This time, I didn't bother to tell them to be careful. There were already ugly gashes on the wardrobe, especially right above the keyhole where the knife had gone in, and inside were scratches from my fingernails and deep gouges from the belt buckle. There was also a dark, discolored spot. Probably from when I'd wet myself. The drawers still didn't slide out smoothly. In the top drawer were my journals and graduation album, just as I'd left them.

When the wardrobe was placed inside my bedroom, there wasn't enough space for even a twin bed, so it had to be moved to another room. I thought then the wardrobe would have been better at eight feet.

By noon, the sun streams in through the pharmacy window. I doze off, my arms folded on the glass counter filled with antibiotic ointments, mouthwashes, and birth control pills. Then the living room of a white wooden house brimming with light spreads before my eyes. The trolleybus. Parnell Village lined with its quaint, Victorian-style restaurants and boutiques. The bumpy hills of Auckland. The Waitemata Harbour and the Hauraki Gulf, teeming with yachts. When these scenes sparkle outside the window of the pharmacy, I think long and hard, and wonder where my life went wrong.

Flies

There was an unusual amount of gravel. He could feel every
rock through the thin soles of his tennis shoes. He slipped and
stumbled repeatedly. He stopped to light his cigarette, as well as to
rest his legs. Everywhere he looked was gravel.

The bathroom at the bus terminal didn't even have urinals. He
stepped onto the cement ledge and finally relieved himself on the
cement wall, which was encrusted with yellow and white stains.
When he looked out the small window and saw his bus pulling away
from the terminal, he rushed out without even zipping himself up,
but the bus was already beyond reach.

He paid for a bottle of soju and a pack of cigarettes at a nearby
corner store, and waited at a table under an umbrella set out along the
gravel path. His plastic chair rocked on the uneven surface. An elderly

woman in baggy nylon pants brought over a bottle of the local soju and some coarsely chopped cubes of radish kimchi. The soju wasn't the brand he liked. He drank straight from the bottle. He'd better get used to the taste anyway.

In one corner of the backroom sat a pile of cotton work gloves. As the owner mended a hole in a fingertip, she asked listlessly if there was anything else he needed. Bits of loose thread clung to her tired, frizzy hair.

"When's the next bus to Ungok-ri?"

She bit off the thread and motioned with her chin in the direction the bus had gone. He couldn't make out her words whenever she bit off some thread, but the gist was that he'd just missed the last bus, and the next one wasn't coming until early morning, so he should get a room, and if he was interested, she knew a decent place.

He swung his backpack over his shoulder and set out blindly down the road the bus had taken. The woman came outside to wipe the table.

"You plan to walk?" she shot toward his back. "The sun's gonna set soon. Like I said, there's no other place to spend the night except here."

The rice paddies were brimming with water, and the bean and sesame fields were green. After walking on the gravel road for half an hour, he wished he'd listened to the woman. He'd come across only one boy herding a pair of black goats. Even from afar, the boy had been able to tell he was a stranger and had kept his distance.

He sat down by the side of the road to have a smoke. He wasn't in a hurry. And nothing was waiting for him in Seoul. He peered at the furrows, dried up from the recent drought. It grew dark quickly in the mountains.

Just as he was settling into a furrow for the night, he glimpsed a set of headlights bobbing through the dark. He jumped up and ran toward them. He forced his cramped legs to move. He stood in the middle of the road, blocking the pickup truck's path.

"You headed to Ungok-ri by any chance?" he asked.

From out of the glare came a man's voice. "No, we're going to Maehyang-ri."

He slowly moved out of the way. The truck pulled up next to him. The window rolled down to reveal the driver's face. He smelled faintly of alcohol.

"We've got to pass through Ungok-ri, though," the driver added. "But there's no room up here in the front, as you can see."

A woman and her two boys were squeezed in the passenger seat. She had her arm around the smaller one, his limbs splayed limply as if he were in a deep sleep. Judging by the boys' age, the woman was probably in her early thirties at most, but without a trace of makeup she looked over forty. Her eyelids were puffy, as if she'd been sleeping as well. Her small, suspicious eyes flicked over him. He was no stranger to those kinds of looks. When she found him staring back, she hurriedly repositioned the child on her lap.

The back of the truck was loaded with all kinds of odds and ends. He sat squeezed in between pesticide containers and some plastic plates. The truck had to go slowly because of the gravel. Rocks flew out from under the tires like oil splattering from a hot pan, while some popped out unpredictably, scattering in all directions. When the truck rolled over big rocks, the man bounced into the air. His tailbone grew sore.

If the driver were to lose his grip on the steering wheel for even a second, the truck would dash straight into the paddies. He kept a firm grasp on the wheel and glanced into the rearview mirror at the 14-inch window between the front seat and the back of the truck. The man was sitting with his back toward the driver, his shoulders filling the rearview mirror.

He wasn't very tall, but he was stocky with a short, thick neck. He had grabbed onto the side of the truck bed and swung himself into the back in one motion. He was now smoking a cigarette, gazing out at the paddies and bean fields buried in darkness. The driver rolled down his window halfway and shouted at the top of his lungs, "So what's your business in Ungok-ri?"

The man twisted around and just laughed toward the window.

"I'm a farmer in Maehyang-ri," the driver said. "We used to live in Seoul. It's been four years since we left."

The wife glared at her husband. "Why'd you pick up a complete stranger? Who knows what kind of person he is?"

"Well, did you expect me to just leave him back there in the middle of nowhere?" the driver hissed in a whisper, in case the man should hear. "How could I pull something dirty like that?"

Ungok-ri was submerged in fog—fog so thick it was impossible to see more than a meter ahead. The driver switched off the headlights and turned on his hazards. He put the truck in low gear, crawling to a stop in front of some flickering lights.

"We're here."

From the back came a soft thud as the man's feet hit the ground. In an instant, he was standing by the driver's window. He raised his hand in a salute and disappeared into the fog. The words *Building a Just Society* on the back of his jacket were barely visible in the faint light.

The woman looked at her husband and muttered, "'Building a Just Society'? See? I knew something wasn't right."

"Keep your mouth shut—you don't know anything," he snapped, as he turned the truck toward Maehyang-ri. "You ever see a thief walk into a police station to turn himself in? Jeez, you're slow. Can't you tell? He's obviously the new police officer—the *police*, woman."

He turned his head and spat. His saliva dropped onto the window instead. "Why is this place always so goddamned foggy? I wonder why he had to leave Seoul to come to this hole."

"So you think he was pushed out of Seoul?"

"Did you forget we were pushed out, too?" he berated her, checking both side mirrors. "If you can't stop talking, tell me if there's anything on that side."

Their son started to whimper, startled awake by his father's voice.

•

In the police station, an officer on night duty was boiling some instant noodles for a late-night snack. The man pushed open the door, letting in the fog. The officer seemed to have been expecting him. He stuck out his hand in greeting, still gripping the chopsticks he'd stirred the noodles with; then he burst into laughter and hurriedly transferred the chopsticks to the other hand.

"The name's Lim," the officer said. His hand was moist, but he had a solid grip. The police chief had already gone home.

Three metal desks and two filing cabinets lined two walls of the station. On a third wall was a map. Maehyang-ri, where the truck driver lived, was located northwest of Ungok-ri. Surrounded by mountains, Ungok-ri was made up of a number of villages, each a cluster of about a dozen houses. There was a bridge over a stream that flowed southeast. The farmer's truck was probably crossing the bridge at that very moment. The rest of the map was marked here and there with the "山" sign—most likely all fields.

"What's there to see?" Officer Lim said, slurping his noodles. "It's just paddies and fields. This town's just like this pot. We're basically buried in between the mountains, and when the fog rolls in, we're stuck inside as it boils. Still, this place has everything a man needs, if you know what I mean. You can't tell from the map, of course, but you'll see when the fog clears." Lim snickered, and then choked on his laughter.

The man unpacked in the night-duty room attached to the station. There was just enough space for an average-sized man to lie down. There was no furniture, and instead of hooks there were some nails hammered into the slate wall. He took off his jacket and hung it on a nail, but it was loose, and both nail and jacket fell to the floor. A grimy pillow and quilt sat folded in the corner. The pillow smelled of cheap hair product. Once he lay down, he saw through the small window a naked bulb dangling from a ginkgo tree.

At a little past nine, all was quiet outside. He heard a clatter through the wall; it seemed Officer Lim was rinsing out the pot. The small town was a far cry from Seoul, where he'd been until that morning; he felt as if he'd crossed over into a different dimension. He imagined walking down a Seoul street flashing with neon signs. There, he couldn't stop walking for even a second to light a cigarette, for example, because people would bump into him from behind. Seoul was filled with noise, and drunk men were dragged into the police station all night long. Dozens of incidents were reported every day. But at the Ungok-ri station, the phone didn't ring at all; he hadn't heard it once in the past half hour. The place was graveyard-quiet. He closed his eyes, but the quiet kept him awake. He pulled out a notebook from his backpack. The pages, covered with writing, curled up at the edges. Lying on his stomach with the pillow under his chest, he wrote by the light of the bulb that came in through the window. He scrawled down a few words and then erased the whole thing. He heard the first bus as it rolled into town. Only then was he able to fall asleep.

•

The night-duty room was only a temporary lodging place; he couldn't expect to stay there forever. There were thirteen houses in the village of Cheongbong. The houses were simple, not all that different from the way they looked on the map, like something kindergarten children might draw using squares and trapezoids. People lived under tile roofs, and cows and pigs lived under tin roofs. They arrived at the house Officer Lim had recommended. Nailed to one of the gnarled wooden posts was a nameplate engraved with Chinese characters.

"Doesn't matter how many times I look, they all look the same to me," Lim muttered, peering at the Chinese characters. He then glanced at the man and laughed. "Everyone in this village is from the same clan, so they all have the same family name. On top of that, their first names are so similar it gets really confusing."

The gate was wide open, but no one was home. Officer Lim strode into the courtyard. Pollack were hung out to dry on the clothesline that cut across the yard, their mouths strung together with a nylon cord. Officer Lim pushed open a door as though it were his own house.

"These people can't sit still for a minute. They must've gotten tired of waiting for us and headed out to the back fields."

While Officer Lim went to find the owners, the man peered around the house. Every piece of furniture was old and shabby. He walked back out to the yard where the pollack hung. He caught a whiff of something foul. Although the fish were split down the middle to dry, and held apart with a bamboo skewer, the parts deep inside where the sunlight couldn't reach were rotting. Something writhed and squirmed within the crevices. Maggots. The bellies of all twelve pollack were teeming with fat little maggots that bulged and shrank ceaselessly as they ate through the fish. Some had squirmed out and clung to the scales.

The husband and wife were holding hoes, the blades covered in dirt. They wore towels over their wide-brimmed visors, so that everything above the nose was buried in shadow. The man felt their eyes move over him from within the shadows. Officer Lim must have filled them in already. The woman finally spoke, pushing open the bedroom door closest to the front gate.

"I hear you're from Seoul. I'm not too sure the food will be to your liking. Don't know when you plan on heading back, but make yourself at home while you're here."

She said the room had belonged to their eldest son, who had left for the big city. All that remained was a low desk and a few books.

The couple was rarely home during the day. Their bedroom light came on briefly in the evening and went out shortly after.

When the man returned from night duty, he would stay up for a little while and then go to bed late, waking up past noon. Set out on the wooden floor of the living room was his meal tray, consisting of rice—the ceramic bowl painted with the Chinese character signifying *long life*—kimchi, marinated greens, and pickled pollack. The clothesline was bare except for two pairs of coveralls. Recalling the pollack that had been writhing with maggots, he stayed well away from the fish. The maggots had probably matured into flies by now, soiling the walls of some house with dung. When the pollack went untouched for a few days, it ended up going to the pigs.

The streets remained empty during the day. Once in a while, teahouse girls sauntered along, carrying flasks and teacups wrapped in cloth. On his way to work and back, he saw people squatting in the fields, pulling out weeds. If their eyes happened to meet, they awkwardly got to their feet and nodded to him.

Even the path from his rented room to the station was entirely of gravel. Who had brought and laid it all? With each passing day, he grew used to walking on the rocks and his calves grew stronger.

The days passed quietly. Disputes were never brought to the station. The village elder gave the verdict and everyone seemed perfectly happy to go along with the decision. Ungok-ri was as quiet as the inside of a fishbowl. His daily routine consisted of keeping watch at the station and patrolling the teahouse and market. He signed a couple of patrol books and came back to the station; this went on. No one spoke to him.

He was passing the bean field on his way home when he came across an old woman. She had flattened herself on the ground as soon as she'd seen him, but she hadn't been able to conceal herself completely in the shallow field. Initially he'd intended to keep walking, thinking she was merely weeding, but something stopped him. Assuming he was gone, the old woman got up and resumed digging with a hoe. There were several small holes along the path behind her. They were full of beans; she'd probably picked them from the field. There were beans even in the folds of her dirty clothes. She was dressed in a thin, traditional dress not suitable for the weather, and wore a half-slip over the skirt. She also had on a men's fur vest. She dug quickly. She slipped some beans in the hole, as well as in her mouth. She had trouble chewing with her two remaining teeth. Half of the beans spilled onto her skirt.

"Halmoni, what are you doing?"

"What does it look like? I'm burying my gold." Sounds escaped through her gummy mouth.

Her breath reeked. She grabbed a fistful of beans, along with some of the half-chewed ones that had fallen out of her mouth, and put them in the hole, covering them up with dirt. Her eyes, crusted with sleep and boils, met his, and glinted suddenly. There was a flash and something struck his forehead. He felt a sticky warmth trickle down his face.

The old woman was already past the field, fleeing toward the mountain. In the furrow among the scattered beans shone the hoe she'd hit him with. As he stood up, pressing his palm to the wound, he stumbled and tripped into one of the holes.

•

The path was always foggy. The fog rolled in regardless of the season or time of day. He kept losing his sense of direction. There were no signs or buildings that could serve as markers. Everything looked the same. He groped along toward the station in the thick fog. He couldn't even see his feet, but he heard the gravel crunch under his feet. When he heard light footsteps over his own, he stopped. Steps approached, and then a form materialized right before him. It was a young woman, barely twenty years old. Her eyes widened in surprise. He hadn't come across a young woman in the village until now, other than the ones who worked at the teahouse. Her hair looked damp, as if she'd been walking in the fog for a long time.

He meant to step out of the way, but got in her way instead. In Seoul, he'd frequently bumped into people, because he'd reacted too quickly for his own good and they'd ended up misreading his movements. Although he possessed outstanding marksmanship and an unusually quick reaction time—all requirements to be a police officer—these turned out to be disadvantages in this case.

It was best to stand still. She nodded at him and passed by. Quickly, the fog wiped away every trace of the girl, as if he'd dreamed her up.

He couldn't just wait for the fog to clear. He was forced to rely on the gravel. All he had to do was make sure he stayed on the gravel, since the path led to the station.

By the time he arrived at the station to begin his shift, he was wet, as if he'd been caught in a drizzle. The station was empty, save for a few reservists guarding the armory. The door to the night room was in the back. Though its small window looked out to the front of the station, the door opened onto an empty field. A pair of shoes—Officer Lim's, he was guessing—lay outside the door. He knocked. "All right," Lim said from inside a moment later. "Why don't you go wait in the station?"

He went into the field, sat down, and took out a cigarette. He was about to light it when the night-room door opened a crack. A hand reached out to set a pair of women's shoes by the door, followed by a pair of legs that fumbled for the shoes. The woman then said something into the room, causing Lim to laugh. After making sure no one was around, she got to her feet. Her eyes were bloodshot and her lipstick was smeared as though it had been rubbed out with an eraser. The night room wasn't big enough for two adults to lie next to each other. Her footsteps faded into the fog. She disappeared in the direction of Cheongbong village. He could tell, even though the fog was thick. The door opened once more and this time, Lim put on his shoes. He stretched lazily. To the man, Lim was like the fog—a natural part of the town.

As the fog cleared and the day went on, the scene outside the station window came to life. He could now see the post office, and even all the way to the market entrance. The girls returned to the teahouse on their scooters and once again hid themselves inside.

When Lim came back to the station around 6 P.M. to relieve him, the man led him to the bar across from the station. Scattered around the bar were several stainless steel tables with little fire pits in the center. The man ordered a green onion pancake and a bottle of soju. Only he drank, since Lim had to be on duty soon. Lim patted him on the shoulder, as if he understood all too well.

"I know it can get lonesome being stuck in a place like this. It must be completely different from what you're used to. You're too good to waste away here."

The soju disappeared quickly. He tipped backward on his stool. The other customers stared at him. He struggled to get up, but couldn't. "Damn it, what's wrong with this soju?" he slurred. "Tastes like shit."

The customers whispered, leaning toward one another. *Should the police be drinking like that? Who knows? But why did he even come here in the first place? Isn't it obvious? This was the only post he could get.*

"I had no idea you were having such a hard time," Lim said, pouring him some more soju. "Other people might not understand, but I do."

He couldn't remember how he managed to get home. At the entrance of Cheongbong, he vomited up everything he'd eaten.

It seemed that the commotion he'd caused at the bar had already spread to the village women. Although they'd never smiled at him or even spoken to him, they had at least acknowledged him. But now the women who had been joking and laughing while weeding suddenly fell silent and turned their backs on him. He walked past them as he headed to the police station. The next day, he discovered maggots squirming in the pile of vomit that he assumed was his.

·

It was after lunchtime, so everyone was working out in the fields and all the houses were empty. If she hadn't been humming, he would have walked past the neighbor's house without a second glance, like all the other times before. He was exhausted from the night shift. Through the wide-open front gate, he saw a tap and rusted pump in one corner of the yard. A young woman squatted beside it, washing her hair. It seemed the soap wasn't rinsing out easily. Because of the tangles in her hair, her comb got caught midway. She swore all of a sudden. She'd rolled up her skirt at the hem, knotting it above her knees so that it wouldn't get wet. The pale legs peeking out from beneath her skirt didn't look like the legs of a farm girl. She filled the basin with clean water, keeping her eyes tightly shut to prevent soap from getting in them. He stood rooted to the spot, planning to leave before she opened her eyes, but he kept delaying. She grasped her hair in both hands and wrung out the water. She then took down one of the towels from the clothesline and wrapped it around her head like a turban. He took in her narrow chin. She slowly opened her eyes.

She walked toward the narrow living room porch, feet squishing in her wet rubber flats. All of a sudden, she looked back and glared out at the gate. Their eyes met. Hers widened in shock. It was the same girl he had met in the fog.

He fled. Rubber shoes squeaked behind him and the gate slammed shut. Still, he kept running. His heart didn't stop racing even after he'd shut himself in his room. He liked feeling his heart race.

•

Whenever he'd search for a target among the pine trees, he broke out into a sweat. For the first time in ten years, the hunting ban had been lifted. The police chief took down the rifle he'd laid to rest a decade ago and cleaned it. He called the man over. "I heard you're a dead shot," he said, handing him a rifle.

The chief liked to shoot birds, but the man preferred to keep his senses alert and sneak through the woods looking for game. Silent hunting, they called it. A rabbit jumped out from behind a bush. He took a shot, but the bullet hit the base of a pine instead. He reloaded the double-barrel gun. Luckily, he was standing in a headwind; the rabbit wouldn't be able to pick up his scent. He waited for it to come out from the bush again. It finally appeared in his range. He counted to a hundred in his head. *Run, Rabbit. I'll give you to a hundred. After that, I won't go so easy on you.* It scampered off into the woods. His eyes tracked the rustling noise. It couldn't be too far. He held his breath and took aim. Right then, a gunshot rang out that shook the forest, and the rabbit hid somewhere else.

The cock pheasant that the chief hit fell out of the sky, crashing down into the branches. But the rabbit wasn't the only thing spooked by the gunshot. A woman's head popped up from a low hill covered with bushes. Several buttons on her blouse were undone, her bra dangling loosely beneath it. Dried grass clung to her tangled hair, which was flattened to the back of her head. A man's hand sprung out of the bushes and pulled her back down. Just by a single glance, he could tell it was the same woman, who had come out of the night room and walked into the fog with short, mincing steps. He heard the police chief draw near, running toward the fallen bird. His flushed round face appeared between the pines. He poked the pheasant with the muzzle of his gun.

"You enjoy the meat, since I enjoyed the hunt."

The man shoved the dead pheasant in the gunnysack he'd brought along. He slung it over his shoulder and trudged toward his lodgings. When he was almost there, the girl from the other day stepped out through her front door. Her socks, which were folded down at the ankles, were blinding white. He looked at her in greeting.

"I heard shots coming from the woods. Was it you?" She glanced at the sack he was carrying. "What did you catch?"

Her eyes brimmed with curiosity. He put the sack on the ground and untied the rope. She looked inside.

"Poor thing! So you're a crack shot?"

"Nah, I was aiming for a rabbit, but it got away."

"Why were you spying on me the other day?" she said, as she peered into the bag. "Is a police officer supposed to do that?"

She was so close he could hear her breathing. He had no time to respond. She turned on her heels and brushed past him.

•

There was a long line of trucks loaded with goods. These trucks, which occupied every corner of the market, were instantly transformed into shops when their tailgates were opened. When it started to grow dark that evening, a driver came running into the police station. The man followed him to the market and found the old woman lying on the ground right in front of the truck's front tires. Based on the clothing that littered the ground, it seemed she had caused quite a commotion already.

"It's no big deal about the clothes, but how am I supposed to go home if she doesn't get out from under there . . ."

The old woman gave off a piercing stench. He crept up to her. "Halmoni, why are you lying here? What happened to all your gold?"

Her eyes snapped open. He pointed at the scar on his forehead to remind her who he was.

"You're the one who stole my gold! You saw where I buried it, didn't you!"

She jumped to her feet and lashed out at his face, catching him off guard. His head snapped to the left, and his hat was knocked to the ground. She seized him by the collar. He could hardly breathe. Where did this old hag, withered like some ancient tree, get that awesome strength? She wouldn't let go, shrieking at those passing by. She lost a tooth in the racket, leaving her with only one bottom tooth. Her foul breath hit him in the face.

"This bastard took all my gold! Call the police, call the police!"

"Old woman, I *am* the police."

It was only then that she noticed his uniform. Her grip loosened. A crowd had gathered around them, but no one tried to help. He heard a whisper: *She might be crazy, but she wouldn't accuse just anyone, right?* He gazed at the faces around him. Not a single person was on his side.

The truck driver pulled the old woman off him. She swung her arms wildly, clawing the truck driver's cheek. Blood began to seep from the wound. In a panic, she picked up her rubber shoes and scampered away. One by one, the onlookers began to leave.

"Three years I've been coming here, but I just can't figure these people out. You noticed there aren't any dogs around here? Know why? 'Cause you don't need them, that's why. This whole goddamned place turns into one big, nasty dog when a new person shows up. There was a man from Seoul who moved here to start farming. He couldn't make it and eventually had to leave."

The man brushed the dirt off his uniform and picked up his hat. He bent the brim and set it back on his head. He made eye contact with the girl, who had been peering at hairpins on display. She picked up a few and put them back, as though they weren't to her liking. Right then, the woman trying on a pin next to her looked up. It was the woman he'd seen coming out of the night room, the same one he'd seen in the bushes when he'd gone hunting. She followed the girl's gaze and saw him. The two women exchanged glances and whispered to each other. The woman moved onto another display case and the girl hurried into the post office. He realized then the girl must work there.

•

The old woman's body was found in the bean field. The cause of death was a gunshot wound in her leg. A farmer who had gone out to the field in the early hours had discovered blood dotting the gravel, ending at the woman's corpse. The furrow was dark with her blood. Although Ungok-ri wasn't known as a hunting site, hunters did sometimes come by. For the past few days, the fog had been heavy. The old woman often wandered through the woods, and hunters could have mistaken her for an animal. She'd been alive until she came to the furrow. If she'd been discovered earlier, she could have been saved.

Something needed to be done about the body; they couldn't simply wait for her son to arrive from Seoul. The people from the neighborhood began the funeral preparations. Together with Officer Lim, the man paid a condolence visit. He noticed that the people's stares weren't so friendly. They sat at a table in a corner of the yard.

"They think maybe you shot the old woman. No one does any hunting round here except you and the chief. Plus, there was the incident at the market the other day. This is a small town, and news travels fast. There's nothing you can do once you get on their bad side. Why didn't you try to get to know them a little?"

Lim poured him drink after drink, and he gulped down several shots in a row. Because he drank so quickly on an empty stomach, he was drunk in no time. "I don't get it—I can't seem to handle the liquor here," he muttered.

But Lim didn't hear what he said. He was too busy swatting at the flies that buzzed around his face.

•

The fog had settled heavily over the whole neighborhood. He slipped on the gravel and fell down several times. When he pulled himself together at last, he found himself standing in front of the house where the girl lived. He tried the front gate; it wasn't locked. The rubber flats she'd been wearing sat on the stone step outside a bedroom door. Because there was only one pair of shoes, he was certain she didn't share the room with anyone else.

The bedroom door was also unlocked. His courage bolstered by alcohol, he crept inside, removing his shoes and putting one in each coat pocket. He heard her steady breathing, and glimpsed even teeth gleaming between parted lips. He quieted his breathing and peered into her face, but thick fog covered the moon, and he couldn't make out her features. He moved his fingers over her face and found her mouth. He'd planned to leave after listening to the sound of her breathing. He was about to put his ear next to her lips when she reached up and dug her fingers in his hair. He was overcome with sleepiness. She pulled his face toward hers, and her hot, moist tongue thrust past his chapped lips.

•

It was his landlord who woke him up. His wife was probably out in the fields already. The man had come back from the girl's room at dawn, when the fog hadn't yet cleared. He sluggishly put on his clothes. The landlord told him to come to the house next door and left. The man's head ached from the drinking. But the memory of what had happened the night before was vivid.

Many elders from the neighborhood sat smoking in the main room. The air was thick with smoke. He kneeled before them. The girl's father, with his back turned, sucked on his cigarette impatiently. The man's landlord, who was the girl's uncle, spoke quietly.

"This is a very small town. How could you, to a girl who isn't even married—" He pursed his lips together, as if he found it shameful to even speak of the matter.

The elders glared at the man. When a rabbit gets cornered in a dead-end, it somehow senses its predicament and freezes.

"I guess it's too late now, since what's done is done," said a man he'd sometimes seen working in the field. "We have to take care of this before word gets out. I'm sure you had some kind of plan when you snuck into her room."

Right then, he heard a woman burst into sobs in the adjoining room. He figured that the village women had gathered there.

"Stop that!" shrieked an older woman's voice. "You did nothing to deserve any sympathy. There's not enough men around that you'd go and be intimate with someone you barely know? What are you going to do now? How's your father going to show his face around here?"

Amid the shrill cries, the man heard someone console the weeping girl. "Sister, don't cry. Everything will be all right."

He recognized that voice right away. It was the girl from the post office. In that instant, he realized something was very wrong. The girl from the post office should have been the one who was crying. She was the one he'd spent the night with.

He'd never heard the voice of the weeping girl before. His land-lord stepped into the adjacent room and dragged her out. The girl who stood before him now was the one who had snuck out of the night room with bloodshot eyes and fled into the fog. The one whose head had poked out from the bushes at the sound of the gunshot. He choked back the scream that threatened to escape from his throat.

•

Officer Lim tugged on his trousers lazily. The night room was too small for two people to sit and talk. The man told Lim to come to the woods, where they had heard the gunshot. Lim nodded. Lim's eyes were red, as though he'd been drinking on duty. He came sauntering up to the pine grove, his hands in his pockets. He snickered, flashing his yellow, nicotine-stained teeth.

"I knew you were different, but I never guessed you'd act this fast."

"Something's not right. You know that."

Instead of answering, Lim put a cigarette in his mouth.

"I saw her come out of the night room," the man said anxiously. "Are you still going to pretend you don't know what I'm talking about?"

"Oh, I didn't know you saw that."

"After seeing her with you, how could I sleep with her? I never touched her!"

"Come on, you expect me to believe that? Everyone will know by tomorrow. I warned you, didn't I? I told you how small this place is."

"You honestly think I'd make a move for your woman?"

Lim dropped the cigarette butt and ground it out with his shoe. "Who says she's mine? She was no virgin, that's for sure. I bet even her parents know. I couldn't care less what she did while she lived in the big city. The only reason word hasn't gotten out is because of this place. It'd be a shame if a young woman with a bright future couldn't blossom because of a few rumors . . . I had a few drinks with Mr. Kim from the electronics shop last night, but damn, this hangover isn't going away. I was wondering where she was last night. Turns out, she was with you."

Lim started down the mountain, but came back. "Hey, it's not such a bad deal," he whispered, as if letting him in on a secret. "She's a good girl, and she isn't bad-looking. But you should've been more careful. You want to know the difference between us? You got me, but the folks here got you. Your mistake was going to her house. You really shouldn't have gone there."

•

He waited outside the post office until she got off work. He grabbed hold of her wrist and dragged her into the police station. She tried to shake him off, but followed without a word. He ran his fingertip over her face. He was sure she'd been the one in the room that night.

"You think I'm stupid? It was you last night! It was you in the room! So what the hell is going on? What are you guys trying to pull? Tell me right now!"

The girl raised her face and glared at him. "What kind of girl do you take me for? You think I'd sleep around? I wasn't even here yesterday. I had to go to town and I missed the last bus so I ended up spending the night at my friend's house."

His fingers had left a red mark around her wrist. Massaging it, she looked around the station.

He sank into a chair. "It'd be different if it had been you," he mumbled. "I would have stayed here for you."

She whipped around and gazed down at him. "Thanks, but no thanks. I hate this stinking place. You expect me to grow old, stamping mail? No way. I'm moving to Seoul soon."

"You can tell me. It was you, right? It was you last night, wasn't it?"

She gazed out the window, her arms crossed. "The only reason I'm talking to you right now is because of my sister. Do I have to spell it out for you? You were with my sister last night. So please stop harassing me."

When he came home from work, his room was bare. The landlord's wife, who was carrying out the pigs' fodder from the kitchen, looked at him and said casually, "They came this morning to take your things next door."

All his things were in the room he'd barged into that night. The woman, who had been ironing his uniform, got to her feet and greeted him.

•

He now came home drunk every night. Whenever the post-office girl saw him, she greeted him with a smile, calling him *hyeongbu*—brother-in-law. The people whispered when they saw him going to and from the police station. *The law, my ass. They're all corrupt. Just look at him. He shacks up with her, but doesn't even have the decency to marry her. And he shows his face around here like nothing's wrong.*

He had changed. When he got drunk now, he picked up a club and smashed the furniture. The mirror in their room broke in weblike cracks. He avoided looking directly at her.

He was supposed to be on night duty that night. He forced himself to nap, even though sleep didn't come. She sat near him mending clothes. He had his eyes closed, but he could sense she was walking on tiptoe so as to not disturb him. She appeared demure, a completely different girl from the one who'd snuck out of the night duty room that foggy morning, or the one who'd been hiding in the bushes. He sometimes felt her breath graze his nose and cheeks, as if she'd crept close to peer at his face. He hated everything about her; he couldn't even stand the sound of her breathing.

Right then, a fly flew in. It landed on the back of her hand as she was sewing. She shook it off, but it whirled once around the room and settled on the wall. She crept on her knees and swatted at it. But it was no use. This time, it settled on the man's chest. Her hand came down on him with a thump. At that instant, he heard something shatter inside him. What broke the ice in the end wasn't a pick, but a needle.

He bolted to his feet and punched her square in the face. Blood gushed from her nose, covering her mouth and chin. The commotion caused her parents and sister to come running from the main room.

"It wasn't enough for you to get kicked out of Seoul and take advantage of a perfectly good girl—you had to start beating her?" cried the mother. She bared her teeth and leapt at him.

He dodged out of the way, and the mother crashed into the wall behind him. In the broken mirror, he saw a complete stranger looking back at him. The shattered glass looked like a giant fly's eye, made up of countless lenses.

"It's clear he doesn't care what anyone says!" the post-office girl said. "What kind of man refuses to do what's right and continues to live in sin?"

He struck her across the mouth, stopping her tirade.

He ran out of the house and headed for the bar across the police station, where he downed two bottles of soju. Even after drinking the local soju for several months, he still wasn't used to the taste. The bar owner set a green-onion pancake in front of him and asked when the wedding was going to be. A few customers watched him as if waiting for an answer. They were all in on it. Perhaps they had all planned it from the very beginning.

The police station was empty. The entire village was at his mercy. He took down two M2 carbines. He loaded them with ammunition, slung one across his chest and held the other in a shooting position. Two reservists were joking around, standing guard in front of the armory. When he aimed the M2 at them, they laughed. "What are you doing? Don't fool around."

He fired. Luckily, they managed to move out of the way and the bullet hit the slate wall behind them. They faltered, took a few steps back, and fled.

He walked down the gravel path. The fog was starting to creep in. A light glimmered through the fog—the first house in the village. The hand grenades he had put in his pant pockets chafed his thighs each time he took a step. Every pocket was stuffed with the ammunition he had taken from the armory. He slipped, thrusting out his hand to steady himself. As the fog rolled in, the crunch of gravel under his feet and the bullets rattling in his pockets were the only things he could hear.

Night Poaching

The detective in charge of the investigation had turned over every last detail to me, so the town coming into view through the bus windshield didn't seem all that unfamiliar. According to him, wherever people lived was pretty much the same. But what struck me immediately were the specialty restaurants lining the small street outside the bus terminal, with enormous pressure cookers out front. If the hunting grounds were in operation, those pressure cookers spewed sticky steam all day long. The grounds were open this year. But it was past midnight, and the restaurants were dark.

"Turn left where the specialty restaurants come to an end. You'll see a mailbox right away. Then inquire at the rice shop across the street."

The detective's information tended to be accurate, and sure enough, I saw the mailbox as soon as I turned left at the end of the street with the specialty restaurants. Across the street, the rice shop was dark, but through the frosted glass I saw a gleam of light coming from the living quarters at the back. I could even hear the drone of the television.

A man looking as if he'd just crawled out of bed helped me find a truck that would take me to my final destination. There was no regular transportation between this place and where I was headed, which meant people had to rely on delivery trucks that weren't in use at the moment.

Since all the cab seats were already occupied by other passengers, I had to ride in the back of one such truck, but I was in no position to complain. "Forget about traveling comfortably in the passenger seat. Just count it a blessing if you don't have to squeeze into the cargo bed with a bunch of the village women," the detective had added.

When we left the town behind and had been speeding along for about twenty minutes, the occasional streetlight disappeared altogether. So did the glow of distant houses, glimmering in the darkness like clusters of stars. The asphalt road came to an end and was replaced by a narrow, unpaved road just wide enough for one car to pass. Mountain shadows pressed in from all sides.

"If you can't get yourself a jeep, forget about taking your own car," the detective had said, shaking his head. He'd made the mistake of driving his new sedan to the scene of the accident. "Trust me, it won't make things any easier. You'll just end up with a big hole in your gas tank."

Just as he'd warned, the truck bounced nearly half a foot off the gravel road. Even after the driver turned on his high beams, you could see only a meter or two ahead. Outside the cones of light was total darkness, and for someone like me, who was traveling this way for the first time, it was like stepping through a black curtain into an unknown world. The truck, carrying five people including the driver, raced through the woods for about an hour. Human beings are a strange bunch. They laid railroad tracks across Niagara Falls, or transported materials up a steep mountainside just to build a snack stand, or they built a village deep in the woods, like this, when there weren't any proper roads.

Although it was early November, the temperature in the mountains fell below zero at night. I had on the jacket I usually carried around in Seoul, but it didn't help. I had to clasp the side of the truck bed to keep from falling out, and my hand stuck to the metal like to ice. *Goddamn.* The previous detective, who had described every tedious detail, like the exact location of a tearoom, for example, had forgotten to mention the most important thing: the fickle mountain temperature. There'd been another thing; he'd also stayed quiet about his reasons for suddenly quitting a case he was so close to cracking.

Maybe it was because of the cold, but I had to take a piss. The truck's bouncing and rattling made it worse. In the end, I had to tap on the rear window. The driver stopped the truck, but didn't get out. I hopped out from the back and walked up to his side. He stuck his head out the half-open window and threw a nervous glance toward the woods. I heard a stream flowing somewhere in the darkness.

I was crossing the road to find some privacy behind a tree when the driver leaned out the window and shouted, "Where you going? Just do it there, right there!"

He was pointing to a spot right in front of the headlights. Among the passengers was a young woman. No matter how desperate the situation, I couldn't pull my pants down in front of her. Though I couldn't see inside because of the lights, it was the opposite case if you were looking out. I couldn't urinate on a lit-up stage. But the driver didn't give me a chance to protest.

"Don't you understand Korean? I told you not to go in the woods."

I didn't blame him for acting this way; it was understandable after an accident like that. These people were going to be afraid of the woods for a long time. I turned my back to the truck and urinated toward the middle of the road. The detective had said it was a peaceful village, not at all the kind of place where you'd expect an accident like that to happen. Still, something told me I shouldn't blindly trust everything he said.

When my tailbone was throbbing and the hand gripping the side panel had gone numb, the truck's headlights swept over the jangseung totem poles marking the village boundaries. It seemed we were finally at our destination. The driver, who had taken the detective to this village numerous times, dropped me off at the house of Mr. Kim, the head of the Kim clan, and sped off into the dark.

"It'd probably be best to stay with them. They're not so uptight because they're used to taking in lodgers from out of town. It's just him and his wife, and they'll stay out of your hair. He limps a bit. He's the cousin of the deceased—their mothers were sisters. Make sure you prepay, and slip them a few thousand won more than what they ask for. Might be a little late in the season, but if you're lucky, you'll get some pine-mushroom skewers for breakfast."

His words would have made anyone curious about this place.

Maybe it was because I'd called before leaving Seoul, but the front gate was halfway open and the light bulb in the yard was burning hot, as if it had been left on for a long time. The dog barked at my footsteps. A door opened and Mr. Kim stuck out his head.

Except for the size of the doors themselves, the layout of the house was similar to any house in the country. The furniture was an odd assortment of new and old, some from the time of the Saemaeul Movement when homes in rural communities had been revamped. The doors to the rooms were more like pet doors, barely big enough for a grown person to pass through.

"It's probably because of the cold. The bigger the door, the more it lets in the cold. Or maybe those rooms were used by women before and people wanted to prevent easy access inside? Anyhow, make sure you watch your head."

Despite the small door, the room was spacious. Near the corner where the floor wasn't heated, recently harvested rice in burlap sacks was stacked up all the way to the ceiling. A low desk was the only furniture in the room, and above that was a tiny window the size of a sheet of paper. The room smelled faintly of old grain. The woman brought me a freshly basted sleeping mat and blanket. The starched sheet chafed my skin.

The house of Park Gicheol, whom everyone had called The Deer, was located outside the village. On a mountain path where trucks and jeeps were useless, it was best to travel on foot. I backtracked the way I'd come the night before, and saw the totem poles once more. The colors were faded as if they'd been standing there for a long time, and the noses and eyes had become a pale clump.

Even the detective had trouble describing the exact location of Park Gicheol's house. All he'd said was to get Mr. Kim's help. Since there weren't any signposts, I had to simply eyeball the distance and fumble along. When I walked through a carpet of leaves, I left behind footprints filled with water. I climbed until I was out of breath, until the larch trees had disappeared and were replaced by pines. In the shadows of the trees, I became cold as my sweat dried. I continued between the pines on what looked like remnants of a path. Finally, the woods opened up and I saw a wide field. Park Gicheol's house was situated at the edge of the field a little ways up the hill. I was lucky it was winter. If it had been summer, his house would have been completely hidden by all the bushes and the deciduous trees. The long, narrow house seemed to be clinging to the ground.

It was early morning, but the house was empty. There were two small rooms and a large kitchen all on one side. It seemed an animal pen had once stood across from the blackened wood-burning stove where the lid of a cast iron pot hung, covered with a thick layer of dust. I pushed open one of the bedroom doors. In the middle of the room was a low aluminum table; on it was a porcelain bowl of water with grains of rice floating in it, along with a dish containing several pieces of pickled radish.

I went out through the kitchen to the back yard. An unpicked squash lay rotting in the soil. Dust covered the edge of the porch. Perhaps because the house sat a little up the hill, I could see past the yard, far into the distance. Two jeeps were driving into the village along the road I'd taken last night. Hunting season was in full swing. Hunters from all over the country will flock here, and shots will ring out non-stop until the season ends next February.

"Park Gicheol's elderly mother picks pine mushrooms. Folks from the village collect a nice profit from picking them in the fall. She usually eats lunch up in the woods, a rice ball seasoned with some salt and pepper, and then she makes her way back down in the evening."

But it was November and the season for picking pine mushrooms was over, so where was she? Even if there were any mushrooms left in the woods, they would have frozen by now, since the temperature had dropped below zero for the past several days. And frozen mushrooms weren't worth much. But the villagers wouldn't have missed any, would they?

A frame hung between the door and the eaves. It wasn't difficult to find the man I assumed was Park Gicheol. True to his nickname, his large, droopy eyes, not to mention his long neck and pointed chin, resembled those of a deer.

But there was another reason Park was called The Deer. No one in the village knew the woods as well as he had. He'd even moved like one, leaping through the woods and valleys with his strong, nimble legs. The detective shared some of the stories he'd heard from the villagers. "A hunter saw Park in front of a shop in town. He said the shadow cast on the wall behind Park wasn't that of a human! What else could this mean except that Park is more deer than human?" The detective knew how to mix just the right amount of hyperbole with facts; he had a certain flair for storytelling.

I wandered around the house, killing time. I waited for more than an hour, but Park's mother didn't come. Under the narrow porch I saw a pair of rubber boots I assumed had belonged to Park. The black boots were caked with mud up to the ankles. I hadn't seen a single spot on my way over here where you would get that much mud on your shoes. Judging by the boot size, he seemed to have been rather small.

Last month around mid-October, Park Gicheol was discovered by a villager who had gone into the woods to pick pine mushrooms. He'd already stopped breathing by that point. His body was covered in dew, and his pants were soaked with blood from a wound in his right thigh. Flies, their wings still wet with dew, swarmed over his body. The cause of death had been ruled as blood loss due to a hunting accident. Since the accident had occurred before the start of the hunting season, it meant the bullet that had killed Park had been fired from an unregistered firearm. It was, no doubt, the work of a poacher.

Poachers had been causing a lot of trouble. Usually in groups of three, they prowled the deserted trails in jeeps. While the driver circled the base of the mountain, the second person shone a powerful searchlight into the woods, and if an animal was spotted, the third person fired.

Those overhunted creatures were then sold off to specialty restaurants. Perhaps Park Gicheol, bounding through the woods in the dark, had looked like a deer. Hunting accidents like this happened sometimes. Though he had been shot in his right leg, he should have been able to make it home on his one good leg. So why, then, had he been discovered at the edge of the hunting grounds, in the opposite direction of his house? Park, who knew the entire area like the back of his hand, would never get lost, even in the dark. Then was it a suicide disguised as an accident? Park had left his mother, his only beneficiary, with a tidy sum when he died.

I didn't head down to the village. Instead, I walked through the woods. The deer farm where Park had worked wasn't very far from his house. Two months before his death, the farm had burned to the ground when an electrical short circuit sparked a flame in the middle of the night. Park saw the fire and rushed to the farm, but all the deer pens were already engulfed in flames. The previous detective seemed to have believed that there was a connection between Park's death and the fire. The detective had met Ahn Seongman, the owner of the deer farm, numerous times. Ahn lived in town. He may have been the owner, but all he'd done was drop by the farm occasionally. It was Park who'd managed everything.

The yard was scorched in places. When Park had opened the gate, flaming deer had dashed around the yard, spreading the fire. Now, the charred wreckage of the pens were all that remained of the farm.

After waiting nearly an hour for a car to drive by on its way into town, I was finally able to hitch a ride with a truck. Unlike the previous night, I saw many jeeps entering the village from all parts of town, headed for the hunting grounds. The truck driver was another Kim, and owned a corner store back in the village. He sometimes took supplies into town. He didn't open his mouth unless he was asked a question. We ran across many jeeps heading in the opposite direction on the narrow road. Each time, the truck driver backed up and moved out of the way. Besides the fact that both men were quiet and reserved, Mr. Kim, the head of the Kim clan, and Kim, the truck driver, had something else in common. Even the young truck driver who'd first driven me to the village had been the same. They all had an unhurried way about them, with sharp jawlines and large, serene mouths, big eyes that drooped at the corners. How could I put it? They resembled gentle herbivores, animals that would chew cud, moving their jaws slowly.

Unlike the village, the town was bustling. Elementary school students were heading home after school, illegally parked jeeps were everywhere, their drivers honking their horns, and the pressure cookers set out in front of specialty restaurants hissed their sticky steam. Music blasted from every store. In the city it would have sounded like white noise, but here, the commotion added to the gaiety. I didn't need to search the whole town to find Ahn Seongman. According to the detective's notes, Ahn would be at Mother Earth Tearoom at this hour.

Ahn had smooth skin for someone his age. In fact, he'd make the perfect Santa Claus, if he'd had a white beard and a red costume. But unlike Santa, his eyes were bloodshot and veiled. Though he had lost all his deer, the girls at the tearoom still referred to him as the owner of the farm. He glanced up at my face and spoke informally right away, saying I was young enough to be his son. Even so, he was far from grandfatherly to the girls at the tearoom, who were young enough to be his grandchildren. A girl who'd been bantering with him moved to another table to give us some privacy. Though she was wearing false lashes and heavy makeup, she looked barely twenty. Ahn smacked his lips.

"How many times do I have to say the same thing? If I'd had all that time, I would have found the perpetrator by now."

"This is all so that we can find the shooter. Help us out just one more time, won't you, boss?"

People are the same. If you humble yourself, they relent. The thing is, we couldn't care less who the perpetrator was. That was another department's responsibility. All I had to do was determine the manner of death, if it was a suicide, homicide, or accident.

"What does a fire on a deer farm have to do with a shooting accident?" Ahn said, picking up his cup and sipping his now-cold tea.

Though I could read greed in his eyes, he was still choosing to adopt the role of Santa Claus. He had picked up the teacup to avoid my eyes. At times like this, I just had to be straightforward.

"I believe you were raising deer not for their antlers, but for a different reason."

Ahn called over a girl and ordered another cup of tea. He thrust his flushed face up to mine. I caught a whiff of stale breath and medicinal herbs. He admonished me, as he would a son.

"Look here, poachers have killed off nearly all the wild boars and rabbits out there. Have you even gone into the woods? You got to be careful because of all the illegal traps they've set up. You know Mr. Kim, don't you? He stepped on one, too. And those poachers don't even collect the animals they've trapped. The woods are full of carcasses. Game reserves raise animals like pheasants and release them during hunting season. Even here, they just released two thousand pheasants. So what's the big deal? I'm releasing deer already paid for so that people can hunt them. I'm not breaking any laws. Plus, this offsets overhunting by half."

Ahn let slip more information than he realized. He rinsed his mouth with the tea the girl brought and smacked his lips again. I'd seen the wound on Kim's leg. Though it had since healed, the scar was distinct enough to count the spikes from the trap. Ahn had revealed Park Gicheol hadn't only been in charge of looking after the deer. During hunting season, he would have accompanied the hunters. After all, no one knew the area better than him. Plus, Park was nimble. Someone like Mr. Kim with his limp wouldn't have been able to do what Park had. The hunters may have been the ones to give Park his nickname, not the villagers.

"By the way, do you happen to know a Kim Jinseong?" I blurted.

I'd only remembered the name as I was walking out. It had been included in the information the detective had transferred over to me, and for some reason, it occurred to me just then that Ahn might know who he was. Though he was sitting with his back to the entrance, I saw his shoulders go stiff.

"Hmm, doesn't ring a bell," he said.

The girl, who had been sitting next to Ahn with her legs crossed, cut in. "Boss, maybe he means Mr. Kim from Seoul?"

"W-w-well, maybe," Ahn stammered. "How can anyone keep track of so many Kims?"

The name Kim Jinseong had been written at the very end of the detective's report. But unlike the other names, there was no other information about him. And then just as he was starting to investigate Kim Jinseong, he'd resigned from the case.

Since I was in town, I went into a store and bought a padded parka. I even bought a pair of hiking boots. At the stationery store, I picked up some instant heat packs and a flashlight. If I wanted to move ahead with the investigation, I had to go in the woods in the middle of the night, just as Park had. What exactly happened there at night?

It was easy to find my way back into the village. I just hitched a ride with one of the jeeps heading into the hunting grounds. My companions were two middle-aged men and a third man probably twenty years younger.

"So how's it looking out there?" asked the young man, who was driving. He seemed to have mistaken me for a local. "Lots of game around? It's our first time here."

"They just released two thousand pheasants into the woods." I simply repeated what I'd gotten from Ahn Seongman.

"Since they have wings, you can't guarantee they'll all stay in the woods," said one of the middle-aged men in the back, who'd been stroking the stock of his double shotgun. "I much prefer land animals. Like deer and wild boar."

The other middle-aged man snorted. "Hey, you don't know what you're talking about. Double shotguns are the best for hunting pheasants. Don't take a bad shot at the wrong animal and make it suffer for nothing. Forget everything and just set your sights on a pheasant."

The two men snickered like boys and jostled each other. Park Gicheol had roamed the woods all night, a gunshot wound to the thigh. It seemed Ahn had made quite a profit off his farm until now, since his seemed to be the only one near the hunting grounds. Park had accompanied the hunters. If a deer got shot and disappeared into the woods, he would have tracked its prints to find it. Or if a hound found it instead, maybe Park would have slung the deer over his shoulders and taken it back to the hunters. He may have even skinned the deer himself, and connected the hunters to the restaurants in town that would cook the venison. But two months before Park's death, the deer farm had gone up in flames. The hunters coming to hunt this season would have to be satisfied with pheasants and ducks, and possibly wild boar, if they're lucky.

Back at Park's house, his elderly mother barely managed to sit up and drink the water by her bed.

"Since he died, I've been going into the woods every day. I think it's going to rain. My whole body's sore . . . The gods must be crazy. They leave the person who's supposed to go and take the one who's supposed to stay."

It was difficult to understand her. Her words tumbled past her few remaining teeth. It seemed she'd run out of tears to shed. Time had sucked all the moisture from her body and left her with wrinkles.

"I've combed through every corner of the woods, but I can't find it. There's a pine mushroom patch only he knew about. When the mushrooms were in season, he'd take me there and we'd bring them back by the bagful. I keep thinking about that spot. Just one more time, I want to see it before I die. I know these woods pretty well myself, but I can't find it . . . Now he's gone, and somewhere out there, there's a place filled with pine mushrooms."

Her cloudy eyes skimmed the yard, as if she were seeing the mushrooms. The fireplace was damp, as though it hadn't been lit for a long time. As I started up the fire, smoke filled the kitchen. I slipped my hand under the mat where she lay and felt the floor starting to grow warm.

"Do you know a Kim Jinseong by any chance? Have you heard of him?" Weakly, she shook her small head. ". . . I didn't think he would die. I should have put a stop to it when he started bounding through the woods like a deer. Now he's died like one, too."

I was left with no choice now but to start where the other detective had left off. Who was this Kim Jinseong?

I arrived at Mr. Kim's house to find the yard filled with people. They were from various parts of the village, all members of the Kim clan. In other words, they were also related to Park. They asked how big of a settlement Park's mother was going to receive. They also wanted to know who would be next in line if, for some reason, she was unable to receive it. The other detective had mentioned experiencing something similar, and that it had made him think again about human nature. Maybe it was a good thing he had quit the investigation. On the other hand, there's a category of people who remain unfazed by these types of situations, not because they've grown numb, but because they tend to be more objective. And those kinds of people respond this way: "Please wait until the investigation is complete."

The real ugliness will begin after Park's elderly mother gets the insurance money. I pushed my way through the crowd and climbed onto the stoop. It wasn't easy to remove my boots. While in the middle of untying my laces, I happened to look down and see the faces in the yard. With a start, I realized they resembled a herd of deer. As soon as I saw their fearful gazes, full of suspicion, I swallowed the question I'd been about to ask. Just as Ahn Seongman hadn't, I knew they wouldn't tell me about Kim Jinseong. Though I didn't know who Kim Jinseong was, I could tell they were all afraid of him.

.

I sat on the bench in front of the pharmacy, waiting for the girl from Mother Earth Tearoom to come back from her delivery. Buses constantly pulled into the terminal and left. Even more jeeps had taken over the sides of the road than when I had come to town several days earlier. I called to the girl as she pulled up on her scooter. She was wearing long boots over a short skirt.

"What brings you back here?" she asked, recognizing me right away.

Though she wasn't even chewing gum, it sounded as if she was.

"You know Kim Jinseong well, don't you?"

"You expect me to share that kind of information for free?"

Each time she blinked, her false lashes folded and opened like a fan.

"You know what? I like you, so I'll tell you, but I don't actually know him that well. All I know is that he lives in Seoul and owns a small business. He's got all kinds of connections, though. Who cares if none of that's true? The important thing is, he's generous to everyone here."

Opening day of the season was November 1. The hunting areas rotated every year, but according to the girl, Kim Jinseong came to this place even when the grounds weren't open. Why would he come here in the off-season, when hunting was illegal? The girl grinned. Each time she grinned, a dimple formed in her left cheek.

"Are you asking because you really don't know, or because you're naïve? They came here last year around this time. Closed season?

Who actually follows those rules? You think I actually have a motor-cycle license to drive this scooter? Every time they come here, they drop a lot of dough, so people just keep their mouths shut and pretend not to notice anything."

Young or old, it didn't matter—everyone was always trying to teach me something. Her cell phone rang, and she answered it.

"I gotta go. I'm behind on my deliveries. They're all Seoul cus-tomers. Can you believe all the motels and hotels around here are full? Stop by the tearoom later. Don't just order a coffee and take off, okay?"

Her scooter puttered across the road. A jeep trailed her from behind and honked its horn, pulling up next to her. She leaned in close to the open window on the passenger side and exchanged a few words with the driver. Shortly after, the jeep pulled into the left-turn lane to wait for the signal. The girl looked back at me and pointed toward the jeep. It wasn't hard to read what she mouthed: *Kim Jinseong.*

Kim Jinseong's party, which consisted of three jeeps, went in and out of the woods ceaselessly. He looked different from the other hunt-ers. Though in his late-forties, he was fit and lean. He'd registered at the local police station as soon as he arrived, and was also using registered firearms. His was a pump shotgun. The other members in his group used double-barreled shotguns, either the side-by-side or the over-under. Even with a more classic gun, where he had to pump the gun to reload after each shot, he easily caught five pheasants, which was the daily catch limit. As per the law, he stopped hunting at sunset, and stored his guns at the police station. He abided by every law. He seemed to be doing nothing wrong.

I put on a sweater underneath my parka and slipped out of my room for a quick stroll. I had intended to head back before the night grew deeper, but I changed my mind midway. After all, I had my flashlight. A large disk of light lit the darkness ahead. It was slow-going, since I could only see what was directly ahead of me. I passed the totem poles and walked up the mountain path that led to Park's house. Though I had traveled this path many times now, the trees looked bizarre and even grotesque in the dark. I walked quickly. I started to sweat.

It seemed Park's mother was still awake. Light spilled from her window. She'll receive the insurance money soon, and she will see a fortune she has never known. Her peaceful life will come to an end. The fog surged in from the edge of the hunting grounds, across the river and past the field of reeds.

When I was between Park's house and the deer farm, it started to rain. I needed to get back to Mr. Kim's house before the rain got worse. The wet leaves became as slippery as ice. After I slipped and fell twice, I took my hand out of my pocket. In the beam of my flashlight, the rain pierced the forest like silver arrows. The woods started to grow pungent.

It was when I'd finally reached the road leading to the hunting grounds: the headlights of a jeep flashed through the trees. Gravel popped out under its tires. Its headlights swept across the woods, exposing more than what daylight revealed. The rain was coming down hard. Gun shots rang out.

On this night, another kind of hunt was underway. Even from where I stood, I could see the jeep lights. I turned off my flashlight, ducked, and made for the lights. The rain streamed into my eyes, blurring my vision. I moved quietly under tall trees. Another shot rang out. This time, it came from a different direction. The rain covered the echo of the shots, but I could tell they weren't using pump or double-barreled shotguns. It occurred to me that if I went down to the road, I could very well get shot. I had no choice but to walk through the woods toward Mr. Kim's house. I just wanted to get back to my warm room.

Two jeeps were stopped on a narrow, deserted trail. The interior lights were on, but I couldn't see inside because the windows were fogged up. The door of one of the cars flew open and a girl in high heels and an ankle-length parka scrambled out and made a run for the woods; she didn't get far. She slipped and fell backward. Even in the dim taillights, I could tell who she was. Though her eye makeup had smeared down her cheeks, it was the girl from Mother Earth Tearoom. Someone inside the car swiped at the fogged-up window. Through the small opening that formed, a face appeared. It was Kim Jinseong.

He climbed out of the jeep, zipping himself up, and then with a shotgun slung over his shoulder, he went after the girl. Judging from the way he staggered, he was very drunk. Even the girl, who'd fallen on her rear-end and was now backing away, was just as drunk. He aimed the shotgun at her face. "Bang!" he cried.

The door of the second jeep opened and a middle-aged man snickered at them. He was drunk, too. The girl meekly climbed back into Kim Jinseong's jeep. She was like a bird caught in a snare. All of a sudden, the headlights of the jeep flashed on and off. I blocked the blinding light with my hand and quickly ducked. Kim Jinseong, who had been climbing into his jeep, turned and looked in my direction. He yelled to the other jeep, "Hurry! The searchlight!"

"You crazy? What if we get caught?"

"Do what I say. I just saw a deer!"

"The Deer? What's the matter with you? He's dead. Are you that wasted?"

"No, a real deer! I just saw the scared-shitless eyes of a deer! I told you to turn on the searchlight!"

The drunk Kim Jinseong was reckless. Even before the searchlight came on, he fired a round in my direction. I hid in the ditch. The bullet tore through a branch right above me. Water seeped through my clothes and soaked my chest. The searchlight was blinding.

"Shit, I lost him! Lee, turn it that way! There!"

I army-crawled along the ditch. My face became covered with mud. I tasted mud. I couldn't move quickly. My body had grown sluggish since completing my army service eight years ago. I wanted to shout for help, but I knew no one would hear me. The houses were too far away. I recalled the faces of all those who had gathered in Mr. Kim's yard. Their angular jaws, large eyes, and thick lips—spooked deer, every one of them. In moments of danger, deer duck their heads. All of a sudden, I thought of something. The man who'd first given me a ride to the village in his truck, he'd been terrified of the woods at night. His reaction had been almost exaggerated. Even Mr. Kim had told me many times not to go walking around at night. They all knew. They all knew how The Deer had died. Another gunshot rang out. Gravel exploded. I knew those guns weren't registered. So even if there were another hunting accident, they wouldn't be able to trace the crime back to them. The girl from the tearoom was there, but she was drunk and scared. The searchlight whipped across the woods.

"There! It's a wild boar! It had yellow eyes!" shouted Kim Jinseong.

They were experts. But they weren't just any experts. They could tell what kind of animal it was just by looking at the eyes. They went the other way into the woods to chase after the boar. I had to flee to where the jeeps couldn't go. Park's body had been found in the opposite direction from the village. He must have thought the same thing and fled deep into the forest where the jeeps couldn't follow him. And while he'd run further away, his life had drained out through the small wound in his thigh.

The cotton padding of my parka sagged with rain. Walking became more difficult under its weight. But I couldn't just discard it here. They would roam through the forest all night, and if they learned that someone had seen their faces, they wouldn't stop until they caught me. I broke out into a cold sweat under my drenched underclothes.

In the rain and the dark, I lost my bearings. I had no choice but to press even deeper into the dark. Maybe I was hearing things, but there seemed to be footsteps coming after me. I tripped and rolled down a knoll. I hit my head on the base of a tree and cut my forehead open. The blood from the gash mixed with the rain and trickled into my mouth. It tasted salty and fishy.

I seemed to be stumbling around in circles. Another shot rang out behind me. I had to keep moving to avoid getting hit or dying of exposure.

It was only when I tried to lift my foot that I realized it was stuck. The miry mud clung to my ankle and wouldn't let go. When I tried to pull my boot free, my foot slipped out of the boot instead. I'd lost all feeling in my wet feet a long time ago.

After barely managing to cross the muddy field, I started to climb a low hill, but stepped on something slick and slipped again. I tried to get up, but my palm, which I'd thrust out, slipped as well, and I fell back. When I lifted my hand, something soft and mushy came away between my fingers. Though it was dark, I could tell what they were. I groped the ground. Everywhere I touched was covered with pine mushrooms. I recalled the muddy boots that had been sitting under Park's porch. Park, who knew these woods like the back of his hand, could have avoided the mud. But the only way to get to the mushroom patch was to cross the mud field. I had stumbled upon the mushroom patch that had eluded even his mother. The mushrooms were so big that some of them were fifteen centimeters long. I started laughing. I couldn't stop laughing.

It was around dawn when I finally made it to Park's house. The rain had stopped, too. Far below, several jeeps were slipping out of the village along the lower road. Sensing my presence, Park's elderly mother opened the door to her room and peered out. I could tell from her expression how frightful I must have looked. She told me later that she'd thought I was a rebel fighter. My legs gave out and I collapsed onto her living room floor, saying the same words over and over again. "I found it, I found it!"

Early in the morning, two days later, I was sitting in the back of a truck heading to town. I would be back in Seoul by evening. I liked nights in Seoul, because they weren't pitch black. Jeeps were heading into the hunting grounds in single file. A heavy fog half-shrouded the woods I'd blindly roamed two nights ago. Had it really been a hunting accident? Two months before Park's death, the deer farm had burned to the ground. There wasn't a single deer left to hunt. Park was helping the hunters. When they became drunk out of their minds, they had probably started to go after a human deer. The police will uncover the full story. That night when I was fleeing through the woods, it wasn't the boar, bear, or tiger that I most feared. I'd only wished that I wouldn't come across another human being.

Never go for a walk in the woods at night. Especially when it rains. An accident could happen at any moment. A creature spewing double barrels of fire could come and set off a deafening roar. Rabbits, raccoons, boars, roes, and deer are slaughtered all through the night. But an entirely different animal could end up dead.

The truck bounced up as if it had rolled over a big rock. I bounced up, too. My tailbone started to ache. The gash ran through my eyebrow and stopped just above my eye. The other detective had known everything. He'd quit after he'd gotten spooked in the middle of the investigation. He'd known exactly what went on in the woods during those rainy winter nights. That sneaky motherfucker. He'd given me every detail about the case, except the most important thing.

O Father

B ack then, I had two fathers. One was my biological father, who, on a whim, quit his job at the company and lounged around all day, lying on his belly on the heated floor, while thumbing through slim Japanese magazines or books like Shintaro Ishihara's *Season of the Sun*. Then there was Father God, whose countless eyes roamed the earth, watching over his people's every move from heaven above.

Father number two gathered all the neighborhood children every Sunday and gave out Kool-Aid drinks, candy, and fistfuls of sour plums. Father number one passed onto me his fondness for seafood and trained me by supplying just enough hardships to overcome. It was also thanks to him that I ended up with my secret, unusual complex.

•

The Baptist church stood in the middle of a large, undeveloped field. I went there every Sunday, rain or shine. Sometimes my mother put my youngest sister on my back and forced me to take her. There was nothing but vacant land past the residential area with its clusters of houses, no shelter whatsoever to escape the harsh wind during the winter, or the scorching sun during the summer. When I look back now, I don't know why I persisted in going week after week without ever missing a Sunday, but I can still see the red brick building, standing in all its glory like a mighty fortress, its gigantic cross surging into the sky as if to pierce it. At seven years old, I was completely awestruck. The church was the largest building in our neighborhood at the time.

It took about forty minutes for me to walk to the church, and by the time we got there, my youngest sister would be dangling from my rear end, having slipped from her wrap. My middle sister would have lagged behind, complaining that her legs hurt before we even arrived at the church.

My middle sister was sickly and always fell asleep during the sermon, missing the snack time that followed. When the teachers hauled over the plastic bucket sloshing with Kool-Aid, the children climbed onto the wooden benches in excitement. We drank out of a plastic bowl one at a time, but because of all the waiting mouths, we were forced to empty the bowl quickly without taking the time to savor the taste. My sister didn't wake up, even though her turn had come. One teacher, out of a sense of duty to give every child a taste, brought the cold bowl to her lips, but she only whined and turned away to fall back asleep.

When many children showed up at the church, the teachers added tap water to the half-empty bucket. Those in the back got a watered-down version, but no one complained. Food was scarce back then.

If there were rumors that candy was being handed out somewhere, children didn't think twice about walking an hour to get there. The church couldn't afford to skip giving out snacks for even one week. If it did, half the children would be missing the following week. This was the situation only thirty years ago.

My middle sister would wake up only after the bowl had gone all the way to the end. She would then start to cry, thinking of what she'd missed. We were only a year apart, but she looked about three years younger than me. She was far below the average weight and height. When she started to cry, I took her by the hand and got her in line to drink the Kool-Aid at the bottom of the bucket.

She first became ill when she was in second grade. She'd gone on a school field trip and bought ice pops that cost ten won for two; from that point she suffered from chronic stomach pain that lasted until she entered seventh grade. Because she was always clutching her stomach, she became permanently hunched over by the time she entered middle school. Purple antacid bottles, which smelled of mint, rolled here and there around the house. She stayed behind in the classroom during gym class, and on sports days, it was our mother who participated instead, entering the mothers' race to perhaps win something like a wicker basket, while my sister remained inside.

After eighth grade, my sister grew as tall as me, and went on to surpass me. She, who'd cried at the drop of a hat, became even defiant at times. At some point, I found myself gazing up at her. When she started to tower over me, my words no longer had any effect on her. I tried threatening her, but it was no use.

·

Our whole family, minus our father, got baptized. We were all in high spirits as we loaded the food onto the rented bus; it felt as though we were going on a picnic. The bus stopped near a river in Daepyeong-ri.

There was a red tinge to the water from the recent rains. We kneeled in the water before the reverend, who stood with water up to his knees, and were baptized in the Baptist tradition. They said that when you went into the water, your sins were washed away and you died to the old way of life, and when you came out of the water, you started a new life as God's children.

My youngest sister was only eight months old then. With my sister in her arms, Mother waded into the water and kneeled before the reverend. The reverend took the squirming infant and raised her high in the air. Later on television, I saw a similar scene from Alex Haley's *Roots*.

The reverend plunged my sister into the river, then pulled her out. The shocked baby screamed belatedly. My middle sister and I, who'd swallowed some water just before, gazed at our baby sister, who wouldn't stop bawling. I didn't have the energy to go to her.

My middle sister kept coughing and jabbed me in the side. With her hair and clothes sopping wet, she looked exhausted. She frowned and clicked her tongue, as if the whole thing was completely absurd.

"So even a small baby like that has sin?"

She still seemed upset for having been forced underwater for no apparent reason.

"Be quiet if you don't understand," I scolded her. "It's because of original sin."

I was simply repeating the words I'd picked up somewhere; it was before I knew what *original sin* meant.

From the time I was five to eighteen years old, we lived in a new housing development, built quickly to be sold for a handsome profit. They were Western-style bungalows, identical in everything from the number of rooms to the locations of the windows; even the door-knocker mounted on the front gate—a lion head with a ring in its mouth—was the same. There were two rows of ten houses that faced each other, and our house was the very last house on the small street.

My father, coming home late after drinking, sometimes opened the gate of the house next door and hollered for me.

Seven-year-old Mi-eum, whom I'd met and gotten to know at church, lived in the house across from us. We started elementary school together, with identical handkerchiefs tucked into our breast pockets, and as we grew older I noticed his chest broaden, his voice grow deeper, and his Adam's apple jut out. Whenever there was any kind of test or competition, Mi-eum called or stopped by my house to ask how I'd done. He seemed to consider me his rival.

During the summer, the church held Vacation Bible School. On the last day, prizes were given out for attendance and test results. The early morning prayer class started at five in the morning every day; Mi-eum and I never missed a day. We sometimes had to wait outside, because the teacher hadn't arrived yet to open the doors.

Around this time, big and small churches cropped up in the neighborhood, and many children went to two, even three, different churches during the summer. If I heard a certain church was holding a singing contest, I was there, and if I heard another church was holding an art competition, I was there as well. But because the teachers were well aware of what was going on, the first prize usually went to their own congregants. The prizes weren't anything special—perhaps a cheap framed picture of Jesus standing in the midst of a flock of sheep, or David poised before Goliath—but when you had won and were walking home with it in your hands, you were so happy you could fly.

On the last day of Vacation Bible School, we were tested on everything we had learned that summer. The questions were easy enough, but the last question was a problem.

As God's child, what would you like to do or be?

Perhaps I had watched too many television dramas or perhaps it was just my nature, but I wrote without thinking: I want to spread the Good News to the ends of the earth. Even as I wrote, I felt a little ashamed. The Good News? And to the ends of the earth? It's obvious now, but even back then, I had absolutely no desire to do anything of that sort.

The results were announced. The teacher looked around the room and said that two people had received perfect scores on the test— Mi-eum and me. "However," she added. Only one prize had been prepared, so she'd been forced to pick one person. When I glanced over at Mi-eum, he looked tense.

"So I had to use the last question to decide. The prize goes to . . ."

I still remember the way he looked when he realized it wasn't him. He ran home after class without waiting for me. I approached the teacher, clutching the pastel crayons I had won. I wanted to know his answer to the last question.

"Teacher, I feel bad for Mi-eum . . . I was wondering, how did he answer the last question?"

The teacher flashed Mi-eum's paper at me. *I want to come in first at Vacation Bible School.* At the very least, Mi-eum was honest. But back then, I merely laughed at him inside.

•

I saw Mi-eum again in my first year of college. It was the first time I'd seen him in six years, since we had moved away when I was in eleventh grade. He looked the same as he always had. We had dinner together.

His father used to joke and refer to me as his daughter-in-law. Once in high school when I had run into him on the bus, he had mortified me by trying to get me to sit in his lap. Mi-eum and I caught up with each other. At twenty-four, I was only in my first year, but Mi-eum had already gotten his undergraduate degree and was in graduate school.

He had always trailed me, but he was now ahead in every aspect. I had never gone on a single date, even after joining the work force straight after high school, while he'd racked up plenty of experience and was even dating someone. When he talked about his girlfriend—a woman three years older than him from the same university—how he had passed her on campus, fallen instantly for her, and had followed her around for a whole year, I realized he was no longer the Mi-eum I had known.

I thought he would remember what had happened at Vacation Bible School, but he couldn't. Only after I'd described the situation to him in detail did he chuckle, flashing his white teeth. I pretended I didn't know and asked, "What did you write that day anyway?"

"I wrote, 'Please let me come in first.' You happy now?"

Mi-eum was as honest as ever.

·

After we moved, I often dreamed about our old house. Thirteen years isn't a long time, but when you're five, thirteen years is as long as 130 years. Overnight, at the age of eighteen, I found myself in an unfamiliar neighborhood. From then on, time passed very quickly.

I ended up attending church again in twelfth grade, by chance, when I went to a high school in Yongsan to earn my typewriting credit. I sat at the front of the classroom. The girl sitting next to me, who was from another school, sat twirling a pen between her fingers. As soon as class started, the room clamored with the noise of clicking and banging. Although I was concentrating on my typing, I could see the girl out of the corner of my eye. It seemed she hadn't practiced at all. She couldn't even finish drafting up the table, let alone typing the words that went inside.

We happened to be on the same subway home. We even got off at the same stop. It was a Sunday and it was still light out. I didn't want to go home early, and so I went with her to church, for the first time in a year. The service was in full swing. I sat in the back row, and glanced at her hymnbook and mouthed the words. A few seats in front of me sat a young man who looked like a college student. He looked back and we made eye contact. He continued to stare, as if he'd forgotten to look away. At that instant, I remembered a line I had read somewhere: *The first eye contact is like God declaring, "Let there be light!"* He faced forward again only when another student noticed and started to smirk.

He attended a university in Sinchon. But I had started working at a trading firm after high school instead of going to college. One day on my way home from work, the doors of my subway car slid open and there he was, waiting to get on. He seemed just as taken aback. Humiliated that I'd been caught in work clothes, my hair down like an older woman, I ran off the subway without looking back.

Perhaps he'd been hurt by that incident, but he was late coming to the next Sunday service. During prayer time, I had my eyes closed and my hands clasped together, but I wasn't praying. I heard footsteps coming down the sanctuary aisle. They stopped by me, and I felt a light breath on my cheek. Someone was standing close, staring at me. Instead of opening my eyes to see who it was, I squeezed them shut even tighter. When I finally opened my eyes at the end of the prayer, he was sitting in the seat right in front of me. As bland as it was, this was the entirety of my first love.

I stopped going to church around the same time he was drafted into the army. On Sundays, I pulled the blanket over my head and slept. I was still that same girl, who had gone to church only to receive juice or candy.

I sometimes went to Sinchon Station, hoping to run into him like before. But nothing happened by chance anymore. I heard about him through other people. How he'd lost his younger sister in a car accident, how he'd gotten married, how he'd become a singer. What did he know about me? Even if he were to read this, he probably wouldn't realize this was about him. Until I was twenty-five years old, I had the habit of loitering around Sinchon Station, all because our eyes had met in twelfth grade.

•

Furious sounds of chopping came from the kitchen all morning. Stainless steel bowls crashed together. My mother had been in a rage, since my father hadn't come home these past few days. Her anger continued at the breakfast table. According to her, it was all because he hadn't been baptized, because he hadn't received forgiveness for his sins.

But I couldn't afford to pay attention to anything she said. I was completely focused on the radio. The transistor radio, bound to a brick-sized battery with a rubber band, was my most prized possession before we owned a television. I liked the noise of the static that would hiss whenever I twisted the dial to tune into the right station. I liked the dramas most of all. I listened to them every day without fail. It was through them that I came to know the works of Kim Malbong. The radio often broadcasted her novels, which had been adapted into dramas, or dramatized the events of her life.

The transistor had a strap attached to it. I took it everywhere—when my mother sent me to the store on an errand, even when my father called me out to the yard for a family picture. That's why the radio makes an appearance in the few pictures that were taken when I was seven years old, and also the reason I look so serious in them, because even while they were being snapped, I was listening to the broadcast. Park Il was my favorite voice actor. He always played the dashing hero on radio dramas. Even to this day, when I hear his voice in dubbed foreign films, it's like meeting an old friend. His voice seems ageless.

All of sudden, there was a flash before my eyes. My mother had struck me in the forehead with a spoon.

"What are you doing? I called you over ten times."

I knew what she was going to say next. It was: "If you have your head screwed on straight, you'll survive even if a tiger carries you off." Tears came to my eyes, but it was because I had missed the most important part of the drama.

It was impossible to concentrate on the radio because of her nagging that went on for days. I lay on my belly on the warm floor and thought about my two fathers. How could they be so different from one another? I didn't tell my mother, but I had an idea where my father was at that moment.

●

As the oldest of three daughters, I was my father's favorite. Because the second one came only a year after me, she claimed my mother, and so I couldn't be breastfed for long. I fell asleep with my father at night, and he was the one who spooned soup into my mouth or fed me pieces of sponge cake. I followed him around until eleventh grade.

My father could not stay put in one place for long. At the start of every school break, I took the long-haul bus or train to wherever he was, whether it was to Ulsan, Masan, or Pusan. I scrubbed a seaweed called gompi with salt, and set the dinner table. When evening fell, I closed his shop. Once I shut the plywood doors, we had to use the small door punched through the plywood to go in and out. Sometimes my father sent me on errands to bakeries and shops to collect money. Wherever my father lived at the moment, I was known as the student from Seoul. I made friends, too. We got along well, even though I only saw them during school breaks. I would help my father until the end of break and then return home. Although I would speak in dialect with friends all summer, the moment I arrived at Yeongdeungpo

Station, I would thank the station employee in a courteous Seoul accent.

I set up a low table in the small room attached to my father's shop and did my summer vacation homework. The room had only one window, and someone seemed to be peering into the room, but whenever I would turn around, I didn't see anyone. This went on for several days.

Then one day, my father was hauled into the police station. When he was able to return almost half a day later, he was livid. I'd never seen him so angry. Someone had mistaken him for a spy and reported him to the police, but that someone had ended up being his friend. It was the friend who had been peering through the window.

My father had moved to Seoul when he was seventeen years old. He used both the Pusan and Seoul dialects in his speech. This had been one of the reasons his friend had suspected him. It also seemed strange that he was living on his own without a family. In the end, his friend came to the shop and begged for forgiveness. He and my father drank at the shop until late.

My father's restless wandering ended when I was in my last year of high school. When he closed up his store and came home for good, my mother muttered while preparing dinner. *You've come back, now that you're old and useless?* After that, for fifteen years, my father never left home again, except to go on trips with my mother.

·

Whatever I did, whether it was drawing, singing, or reading, I was the best in my father's eyes. And so until I entered middle school I truly believed I was the best. I worked hard to live up to his expectations. When his friends came to the house, I performed a folk song for them called "Seongjupuri." Sometimes when I was out on an errand and grownups would ask me to sing, I'd do it right away without hesitation. Once, my sixth-grade homeroom teacher asked me to sing during free time. Even then, I replied brazenly, "How about a pop song?"

We saved old calendars to draw on the back. On my errands, grownups would hand me a page from a calendar and a ballpoint pen and ask me to draw them something. Their eyes followed every move of my hand. And so what happened in my first year of middle school was a big shock. I had been singing "Spring Girl" during a performance test, when my music teacher, who had been accompanying me on the organ, stopped playing all of a sudden and asked, "Do you have a sinus infection or something?"

·

Because I was seven years old, I was strong enough to walk long distances. My father liked to take me along on his wanderings, and for that reason, I ended up learning all his secrets.

One day I followed my father onto the bus. Because she had my two sisters to look after, my mother welcomed the times my father took me along. We got off the bus and stepped into a narrow street. I clung to my father's hand as I stared around at the unfamiliar surroundings. I saw several dead-end streets, and we turned left and right many times. We crossed a set of train tracks that cut through the street. Once we passed through more small streets, clusters of shabby houses came into view. My father stopped in front of one such house.

Inside, rooms lined both sides of the hallway. The hallway light was on even though it was broad daylight, since the sunlight didn't penetrate that far into the house. The ceiling was shabby, and on one side of the wall was a steep staircase like a ladder, which led up to the second floor. As soon as we stepped into the hallway, a face popped out from the hole above. It was a girl around my age, with a slender face and dark eyebrows. She hurried down the stairs as soon as she saw my father. Her name was Jini. I learned later that she was a year older than me.

Jini's mother looked nothing like her daughter. She was plump all over, and had a husky voice and laughed loudly at everything I said. Jini and I took to each other right away. She was taking singing classes. I followed her there. She ran up to the second floor of a house located back near the railroad tracks. Children around our age kneeled on the floor around the cramped room. A young man with a guitar sat in a chair and signaled to each child; that child would then stand and sing a pop song. The man was temperamental, but to my surprise, the children were well-behaved and quiet, which was unusual for children that age. They mostly sang songs by Kim Serena. A train passed now and then. Jini kept making mistakes, and each time, the man jabbed her in the stomach with the headstock of his guitar.

"He's a real singer," Jini told me on our way back.

"Yeah right," I snapped. I was in a foul mood. "I've never seen him before."

I was jealous of Jini and her singing lessons. She was the child singer who performed during intermission at a local theater. About a year later, I went with my father to see her perform, but because of the tall man sitting in front of me I couldn't see a thing.

That night after Jini's singing class, we all went for dinner, holding hands like one happy family. My father praised Jini the same way he praised me. Feeling jealous, I sang "Seongjupuri" in a loud voice. Jini sang a ballad called "Saetaryeong."

"Well, I have to say, Jini's the better singer."

It was the first time I'd felt my father was cruel.

I saw Jini again when I entered middle school. In the midst of all the girls with bobbed hair playing basketball, I noticed one student with her hair in two braids. She was tall and slim. Though I hadn't seen or heard anything about Jini after second grade, everything came back to me at once. I slowly approached her. "Excuse me," I said. "Do I know you?"

I saw her flinch. "Sorry, you got the wrong person," she said, and tossed the basketball to her friend. But it was definitely Jini.

The next day when I came home from school, a woman was sitting in our living room, speaking with my mother. This time, too, I recognized her right away. It was Jini's mother. After Jini had told her she'd seen me at school, she had made her way to our house. The reason Jini was allowed to grow her hair long was because she was in dance.

How could I describe the relationship between my mother and Jini's mother? When she was no longer seeing my father, she and my mother grew close. Women were confusing creatures. Jini's mother called occasionally and even dropped by our house sometimes. She eventually married a man from the market when Jini left for the United States. My mother sometimes went to go see her in their home, and even visited her at the hospital when Jini's mother became sick.

Jini's mother died two years ago. My mother said she had kept seeing Jini's mother in her dreams and had given her a call, but it was her husband who'd answered. He said she'd died a week ago and had been cremated, her ashes scattered in a river. He mentioned that Jini had come from America and gone back. My mother was crying as she told me the news.

•

The day I'd gone to Jini's house for the first time, I'd come back with purple earrings dangling from my ears; Jini's mother had bought them for me. I'd wanted to go home quickly, but we'd been forced to slow down repeatedly because my drunk father had kept stumbling. He urinated for a long time against a stone wall. As he straightened his pants, he peered at me with bloodshot eyes.

"Hey, this is a secret from Mom, got that?"

Now, thinking back, I knew for certain where he was: Jini's house. He was, without a doubt, with Jini and her mom. Anger surged through me. It just wasn't the right day for radio dramas.

My mother crept closer and peered into my face. "You better tell me everything you know."

It had finally happened. Why was she asking me about my father's whereabouts? What did she think a seven-year-old would know?

"Where did you go last time with Dad? You remember, don't you? Hurry up and get dressed."

My mother put on her "going out" clothes and secured my youngest sister on her back. She left my middle sister at Mi-eum's across the street. I followed my mother to the bus stop.

"What did you and your father do next?"

"We got on the bus."

But all I could recall were the narrow streets tangled together like a spider web and the train tracks cutting through them, and the white building where the singing classes had been held. My mother grilled me for more details, but like a parrot, I repeated the words I had already said: "There were train tracks and the train went by."

I sat pressed up against the window and looked for the spot where I had followed my father off the bus. "Was it here?" my mother asked every time the bus stopped.

That day, my mother and I searched every railroad in downtown Seoul. My legs hurt, and I was thirsty. We sat down on the benches in front of the shops and rested our legs. My mother stood on the side of the street and untied the baby blanket that sagged with the weight of my sister. She fixed it, securing her tightly to her back. I'm

now the same age as my mother. But back then, she seemed so much
more grownup to me.

·

There used to be a troublemaker who lived on our street. Although
he was the same age as me, he only came up to my shoulders. He
always bullied and picked on my middle sister, probably because she
was smaller than him. One day, she came home with a bloody hand.
He had scratched her with a penknife. Anger swept over me. At times
like this, I wanted nothing more than an older brother who would
protect and stand up for us. Although we had Mi-eum, I knew the
boy might harass us the next time Mi-eum wasn't there. My mother
said to my sister, as she put ointment on her wound, "If he tries something like this again, throw a rock at him at least. I promise I won't
punish you."

Broken pieces of concrete littered our little street. When that boy
blocked our way and picked a fight, my mother's words flashed across
my mind. He thrust an iron poker at my sister. She looked at me and
burst into tears. I don't remember what happened after that. The
next thing I knew, the boy was standing in front of me, gripping his
head and crying. Beside him on the ground was a piece of concrete.
My sister's eyes were standing out of her head as she looked from the
concrete to me.

When his mother marched through our gate, pushing him ahead
of her, I grasped the reality of what I had done. We heard her shouting from the street even before she stepped into our house.

"How could you let a girl grow wild like that? You call that a girl?"

My mother didn't say a single word to the boy or his mother.
In silence she dabbed ointment on his wound and covered it with a
bandage. When the boy's mother kept on about how a girl could be so
wild, all my mother said was, "Don't you have any girls of your own?"

As a mother with three sons and no daughter, there was not much she could say. After they left, I was afraid I would get in trouble, but as promised, my mother didn't say a word.

He no longer bothered my sister after that. But because I wasn't sure when he would change his mind, I couldn't put my guard down, even for a moment, whenever I stepped into our street. His family moved away soon after and I could walk around the neighborhood in peace again.

But I ran into him again on the school field. He hadn't changed at all. "Hey, you!" he yelled when he saw me. "Stop right there!"

I took off blindly. I heard him say from behind, "That bitch threw a rock at me. Catch her!"

I looked back to see him and two of his friends chasing me. At this rate I wasn't going to make it all the way home. Right then I noticed that the front gate of my friend's house was open, and so I ran inside. But he didn't go away. He prowled outside the house, spewing every kind of curse. I was finally able to head home in the evening. After that incident, I had to be on alert at school for a long time. But I didn't see him again. It seemed he had moved far away this time. I sometimes wonder if he thinks of me every time he sees the scar on his head.

•

We searched every railroad in downtown Seoul, but I couldn't find the one I had crossed with my father. We finally headed home on the bus. My sister, grimy from being outside all day, had fallen asleep on my mother's back. The bus went around the Yeongdeungpo Rotary. At that instant, I saw the same street I'd followed my father into.

"Mom!" I yelled. "Over there! That's the one!"

My sister woke up from the noise. When we got off the bus, I couldn't afford to wait for my mother, who kept lagging behind. It was exactly where I had roamed about with Jini that day. My mother ran after me, shouting at me to slow down.

The streets were like a maze, but I ran with ease. The train tracks that my mother and I had searched for in vain finally appeared. When I saw the building by the railroad where the singing class had been held, I became excited.

"To think it was so close to home . . ."

It seemed my mother had never once considered he might be so close. Jini's house was only four bus stops away. As the saying goes, it's the darkest right under the candlestick. At long last, I stood in front of Jini's house.

"Go and see if your daddy's there. And if he is . . ."

The rage that had consumed her when we'd first set out was gone. She hesitated by the entrance. I left her standing outside the gate and went inside. The hallway was dark. A light shone faintly from a room down the hall. I shouted toward the light.

"Dad!"

A head popped out from the room. It was him. It seemed he couldn't make out my face from where he was. "Dad!" I shouted again.

He rushed out of the room without putting on his shoes. I saw clearly the expression on his face. He stood there flustered, his mouth open from shock. In triumph I put my hands on my hips and thrust up my chin, while blocking the front doorway—the only opening that let the sun into that house. I had just one thought. *Here I am, your one true daughter* . . .

My heart lurched in my chest, knowing I had not failed him.

Joy to the
World

There seemed nothing wrong with our plans to marry. After all, I knew all there was to know about him. Whenever he gripped a knife or wrung a rag, he favored his left hand, and once a month, he went to a downtown salon to get his hair cut, the same one he had gone to for the last ten years, despite the trouble of transferring buses. I also knew he hoped I would continue to work after marriage. My friends say these things are common knowledge if you've been with someone for three years, but I was sure I knew him inside out. We made the decision to get married around the time our relationship started to feel a little boring.

"Dating for a long time is a waste of time and money," he'd said one day, while peeling a mandarin orange served at the end of the meal.

"Then why don't we just get married?" I said, as I pierced a pear slice with my fork.

Our marriage was settled this way like an afterthought, like some fruit or candy served after the main course. What difference would it have made if it'd been decided any other way?

When we announced the news to family and friends, no one seemed particularly surprised. "Well, what did you expect?" they said. "Did you intend not to, after dating for that long?"

However, something seemed off. Not once had we ever fought, and we even liked the same foods. If anything, the fact that we didn't have any problems seemed a problem. "What would have happened if we'd been from the same clan?" I asked him one day, but he didn't even bat an eye.* "I hate things that are overly complicated," he said. But there was no need to worry about that, since we weren't from the same lineage. Nothing seemed to be the matter.

My fiancé lived in an old rented house at the base of a mountain. After getting off the subway, you needed to walk for another half an hour. It was much worse if it snowed. Where he lived was a different world from the area around the subway station. The house was so old that he had to use coal briquettes for heating, and dust and ash swirled

---

* Fewer than 300 Korean family names are in use today, with each family name divided into one or more clans, or bon-gwan, identifying the clan's ancestral home. Thus people from the same clan are considered to be of the same blood, such that until recently, it was illegal for a man and a woman of the same clan to marry. Despite this change, marriage between a man and a woman of the same clan is considered to be taboo, regardless of how distant the actual lineages may be, even to the present day.

about all day long. But I liked his room in that old, shabby house. There was plastic roofing attached to the eaves to block out the lashing rain, and in the summertime, I loved the sound of the rain hitting the roof. My fiancé taught math at the local all-girls senior high.

That night, I bought a cake and bottle of wine and climbed the hill. It was to celebrate his birthday for the last time as an unmarried couple. My calves strained as I went over the steep hill. The laughter of young men drifted out into the narrow street. The front gate was open and the light was on in my fiancé's room, and strewn under the wooden porch were three pairs of shoes. I opened the door to find three men whom I assumed were his friends, half reclining against the walls. They were complete strangers to me. Under the dim fluorescent lighting, their faces looked tired, and their wrinkled, grimy dress shirts spoke of their busy day. One man's face stiffened like congealing tofu when he saw me.

Although I had opened the door, I wasn't sure if I should go inside, especially when my fiancé wasn't there. But one stood and made room for me. I placed my shoes away from the other shoes and stepped inside.

They seemed to have been in the middle of a funny story, but the room fell silent. It had probably been men's talk, just as there are stories meant only for women's ears. Someone brought up the stock market, but the conversation soon died out. At last, one of them asked me, "So, what do you do?"

"I'm a receptionist," I said. "I'm sure you don't need me to explain what a receptionist does."

He nodded slowly, as if he understood very well.

"How about you?" I asked him.

"I'm a surgeon. I'm sure you don't need me to explain what a surgeon does."

I found myself grinning at his words.

"Oh, you *do* know how to smile. You have nice teeth."

I pursed my lips. He seemed too forward, somewhat pushy. Plus, it wasn't like me to smile so easily at the words of a man I'd just met.

He whispered something to the others. They seemed very close. It was obvious from the way they addressed each other.

I heard my fiancé come in through the gate. I could tell it was him from the footsteps. Of course I'd know. After all, he knew things about me, too, like what shampoo I used. I crawled across the room on my knees and opened the door. He was squatting by the tap in the middle of the yard, washing his hands. I took the towel that was hanging on the wall and crouched by his side.

"You didn't say you were going to invite other people."

He rubbed his hands vigorously with soap and gazed at me as if I were making a fuss over nothing.

"I had no idea they were coming. We've been so busy we haven't had the chance to get together. I think high school graduation might have been the last time we were all together. Consider tonight a fluke, since I don't even know if they can all make it to the wedding."

"You mean you haven't seen each other in fourteen years?"

"No, I saw one of them last week. I'm sure they meet up on their own. I'm just saying all four of us haven't gotten together like this for a long time."

My plans for a romantic birthday were ruined, but he didn't seem a bit sorry.

My fiancé had hardly any furniture; all he had were a garment rack and a low desk piled with textbooks and reference books. We sat in a circle. The room was so small that my knees brushed against the knees of those next to me whenever I shifted positions. Instead of a table, two pages from an old sports section were laid on the floor. On the front page was a picture of a popular actress. She claimed that next spring she would be marrying the young businessman with whom she had been involved in numerous scandals. I stuck candles into the cake, and my fiancé blew them out. They poured the red wine into paper cups and elbowed one another in the ribs, swearing cheerfully like high school boys. The wine disappeared in no time. The surgeon took out a plastic bag from his satchel. It was an expensive bottle of cognac. He poured it into our wine-stained paper cups. As they poured drink after drink, I learned that the man sitting next to me was the assistant branch manager of a bank, and still single. But the man across from me, who sat drinking without a word, offered no information about himself. The cake sat between us, its shape now unrecognizable after being dug at with our wooden chopsticks.

"And what do you do?" I asked.

He tossed back what was left in his cup and made a face. Perhaps it was the burn of the liquor, but he seemed to disapprove of my curiosity. He lifted his left hand and swiped at his brow. On his left ring finger was a large solitaire ring. It was moonstone. He was probably born in June.

"Let's not talk about work."

That was all. While the rest of the men laughed and talked, he hardly spoke. The seating arrangement changed naturally as people went to the bathroom and came back. The surgeon now sat to my right. He was funny. Even though it was a joke I already knew, I ended up laughing when he said it. I laughed a lot. When he complimented my teeth again, I was even able to say, "Are you actually a dentist?"

Maybe it was because of the alcohol, but I didn't flinch when my knees brushed against theirs. When the silent man left to go to the bathroom, I leaned across to where my fiancé sat and asked him what he did for a living. He was about to answer, but the surgeon cut him off.

"All you have to know is that he works for a certain organization. I'm sorry if he seemed rude earlier. Even his parents don't know what he does, so what can you expect?"

When the cognac ran out, the banker said he would go to the store. He stood up, the loose change jangling noisily in his pockets. We all laughed as he stumbled a little and knocked over a paper cup, spilling the contents onto the newspaper. A large gray stain spread on the actress's forehead and the headline from the reverse side soon seeped through onto her face. It was about the grand slam during the Korean Series. My fiancé and the surgeon began to talk about that game. We heard the banker run into the metal basin by the tap as he crossed the courtyard. The basin clanged and rattled clamorously. But no one went out to check on him. After a while the banker returned, holding two plastic bags filled with beer bottles. The coins in his bulging pockets jingled with each step.

By eleven o'clock, we were all drunk. I slid back with my cup in hand and leaned against the wall. Our paper cups were soft now, having wilted as we switched from wine to cognac to beer.

"What do you think happened to her?" the banker slurred, talking to himself.

The surgeon burst into laughter. But I didn't miss the way the muscles in my fiancé's face twitched. The silent man who worked for some institution filled the banker's cup with beer. When the cold beer frothed to the rim, the banker quickly put his lips to the cup so that he wouldn't spill any. He took a gulp and blurted, "You haven't forgotten, have you?" His bleary eyes became fixed on my face.

"Shut up," my fiancé said, staring at the banker. "You drunk already?"

"I want to get drunk. How much do I have to drink to get there? How drunk do I have to get to forget everything?"

All of a sudden, my fiancé seized the banker by his tie and pulled his face close. The banker went pale. My fiancé appeared to have received some sort of assurance, because he let go. Freed, the banker loosened his tie and leaned against the wall. Something unspoken passed between them.

It was close to midnight, but the friends seemed to have no intentions of leaving. I got to my feet and picked up my coat and purse, but the surgeon clung to the ends of my skirt and refused to let go. My fiancé gave me a look that said to stay put. The banker's eyes filled with tears. The night was becoming stranger by the minute.

"How did you all meet anyway?"

I wondered how four men who seemed so different from one another had managed to stay in touch for fourteen years after high school. My fiancé had never once mentioned these friends. The one who worked for the organization looked at me as if he once again didn't approve of this question, and kept drinking. He hadn't softened a bit in the past five hours. The only change in him was the stubble on his face, which showed the progress of time.

"We're part of a group called Faust," the surgeon said.

It was the last thing I expected to hear. Faust? It hardly suited them.

"Are you saying you fell for the devil's temptation? I guess you were real troublemakers."

The surgeon's eyes flashed. They flashed with a different curiosity than he had shown until now. "When he said he was getting married, I wondered what kind of woman he'd met. Now it all makes sense . . ."

I didn't believe they had actually read *Faust*. It was a work that required patience. I glanced at my fiancé. He made no response and continued to drink. Faust aside, this was the first time I'd seen him drink so heavily. Red splotches had spread down his neck. I realized there were things I didn't know about him. I poked him lightly in the side. As though his mind had been elsewhere, he flinched, dropping his cup. His pants got soaked. I wadded up some tissue and dabbed at the stain, but all he did was gaze down at my hands moving busily to clean up the mess. He felt like a stranger.

"Why didn't you tell me about your little group? I had no idea."

"You expect me to tell you every single detail?" he snapped, rolling up his sleeves. "Like when I stopped wearing diapers? Or the first time I ever shoplifted?"

The surgeon snickered again. "You mean you didn't tell her the first thing you ever stole was a pack of Juicy Fruit? This guy has a real gift for stealing. If he wanted to, he could have robbed a bank. But I'm sure he has no desire to steal anything now, since he stole your heart . . ."

My fiancé punched him lightly in the shoulder. The surgeon fell over, pretending to be in pain, and collapsed on top of me. His weight sent me tumbling over and I ended up grabbing my fiancé's thigh to steady myself. I looked up to find his face set in a scowl.

"What kind of perfume are you wearing?"

The surgeon put his nose right up to my earlobe and sniffed. From his hand that grazed mine, I caught a whiff of disinfectant. He backed away only when my fiancé glowered at him. The banker, who sat off to the side, kept drinking. He turned paler. The one who worked for the organization talked less and less, until he'd said nothing for the last hour.

My head was swimming from the liquor. I broke into a cold sweat and the ceiling turned black. My stomach churned from the smell of the smoked cuttlefish jerky, and when I burped, I could taste the cognac I'd drunk earlier. I leaned my spinning head on my fiancé's shoulder and fell asleep.

The banker was crying. When I woke from the noise, I was lying on my side in the corner of the room, with a pillow under my head. I could hear their low voices behind me.

"I still dream about her. But it's someone else lying on the cement where she'd landed. When I get close enough, I realize it's me. My head's split open like a watermelon and chunks of my brain are scattered all over the ground."

"Are you ever going to shut up? It happened fifteen years ago. Her bones have rotted away and turned to dust by now."

It was my fiancé's voice. I lay still, pretending to be asleep. I wanted to roll over but I couldn't. A girl had fallen to her death and there were four men behind the incident. If it had happened fifteen years ago, they had been in eleventh grade. The surgeon laughed; it sounded like a hiccup. The banker seemed to have thrown something at his face. I heard what sounded like a peanut bounce off the ground.

"You assholes. I swear, you're not even human," the banker said. He continued to fret and whine. "How can you sleep at night? How can you act like nothing happened? You're just a bunch of animals. A bunch of goddamn animals."

"You're kidding, right?" the surgeon said, his voice as sharp as a scalpel. "I guess you don't remember, but who was so desperate to hang out with us animals? Did you forget, you stupid prick?"

The surgeon went on. "Why did we let this loser tag along? Didn't I say he was no good? Just look at him pissing his pants like a total bitch. He's been nothing but trouble from the start. He's got a lot to learn."

"Sure she's asleep?" asked the quiet one, finally opening his mouth. He seemed bored with everything that was happening. He had a habit of omitting unnecessary words.

My fiancé crept toward me. I sensed him peer into my face. I kept my eyes closed, making my breathing shallow and even. I felt him wave his hand over my face. Believing I was fast asleep, he returned to his spot.

"We've come too far to turn back," he said in a low, firm voice. "No one forced her to follow us and no one forced her to jump. It was her own choice."

"You think you actually have to push someone off a building for it to be murder?" cried the banker. "She was drunk! Only if we hadn't done that—it was us who made her do it, we made her jump. We're murderers—"

Someone struck the banker in the stomach right then. There was a heavy thud on the wall and the empty bottles that had been lined up on one side of the room were knocked over. He opened his mouth again. "We're not Faust! We can't be saved!"

"You better keep your fucking mouth shut. We have to take this to our graves. I'm not going to jail."

My fiancé sounded strange; I hardly recognized his voice. The wallpaper my nose was pressed against was damp and smelled bad. The voices lulled me back to sleep. I drifted in and out of consciousness. Various scenes met my eyes every time I managed to surface from my stupor. The three men were punching the banker, who had been forced into a corner. Then all of them were smoking, sitting side by side, and leaning against the wall. The last thing I saw was the four of them drinking again, as if nothing were the matter. Every time someone went to the bathroom, cold air struck my forehead.

When I opened my eyes again, it was pitch dark. The room reeked of smoked cuttlefish and cigarettes. Someone lay pressed up beside me. Although I couldn't see, I knew it was my fiancé. Mixed with the smell of liquor, I recognized his scent. Even in my drunkenness, I wondered what had happened to his friends. I assumed they had taken the taxi home.

In the darkness, I felt him touch my bottom. I had no energy to raise my arm. Drowsiness kept crashing in. His hand traveled down to my thigh. With the curtains drawn, I couldn't see a thing, but I could tell it was him. I was sure his friends had gone. This time, I felt his hot breath on my neck. I smelled liquor and something rank. He pressed his hot lips against my skin. I mustered all my energy to turn and felt his face with my fingers. I couldn't even see my own hands as they grasped his face. How could it be so dark? Like a drunk, I kept repeating how dark it was. And I thrust my mouth up to the darkness.

My head pounded all night. When I finally woke, the room was empty. There were empty bottles strewn in one corner of the room. I sat up frantically; I re-tied my hair and examined my clothes. My blouse and skirt were wrinkled badly and I felt something hard under me: a 100-won coin and a 10-won coin. The newspaper was crinkled and warped from spills, and dried bits of food and red pepper paste had splattered on the picture of the actress. The door opened; it was my fiancé coming back from washing up.

"You drank all this last night?"

"Get up. I'll take you home."

"Where'd they go?"

"They went home as soon as you fell asleep. Thank God they've got some manners."

He was lying. But who knows if they had actually left after I'd fallen asleep, just as he said? I drank too much last night. All I wanted was to go home so that I could take a hot bath. Under the porch, my shoes were crushed and were marked unmistakably with footprints, as if the men had trampled on them to and from the bathroom.

The hot water melted away my exhaustion. I sat in the tub until my skin turned red. While soaping my body, I noticed a deep scratch on my chest. It looked as if something sharp had been dragged over my skin. Had a stray cat snuck into the room in the middle of the night? The moonstone ring that the man had been wearing flashed across my mind, but I shook my head. It wasn't like me to think something like that. The scratch stung every time the soap got in it.

·

When I didn't get my period, I recalled the night I had spent with my fiancé. We were getting married next March. Getting pregnant before the wedding wasn't something I had planned, but there was no need to worry, since we were engaged. After all, plans always change.

Though I had intended to work for a while after getting married, I wouldn't be able to continue once I started to show; there were many girls vying for my position as the CEO's receptionist.

As always, my fiancé and I talked on the phone and watched late-night movies on the weekends. I sometimes asked after his friends I had met on his birthday, but he only gave halfhearted answers.

For some reason, I didn't tell him about the pregnancy. One day I changed into my work clothes and my skirt felt tight around my waist. I headed toward the school where he worked and called him. I waited at a café from where I could see the school entrance. Girls in uniform poured out of the gates. The local bus that headed to the subway station came and went, loading students and carrying them away. My fiancé cut across the school yard slowly, his hands shoved inside his pants pockets. Every time students bowed to him, he acknowledged them with a slight nod. I sat by the large window and watched him step through the gates, cross the street, and push open the café door.

He ordered coffee and I ordered a citron tea. I normally didn't drink citron tea. I was hoping he would notice, but he was preoccupied with stirring sugar and cream into his coffee. His thumb and forefinger that gripped the teaspoon were stained with white and red chalk dust.

"I think I have to quit soon." I said.

"It's hard to find a job like that. You know it isn't easy making a living."

He seemed exhausted. He was scruffy around the mouth, as if he hadn't shaved. He continued, "One of my students ran away from home. I couldn't teach all afternoon because I had to go look for her. I'll probably have to look for her tonight. Shit."

"There was something on TV recently, about where kids like that go. I forget the name now. It's cold outside, make sure you dress warm."

"You already gave your notice?"

"No, not yet. The thing is . . . I'm pregnant. I think it was that night. On your birthday."

He'd been gazing out the window, but I saw his face stiffen. Seeing his reaction, I couldn't help feeling anxious.

"If it's because of work, don't worry. I'll look for another job. There must be some part-time work I could do from home."

"It's not mine."

His gaze was still fixed on some point outside the window.

"What are you talking about? You lay down beside me and then touched me. Were you so drunk you can't even remember?"

He sipped his coffee. He then put down the cup and gave a wry laugh. "Sure, I was lying beside you at first. But in the middle of the night, I had to go to the bathroom. When I came back, I just lay down by the door."

The teacup I held in my hand trembled. "That's not funny. Don't joke around right now."

But I could tell by his face that he wasn't joking.

"If it's not yours, whose is it?" My voice rose, despite myself.

He glared at me and hissed, "Hey, I work right over there. If there's even a whiff of rumor about me, I'm canned. So keep your voice down. Like I said, it isn't easy making a living."

All the energy was draining from my body. I slumped back against the sofa.

"When I woke up that morning, I was lying by the door. It was Jinsu who was lying beside you."

It was the first time I'd heard his name.

"The surgeon," he enunciated.

I had believed that all his friends had gone home that night. It hadn't occurred to me that the surgeon might have stayed behind. But in the dark I was sure I had recognized my fiancé's scent. I couldn't move my tongue, as though a tongue depressor were holding it down. I managed to stammer, "I'm not that kind of girl."

"Should I summarize what happened? At first, I was lying beside you. But I had to go to the bathroom. I was so drunk I couldn't find my place. And that's it. I didn't touch you. Everyone else saw Jinsu sleeping by you."

Everyone else? Did he mean that the rest of his friends hadn't gone home, that they had also been in the room?

"Just get to the point. Is there someone else?" I asked.

"You're the one who fooled around with another guy. You were giggling like an idiot, with me right there. Even when he leaned up against you, you just sat there and laughed. If you hadn't told me you were pregnant, I would have married you like a total sucker, knowing nothing. What a joke I would have become then."

When we left the coffee shop, everything had changed; we were no longer two people who were getting married. We parted at the bus stop. Before he left, he hesitated a moment and said, "Can I give you some advice? You shouldn't have it."

My head snapped up at his words like a venomous snake's. He wasn't the man I had known these past three years. "That's none of your business. I don't know how great you think your friendship is, but I'm going to ask him myself."

He seemed a little shocked. I took out my address book and wrote down the surgeon's contact information. I bit my lower lip so that my hand wouldn't shake. When my bus came, I didn't look back. It was full of students from a neighboring school. The students smelled of sweat, dust, and bathroom disinfectant. I gagged and covered my mouth with my hand. My morning sickness had begun.

The surgeon recognized me at once. Dressed in a white lab coat, he seemed more like a doctor. He offered me a canned coffee drink from the vending machine but I refused. He smacked his forehead, as if he had just remembered why. It seemed he'd already been tipped off by my now ex-fiancé.

"I'm not going to beat around the bush. Was it you?"

He laughed silently instead of answering. We walked through the hospital lobby bustling with doctors and patients and headed outside. The December cold cut into my jacket. He stuck a cigarette in his mouth.

"I told you about Faust, didn't I? We've been friends for sixteen years. It's not easy to stay close for that long. Do I look like someone who would fool around with his friend's fiancé? After I came back from the bathroom in the middle of the night, I lay down by the door. When I woke up, you were lying beside me, because the other three who had slept between us had already gotten up. So if they accuse us of sleeping next to each other, I can't say they're completely wrong . . ."

"But you were drunk, like everyone else."

He dropped his cigarette and stamped it out with his heel.

"What are you trying to say? Believe me, there's nothing that'll sober you up like sex. But I slept like a baby all night. It's been a while since I've slept like that. It was all thanks to the alcohol."

"So I guess I'll have to ask the other two then?"

Without a fuss, he gave me the phone numbers of the banker and the one who worked for the organization.

"If things didn't have to get so awkward, you and I could have been friends. Too bad. Well, hope to see you again."

He stood outside until I climbed into a taxi. There was some traffic on the way to the bank. When I arrived, the bank was already closed. A metal shutter was pulled down in front of the main entrance and all the blinds were drawn. I stepped into the payphone booth across the street. A female employee answered. After a little while, she came back on the phone and apologized, mumbling that the banker had stepped out for a moment. I knew that he was avoiding my call. He'd known that I would come looking for him.

I stood by the back door of the bank, waiting for the employees to leave. One by one, they started to file out. He was one of the last to leave. He glanced around nervously as he stepped through the door. Although I hadn't been able to remember his face clearly, I recognized him right away. Each time he took a step, I could hear loose change jingling in his pockets. In a loud voice, I called out to him from behind.

Even after ordering coffee, he perched on the edge of the sofa, his gaze skipping ceaselessly about the room. He was the timidest member of Faust. He was a nervous man.

"Why don't you have some coffee?" I said.

He picked up the cup, but his hand shook so much that some coffee sloshed over the rim. He gripped the cup with both hands. He didn't look like he would have enough courage to touch me. But he would have, if someone had forced him. As if he were thirsty, he gulped the whole thing down. It was pathetic to watch.

"What happened to the girl who fell from the 15th floor?"

He'd been putting a cigarette in his mouth, but at my words, he dropped his lighter. It bounced off my shoe and landed beside the table. I picked it up and flicked it for him. He sucked anxiously on his cigarette.

"Why are you so tense? Do I remind you of someone?"

"I do-don't know what you mean . . ." he stammered.

"I saw the look on your face when you first saw me. And I heard too many things that night."

"This has nothing to do with that. I got up to go to the bathroom. When I came back—"

"After coming back from the bathroom, you must have fallen asleep by the door, since you were so drunk." I didn't have to hear the rest. It was the third time I was hearing the same story. "I guess I have to go see your friend then, the quiet one."

His face turned pale. An invisible hand seemed to be strangling him. He let out the breath he'd been holding.

"You might have his number, but you won't be able to get in touch with him. He's usually the one who calls. It's the nature of his job."

I got to my feet. He looked up at me and said with difficulty, "Don't tell them what you heard that night. You know what I mean."

When I glanced back one last time, he was bent over the table with his face buried in his arms. A cigarette burned on the rim of the ashtray.

I called the last friend several times but couldn't get through. I called once more around 10 P.M. A frail, female voice answered. It was probably his wife.

"Is this Miseon's house?" I blurted, saying a random name.

"Sorry, you've got the wrong number."

After she hung up, I continued to stand in the phone booth for a long time. Even if I managed to meet him, I'd only get the same story. The temperature dropped below zero. I could see high-rise apartment towers in the distance. I raised the collar of my coat and headed for the apartment towers. I crossed two crosswalks. I stood in front of the flowerbed and looked up. Because I was standing so close to the building, I could not see the top.

The security guard was slumped against his chair, sleeping uncomfortably. I was relieved I didn't have to come up with a lie. I stepped into the elevator and pressed the top floor. When I got off on the 25th floor, the corridor was empty. At the far end was a metal ladder on the wall that led to the roof. I climbed the ladder and pushed open the trapdoor. Although there was a padlock on the door, it wasn't locked. Because I kept stepping on the end of my coat, I nearly fell off the ladder a few times. I emerged from between massive water tanks. The ledge was not even a meter high. I put one foot up on it. The flowerbed twenty-five floors below loomed close all of a sudden. A wave of vertigo hit me. On the concrete down below, it seemed I could see the body of the girl who had jumped, her four limbs splayed in different directions. An hour passed, but I could not put my other foot onto the ledge.

I cut across a small park and walked blindly. From somewhere I heard the cheerful strains of a Christmas carol. I found myself standing in front of a small cathedral. Through the lit windows, I saw people singing. It was only then that I realized it was Christmas Eve. Until last night, I had been full of excitement. When I told my fiancé I was pregnant, I had hoped he would say, "What a great Christmas present. You've really outdone yourself this time."

I rounded the building and stepped into the courtyard. Beside the main steps was a statue of the Virgin Mary. Now here was someone who had been shocked by an unexpected pregnancy.

I had been too drunk that night. I still remember the way my fiancé had touched me. The lips pressed against mine had been so familiar. But everything is hazy after that. Sleep overwhelmed me. I was groggy and the room was too dark. The October night was cold, and the room, which my fiancé had forgotten to heat, was chilly. I clung to him to melt away the cold. There was a streetlight at the entrance to his street, but troublemakers often threw rocks at the bulbs to break them. It was too dark that night. If I hadn't been so drunk, I could have smelled the disinfectant on the hand that touched me. The coins I found under my skirt in the morning could have fallen out from the banker's pockets. The scratch on my chest could have been from the moonstone ring the man was wearing. I had never thought that something could go wrong with our plans to marry. I was positive I knew everything there was to know about my fiancé. We drank too much that night.

I pushed open the cathedral door and found a seat near the entrance. The pew felt cold. I'll gradually begin to show. The song they were singing was "Joy to the World." My lips began to move. As I faltered along, the rest of the words came back to me. I slipped my hands into my coat pockets and pressed them against my stomach. I couldn't yet feel any movement inside.

Right about now, the members of Faust have probably gathered again. While they talk about the girl who fell from the 15ᵗʰ floor, the banker will start to cry like a baby. The other three will bully and harass him, and in the end they will once again declare their lifelong friendship. Their friendship will go on for another twenty, even forty years, and the story of the girl who jumped from the 15ᵗʰ floor will never be told to the outside world. She could have left a note on her desk before she jumped. The note would have contained the story of the Faust group. But wishing to protect her reputation, her parents would have burned up the note and scattered the ashes on the apartment flowerbed. The secret will stay buried forever.

My belly seemed a little bigger than before. I whispered to the baby inside. Your dad's name is Faust. Faust falls for the devil's temptation, but in the end he's saved. Baby mine, I love you.

The Dress Shirt

I

Was that one of last year's kites?

The nightscape of the Seoul outskirts stretched on for miles in the smoggy haze, as if a sheet of tracing paper had been placed on top. Car headlights swept between the glow of 24-hour convenience stores, church steeple crosses, and streetlights. The morning would reveal the shabbiness that had been concealed by night—apartment buildings in various stages of reconstruction, residential streets heaped with garbage, and the dark reeking stream that cut through vacant lots overgrown with weeds—but the nightscape was lovely. The high-rises located only five bus stops away glittered like crystal.

Eunok stood on her balcony on the top floor and gazed down at the other six apartment towers, which had been built at varying heights. They spread below her feet like terraces. After a while, the shiny rooftop railings seemed to wash in like the waves, wetting her feet, only to be washed out again. Every rooftop was cluttered with a gigantic water tank with an iron ladder running up its side, a trident-like lightning rod, and large satellite antennas. But what flashed from the end of an antenna on Tower 402 was a kite with a snapped string.

Last winter, kite flying had been popular among the children in the apartment complex. They had dashed through the grounds, trying to get their bangpae "shield" kites or gaori "stingray" kites decorated with cartoon characters to take off into the wind. Cars constantly blasted their horns at the children.

Her husband sat on the ground and fixed the children's kites for them.

"Let's take a look. You see this line here? This is called a bow-string. You know what a bow is, don't you? It's curved, right? But look at this—this is completely straight. It needs to be curved at least 15 degrees. You think it'll fly if you just attach a string? Look here, this string is called the bridle, and below that . . . never mind."

Once he'd fixed the kite, he ran with it against the wind. When he let out some line from the reel and the kite soared above the playground, the children cheered.

"The kites they sell at the stationery store are junk. All they care about is making money. Just think, people who've never made kites before are pumping them out . . . how does that make any sense? Plus, where can you fly a kite here? You need to be on an open hill. That's where you get the most wind. And it has to be in the winter, but parents these days don't want their kids going outside because they might catch a cold . . ."

Her husband kept muttering to himself in the elevator while they rode up to the 29th floor.

"Quit your complaining," Eunok snapped, staring at his reflection in the mirror. "Is that your big grievance? There's no place to fly a kite here, but the subway station is only five minutes away, so what's the problem?"

Her husband became known as The Kite Man among the children, that is, until they lost interest in flying kites altogether. If there was a kite that soared in the sky, it had no doubt passed through his hands. The kites eventually got caught on the rooftop antennas and the strings broke. Sometimes on her way to and from work, Eunok saw one untangle itself and fly up into the sky.

But was there a kite from last year that still hadn't flown away? Eunok narrowed her eyes and stared at the stingray kite that was jerking back and forth in the wind, caught in the antenna. Just then, it broke free and rose into the sky. But because it couldn't catch the wind, it began to nosedive toward the apartment square. She tried to follow it with her eyes, but it plummeted so rapidly that she lost sight of it from about the 15th floor. Its tails got sucked into the darkness.

II

A few years ago, Eunok and her husband had met with four other couples for dinner. After the men had moved the low table strewn with the carnage of fish bones, ribs, and dirty wads of tissue from the living room to the kitchen, they had sat around a small table loaded with beer and nuts. Eunok caught snatches of their conversation whenever she went to put out more cold beer and fruit, but her husband, who had been laughing along without saying much, gazed around at his high school friends and confessed he had always wanted to become a deadbeat.

Because he'd had his back turned to Eunok, she hadn't been able to see the expression on his face. His friends burst into laughter, and her husband said no more. One friend smacked her husband in the back of the head, and someone else said, "You think you're the only one who dreams about doing nothing? We all do. But it's an impossible wish." They filled each other's glasses again and toasted: "To deadbeats!"

The women, who'd been in the kitchen, wondered why the men were laughing and glanced out at the living room. Soon after, when her husband's words were relayed to the women, laughter broke out once more. That night, her husband's confession ended as nothing more than a joke.

Did he really dream of becoming a deadbeat, who loafed around in ill-fitting pants and dragged along cheap plastic sandals everywhere? Who hung out all the time at the local pool hall and the fried chicken joint? Her husband was a diligent worker, who had never been late or absent during his nine years at the bank. However, his diligence wasn't enough to save him. Several years ago he'd made everyone laugh at the dinner party with his comment, but this comment became a reality overnight.

One day when Eunok came home from work, the television was left on in the dark living room and her husband was gone. She walked across the living room to switch on the light and accidentally kicked a comic book he'd borrowed across the floor. While she washed the dishes that filled the sink, splattering water onto the kitchen floor, the phone rang. It was the apartment book-lending shop. She was asked to return the overdue books right away. While she walked down to the shop, her arms filled with over twenty books, she felt her spine was going to snap in two. She waited for her husband until midnight, but he didn't come home.

He was twenty-eight and she twenty-seven when they married. They had dated for about three years, so they hadn't rushed into it by any means. It would be their eighth wedding anniversary this October. Except for a few business trips they'd each gone on, they'd never been apart from each other this long. In spite of all this, Eunok didn't feel any real discomfort or regret over the absence of her husband, who had left the house one day with the television on, never to come back.

Eunok had always done things like changing light bulbs or hanging pictures. Not only had she lost her father at an early age, but she was also the oldest in a family of only daughters. It was easier for her to do these things herself, rather than to clean up after her husband, who would drag out the whole toolbox just to hammer a single nail and leave her with the mess. And it wasn't like she had to worry about the bigger jobs. After all, when the bathroom or kitchen drain had gotten clogged, the apartment handymen were the ones who'd taken care of it, not her husband.

She no longer had to go through the trouble of rewashing certain dishes, all because her husband had noticed a grain of rice or red pepper flake that hadn't come off. Neither did she have to concern herself with his colored clothes bleeding into her white blouses, because they'd been washed together. And when she came home from work and saw that the things she had put away were still in their proper place, she couldn't help but feel happy.

He'd wished to do nothing, yet he managed to last only seven months. He picked fights when she came home late from a work event, and when she told him to quit smoking, he flew into a rage, asking her if he no longer had the right to smoke because he wasn't working. She was tired of walking on eggshells around him and accommodating his sullen moods. But most of all, she hated the bad luck and air of defeat that seemed to ooze out of her husband's room whenever she stepped into the apartment. She was in danger of catching her husband's misfortune if she continued to stay with him.

But now, each day was truly peaceful. She wasn't anxious or upset that he didn't call. All she did was mutter under her breath when she remembered the dinner from several years ago. *Seven months—that's it? What a quitter.* With the act of returning his overdue comic books, she was finally able to cast off the burden she'd been carrying.

Eunok's eyes snapped open at the sudden chill. She saw her husband's white dress shirt, which had startled her awake. Hanging on a coat rack by her feet, it hovered like some foreign object, fluttering limply in the draft from the crack of the open balcony window. Until then, she had never thought that a shirt hanging on a coat rack could be mistaken for a person. As her eyes grew accustomed to the dark and every object in the room began to stand out, she realized once more that her husband had been gone a long time.

After that, she pushed his shirts to the back of the closet, but for some reason, she continued to wake in the middle of the night. A chill, a kind of presence, lingered on her forehead. What had grazed her skin? Eunok went out onto the balcony in her flip-flops. The windows in the apartment tower across from her were dark. Everyone was asleep.

It was unclear why the builders had designed the apartment towers to stand at different heights. From her balcony at the top floor of the highest tower, she could see the entire apartment complex. The rooftops looked like terraced fields, or like the tiered seats of an amphitheater. For a long time, she gazed at the night sky and the darkened windows. The rooftop railings washed in soundlessly and wet her feet.

III

In a panicked voice, the security guard confirmed Eunok's license plate number, saying there had been an accident and that she needed to come down. She hung up the interphone and went out onto the balcony. Only when she had slid open the screen and leaned out as far as she could was she able to see down to the parking lot. The lot was completely full, with a car in every single stall. There was a crowd of people huddled around the front of her car.

High up from her apartment, all Eunok could see was the roof of her car, but there seemed to be something on top of it. Was it a white shirt that had fallen from someone's balcony? She was about to close the window, but she leaned out once more. It wasn't someone's laundry. It was a person—a girl in uniform. A girl in a white blouse and dark checkered skirt.

Even more people had gathered by the time she came down. They were all there—the milkman, students on their way to school, an elderly couple returning from their early morning hike, and every security guard from the complex. The guard speaking animatedly seemed to have been the one who had discovered the girl during his early morning patrol. The police came, followed by the ambulance.

Four paramedics moved the girl off the roof of Eunok's car. She sagged like a gunnysack. The paramedic who had been holding onto her right arm almost dropped her. Someone screamed. A young woman, her face pale with fear, stumbled forward with a hand over her mouth, and bent over the playground flowerbed. Several paper airplanes lay scattered on the flowerbed.

The girl was laid onto a stretcher and covered with a white sheet. Her limp arms dangled out at unnatural angles. Blood had gathered in her hands, making it look as if she were wearing dark purple gloves. Eunok saw the girl's shoeless feet as she was loaded onto the ambulance. Her white socks were folded down to her ankles. The soles were covered with dirt, and the frayed heels revealed torn, bloodstained flesh, as if she'd been cut with broken glass. The toes of her socks were soaked with blood as well. It looked as if she had walked a long way without shoes.

The apartment complex had five parking lots, and the Elephant lot where Eunok parked had a total of 120 stalls. Because every single stall was always taken, cars were forced to double-park, and so announcements requesting certain cars to be moved were made constantly every morning over the intercom. But out of all these cars, the girl had fallen on Eunok's.

"It's the third one already, the third one," a security guard said, as he spat on the ground near his feet.

The guard standing next to him gave a deep nod. "Yup. How are we supposed to stop them when they break the lock to get to the roof?"

"At this rate, our office is going to be moved up there," the first one continued, looking up toward the top of the building. "Our job isn't going to be watching for thieves and solicitors anymore. It's going to be stopping people from jumping. And we'll have to patrol the rooftop now instead of the parking lot."

Once the ambulance left, the people began to disperse. The rest of the guards also returned to their posts, and the only ones left were the police, the security guard who had first discovered the girl, and Eunok. She couldn't complain about her ruined car when a person had just died. The girl's plummeting mass, which had increased as she fell twenty-six stories, had crushed the roof of Eunok's car down to the steering wheel, crumpling it like a piece of paper. The blood had flowed down the windshield and pooled in the middle of the hood. The police and security guard stopped talking and looked up toward the top of Tower 402 once more. They had to tilt their heads all the way back to see the metal railing.

It was the same roof that Eunok had been watching the night before when she had woken from her sleep. From another rooftop behind Tower 402, a stingray kite drifted up. It then caught the wind and did figure eight patterns, the tails whipping wildly through the air. How many kites had gotten tangled in the antennas last year? Just as her husband had said, this was no place for kites. This one seemed to be the last of them.

There it goes. Eunok, who'd been watching the kite fly away, felt a drop of rain on her forehead. All of a sudden, a thought flashed across her mind. The kite that had plummeted to the ground, the one with the broken string she'd seen in the middle of the night—could it have been the girl? Could it actually have been the girl's white uniform blouse, shimmering in the dark? Could the kite tails, which the darkness had swallowed up, have been her pale legs? As the rain fell, the blood that had hardened on Eunok's car started to wash off. The police and security guard jogged over to the security office. The rain flowed along the curb. Eunok's feet became soaked. The rain began to pull down the kite that had been flying in the air.

In her dream, Eunok was flying a kite. She was standing on a flat, open plain. Her hands holding the reel were raw and stiff, but the cold air was refreshing. The kite kept plunging toward the ground.

Stop being so greedy. It's falling, because you're letting too much of the line out at once. Pull in some of the line. You can't make it go up high right away. Be patient for once . . .

It was her husband. She tried to do as he said, but she could barely turn the reel, because she was afraid the string would break. Little by little, she managed to pull the line in, but what she found at the end was not a kite, but the high school girl who had fallen on her car. The girl's blouse was so white it gave off a bluish sheen. There were bamboo spars weaved through her body, and even a hole right below her chest, just like in a shield kite. Through that hole, Eunok saw the dandelions blooming in the field.

Look, the spars are all wrong. That's why it keeps falling. Look here, her husband muttered, as he attempted to fix the spars on the girl's body. Eunok tried to stop him and finally woke from her sleep.

IV

Only when Choi Kisu called again did she remember the message he had left on her voicemail a while back. Kisu was one of her husband's closest friends from high school. She and her husband used to meet him and his wife frequently. Judging by his message, it seemed he hadn't heard about her husband. If Kisu didn't know, it meant the rest of their friends didn't know, either. It also meant her husband and Kisu hadn't talked to each other in over six months.

"You have to come, Boss. You of all people know how long we've been waiting for this child. You have to come."

Eunok couldn't help laughing when he called her Boss.

"You'll be coming by car, right? Then you'll need to take the Dohwa Interchange."

They had said her car wouldn't be ready for another week. "Actually, there's been an accident, so my car's in the shop right now."

"An accident? Are you okay?"

When she had listened to his message, she had wondered whether she should attend without her husband. Eunok had first met Kisu over ten years ago, when she'd been dating her husband. Kisu, who hadn't had a girlfriend back then, often joined them in the evenings, and the three of them would go to a pub or karaoke joint together. Even after they got married, Kisu would barge into their home with a case of beer, without bothering to call first. When he had been set up with the woman who would become his wife, he had introduced her to Eunok first.

Kisu was the one she confided in whenever she and her husband fought. Somehow he knew when they were having problems, and came bearing fruit and drinks to help patch things up between them. But even to someone like him, she could not mention that her husband had left. Nor could she tell him about the seven months he'd spent at home when he'd first lost his job.

"Fine. Even if I end up dropping everything else, I won't miss your baby's birthday."

Kisu laughed and then grew quiet all of a sudden. "Actually, I heard about Sanghyeon. Bad news travels fast."

He fell silent once more. It was unusual for him.

"The truth is . . . someone saw him. On the morning news. You know how they sometimes show all the homeless people camping out at Seoul Station? He didn't look too good, but it was definitely him . . . I can't believe it either. They usually replay the news throughout the day. Why don't you check? That idiot . . . Don't worry, when I see him, I'll give him a good beating and make him come to his senses."

When the news camera was aimed at the man with the sunken eyes and greasy, unkempt beard, he grimaced and covered his face with the army jacket he'd been using as a blanket. The camera took in his grimy pants and ankles, and then moved over other bodies sleeping on cardboard boxes that lined the station entrance. It was a familiar scene. While the camera panned around the station, Eunok kept her gaze on the man. It was easy to see how he could have been mistaken for her husband. The sharp nose, especially the slightly crooked bridge, certainly looked like his. Her husband had broken his nose in a group fight in high school. After all, didn't every boy get in a fight at least once? But the man with the bushy beard wasn't her husband. Even if he had lost a lot of weight during the past two months, the man's cheekbones and face shape were different from her husband's. He simply looked like him. But then, Eunok had never seen him with a beard before. For the past eight years, he had shaved every morning. All she had seen was his hairless chin, as smooth as a pebble.

Because the parking lot was empty during the day, she could see the large elephant painted on the asphalt. After Eunok's car was towed, a white star was added to the spot right below the elephant's belly. It marked where the girl had fallen. People avoided the star, making sure to never park there.

The girl had been eighteen years old and had attended a girls' high school located on the outskirts of Seoul, an hour and a half away by bus and subway. The people in the elevator and at the grocery store, the security guards—everyone was talking about the incident. The guard who had first discovered the girl recognized Eunok and told her that the police were questioning the girl's family and friends about the injuries discovered on her body. The security tape from the elevator revealed that she had gone up to the roof of Tower 402 at eight o'clock in the evening. He also mentioned that homeowners were concerned that the accident was going to cause their apartment value to drop.

The door that led to the rooftop of Tower 402 wasn't sealed off. It was probably because of the ongoing police investigation. She pushed open the small metal door and surveyed the spacious rooftop.

The rooftop railing barely came up to her waist. She faced her apartment tower, which caught the sunlight and sparkled like fish scales. She counted the windows and tried to look for Suite #1703, where they said the girl's family had once lived. But because all the windows looked the same, she kept losing track.

The girl had walked all the way here without shoes. Her socks were reduced to shreds and blood had collected under her toenails, as if she'd stepped on rocks and broken glass. She'd gone up to the roof and sat directly across from #1703, gazing into its balcony window, glowing with an orange light. Although it was spring, mornings and nights were still chilly. What had the girl wanted to see? At that hour, young children in just their underclothes would have been running around in the living room. Their mother would have been reheating the stew for their father, who had come home from work a little later than usual. He would have stepped out of the bathroom, dripping water, and horsed around with the kids. Had the girl noted the new wallpaper and different furniture arrangement? Maybe she'd wondered if the tiny inscription she'd scrawled in the corner of her old room was still there. She and her family had moved out of the apartment a year and a half before. Why had she come this far without shoes, until her toes had started to bleed? The spot on the rooftop directly across from #1703 was strewn with paper airplanes. The girl seemed to have folded them well into the night. More than half of the pages had been torn from her notebook. Eunok spread open an airplane, but the paper was blank, just like the girl's future now.

V

Not only the photographer, but even Choi Kisu, holding the rattle, was having a difficult time of getting his baby girl to pose in front of the birthday table. When she grasped a paper bill during the doljabi ritual, the people laughed and clapped. Kisu's wife passed her to Eunok, but her face turned red and crumpled, as soon as she realized she was being held by a stranger. Eunok cooed and bounced her up and down, but the rainbow-colored hanbok was slippery and the baby kept slipping from her hands. Kisu's wife laughed at how overwhelmed Eunok looked.

Kim Taekyeong, another friend of her husband's, was drinking alone in the corner of the banquet hall. Shortly after her husband had confessed his wish to become a deadbeat, many changes had taken place. Two couples from that night had ended up separating, and one couple had moved out to the country for a job transfer. Only she and Taekyeong had come to the birthday celebration. He noticed Eunok and greeted her.

"Long time no see."

His forehead and nose were already blotchy from the liquor. Since Kisu and his wife were busy greeting guests, Eunok was left alone with Taekyeong. After his divorce, she'd heard he'd started selling cars. He knocked back a shot of soju and thrust the glass at Eunok. He poured until it overflowed, but he was watching her face, not the glass.

"So how's life?"

His bloodshot eyes bored into her. He let out a deep sigh, his breath hitting her in the face. Eunok tipped back the glass and took a sip. The soju tasted bitter.

"Bet life's treating you well, Eunok. Pour me a shot, will you?"

Taekyeong didn't bother to wait. He took the bottle and poured himself another shot.

"You look like you're doing pretty good, a completely different story from Sanghyeon. Goddamn it."

As he got to his feet, he lost his balance and stumbled, his hand sweeping plates off the table. They shattered, and spicy skate fish, pancakes, and soy sauce scattered all over the floor. People stared at Taekyeong. A young man sitting at the next table tried to help, but Taekyeong shook him off. Shoving his shirttail back into his pants, he looked at Eunok, his lips twitching with anger.

Kisu rushed up to them. "What the hell's the matter with you?"

Taekyeong looked from Kisu to Eunok and snickered. "I see what's happening here. You guys think you're too good for me, don't you? I'll leave you to it then. By the way, Eunok, I never liked you."

Eunok picked up her purse and walked quickly out of the hall. She could feel everyone's gaze on her. Taekyeong shouted after her.

"Bitch!"

Kisu followed her out to the elevator. She felt dizzy, perhaps because of the soju.

"Please, try to understand. You know he isn't really like that, don't you?"

•

The apartment Eunok had once lived in for eight years was five bus stops from the banquet hall. She had simply started walking in order to clear her head, but when she looked up, she saw a familiar sight across the street. The apartment complex looked the same as it always had. Because it still hadn't received a fresh coat of paint, the exterior looked ashen, as if it were covered with coal dust. The balcony railings were red with rust. Some were so old that they were barely hanging on. The grounds were strewn with bicycles that children had ridden and flung aside, all pieces of junk no one would think to steal. Even the odds and ends piled high to the ceiling, which she could glimpse through dusty balcony windows, were the same as she remembered. Just like before, she walked past the playground as if she were going for a stroll. Luckily, she didn't run into anyone she knew. The chains on one of the three swings were broken, exactly as they'd been before she'd moved out.

She stood behind her old apartment. A child's clothes hung on the clothesline. The stickers on the balcony window had fallen off, all except for one fish. She couldn't see inside because of the lowered blinds.

Because the complex had been built on the side of a mountain, an embankment stood between the buildings. The first-floor apartment where she had lived was in the shadow of the embankment, so it never got any sunlight, even in the middle of the day. However, if she'd opened the windows and raised the blinds, she'd ended up making eye contact with someone from the building on the other side of the embankment.

The day they had installed the blinds, her husband had gone to the building across from theirs with a flashlight. They'd wanted to determine how much of the blinds they could keep open for air flow without being seen. Every time she lowered the blinds, the flashlight blinked on and off from above the embankment. She adjusted the blinds until you couldn't see into their apartment from the opposite building.

Eunok struggled over the embankment and went up to the rooftop of the opposite building. Fortunately, the door to the rooftop was not locked. The stairs stopped on the 5th floor and a metal ladder ran up the wall. The ladder was so old and rusty that one of the rails dangled loose. Still, she climbed up. She raised the square trapdoor and saw yellow water tanks. Rainwater had collected in empty clay jars that someone had left there.

She drew closer to the railing and was able to glimpse the inside of her old apartment through the bottom crack where the blind wasn't completely lowered. The new owners were still using the same flooring she and her husband had put in. A little girl who looked around five years old was eating noodles with her bare hands; there was black bean sauce smeared all around her mouth.

For eight years, Eunok and her husband had argued a lot. She'd believed the reason for their fights had been their dark, cramped apartment, where they'd had to keep the blinds lowered even in the middle of summer. But when they'd moved into their bright, new, spacious apartment, her husband had left for good. Eunok sat on the rooftop, legs dangling over the edge. She thought of the girl who had fallen on top of her car. The girl, too, had probably gazed into her old apartment for a long time.

She didn't know where it had come from, but there was a dress shirt on the rooftop. It was covered with yellow stains, as if it had gotten soaked in the rain and then dried. White dress shirts were common, but she noticed the third button from the top. One had to look carefully to see that it was different from the rest of the buttons, but it was impossible to fool the very person who had sewed it onto the shirt. Although its size and color were the same as the rest, it had a different number of holes.

This dress shirt, on this apartment rooftop, was definitely her husband's. The sleeves were always the first to wear and get dirty. She'd told him to use arm warmers, but he'd never listened.

Her husband, while getting ready for work, had called out to her, "Hey, where's my shirt? There's none left."

Busy enough herself, she shouted back, not bothering to go in the room. "Look again. An extra one should be there somewhere."

Unable to find a clean, pressed shirt, he'd had to wear the shirt he'd worn the day before.

When one of his shirts had disappeared off the clothesline, she had assumed it had flown out the half-open balcony window. But the shirt had ended up here.

Just as the high school girl had, her husband had probably sat in this exact spot and gazed into their old apartment. Light the color of honey would have seeped through the cracks in the blinds and the little girl's laughter would have rung out. What had he seen here? He would have thought about his selfish wife. About how she'd washed and ironed a week's worth of shirts at a time. About all the times he'd headed to work in his pressed shirt and tie, which was too tight around the neck. And about the dinner a few years back when he'd said he wanted to become a deadbeat.

That night, he had looked around at his closest friends and confessed his wish to do nothing. Because he'd had his back turned to Eunok, she hadn't been able to see his expression. If she could go back to that night . . .

His friends burst into laughter. One friend smacks her husband in the back of the head and another says that everyone dreams about doing nothing. Her husband lowers his head, and brings the beer glass to his lips. Eunok places her hand on his back. He slowly looks up. His bloodshot eyes are glittering with tears. He manages to get his emotions under control. Someone pours more beer into his glass and shouts, "To deadbeats!" The men raise their glasses and cry, "To deadbeats!"

VI

When the kite didn't fly properly, Eunok muttered under her breath the way he'd had. She picked up the fallen kite and adjusted the line before running across the rooftop again. It looked like it was going to rain. She felt the hot breeze. Past midnight, the apartment plaza twenty-nine stories below was as quiet as a reservoir. Though the light was on in the security booth, the guard was sleeping, his head against the back of his chair. There would be no patrol for a while.

She'd washed the shirt a few times, but the stains didn't come out. On the way home from work, Eunok stopped by the stationery store and bought bamboo spars and a reel. The stationery owner pulled out a dusty reel from the back of a shelf.

Look, the bowstring needs to be curved about 15 degrees. Tsk, tsk . . . And there's a correct order for gluing the spars, too. First the head, then the diagonals, then the spine, and then the waist.

Having skipped dinner, Eunok sat hunched over in the living room and made a kite out of her husband's shirt. She could almost hear his nagging. *Are you serious? You've never even flown a kite before? As for the bridle, you're supposed to use just one string.*

The kite caught the wind and shot up into the air. Eunok slowly released the line that was wrapped around her finger. The kite started to spin in circles. The waist spar was too thick. The kite dropped to the edge of the roof. She shaved a little off the waist spar. Once more she ran across the rooftop against the wind with the kite in hand.

It was nearly five in the morning when her kite caught the wind and surged into the air. The line began to unravel from the reel on its own. The kite sailed farther and farther away. When the last bit of line left the reel, Eunok didn't try to hold on to it. The freed kite rattled in the wind and slowly became sucked up into the dawn sky. At last, it became a dot in the distance and disappeared altogether from view.

There were still many of her husband's dress shirts left. Eunok rummaged through the fishing equipment he had bought but never used, and hauled out the fishing chair. Since no one was watching, she sat with her knees spread.

The rooftop railings spread below Eunok's feet like terraces. Her husband had always grumbled at the fact that she couldn't take much time off work to go on vacation to the mountains or the sea. She removed her flip-flops and placed her bare feet on the cement floor. The rough cement was lukewarm. The railings washed in like the waves, wetting her feet. From somewhere she heard the crashing of the sea. She smelled brine and seaweed. The salty wind tangled in her hair.

Eunok found herself sitting on a watchtower with the silvery sand stretching on for miles. She shaded her eyes with her right hand. The sea seemed to loom closer. She turned her head from side to side, looking carefully to make sure no one was lost at sea.

On That Green, Green Grass

The dog thief was careless. In his greed to swipe all the dogs from our block in one go, he kept at his work until dawn, so that it was light out by the time he lured our dog from our house, the last house tucked away at the end of the dead-end street. For the past several years, the paperboy had been delivering the newspaper at the same time. It was bright enough for him to make out the first few letters of the license plate as the truck crept away.

It was a cargo truck, the boy said, a typical one with a Gyeonggi plate that started with the prefix *ba*. He also managed to recall the following two digits, as well as the phrase ALWAYS QUICK, ALWAYS

RIGHT in white letters on the side. As if to conceal the goods it was carrying, a shiny blue tarp had covered the cargo bed.

If the thief hadn't been so greedy, if he had executed the job in an "always quick, always right" manner as the words boasted, nothing could have been traced back to him. Greed will always lead to your downfall.

But weren't we just as guilty of that?

•

In order to find a house with a yard, my husband and I had scoured Seoul's outskirts for three months. There were many things to consider: my husband's commute to his job in downtown Seoul; access to good schools in the area, since our child was starting school the following year; and finances, of course, which played the biggest factor in our decision.

We bought a map that showed the entire province of Gyeonggi, and if a house we wanted to see was an hour and a half away, we got in the car and set out. Even the outskirts were crammed with apartment towers, but the ones standing next to paddies and fields seemed especially ugly. When we'd left the apartment complexes behind and skirted the mountain for about half an hour, the view finally opened out before us.

Furniture showrooms, their entrances flanked by placards and banners, lined both sides of the two-lane road. Small factories lay scattered in the distance, and specialty restaurants serving up things like sumac chicken and freshwater-fish stew huddled close together. We even passed a colony of flashy love motels. Though it was the middle of the day, there were several cars parked in the lots.

My gaze had been skimming the motel signs absentmindedly when I happened to see a sign that said Goryeo Mountain Cabin Inn. I cried out to my husband, who was driving. Though the motel looked completely different from before, its name, the manmade lake out in front, and the old pine tree beside it were exactly the same. My husband and I had stayed there about eight years before.

"Women remember the oddest things," he muttered with an embarrassed chuckle.

As we entered the town, the sudden increase in traffic volume forced us to slow down. Though the old road hadn't changed, shops now crowded either side, making it seem narrower. It was so narrow that cars coming and going out of the bus terminal couldn't complete a U-turn and were forced to put their cars in reverse. I gazed out the window while we waited for a bus to move out of the way. There were several bookstores, as well as a small library. I also spotted a large supermarket and shopping mall, and even plastic surgery clinics and restaurants squeezed between them. The town went on for another 500 meters or so, and fields appeared once more. As if there were a lot of families like us longing for a house with a yard, signs advertising the sale of single-family homes flapped in the wind. I liked the town. More than anything, I liked the fact that it was close to Goryeo Mountain Cabin Inn. To me, the motel felt like home.

When we finally got our yard, we filled it with things we hadn't even dreamed of when we lived in an apartment. We put in sod and purchased a white plastic patio set. We didn't forget to get a parasol for the table. We planted persimmon and jujube saplings, and arranged the rocks we had secretly taken from the river. But the yard was curiously inert, as if something were missing. We tried rearranging the rocks, this way and that, but the yard felt empty all the same.

What we had imagined was a child who would giggle and ride a bicycle, who would play ball on the grass. But our child sat under the parasol like a rock or sapling, more like a still-life object. We needed something full of energy that would make the yard come alive. Only when my husband let loose the mutt he'd bought on his way home did the yard finally become the yard of our dreams.

My husband didn't complain, even when his commute to work was two hours each way. Before our move, he had spent his Sundays napping; after all, there was no need for him to teach our child how to ride a bicycle or play basketball like other dads. But instead of taking a nap, he now trained the dog on Sundays. If I happened to look out while making stew or marinating greens, I saw him in a crouch, tossing the ball. When the dog brought the ball back, my husband laughed as he scratched and rubbed the dog's chest. Our boy sat under the parasol and quietly drew in his sketchbook. Sometimes, when my husband passed him the ball to toss, he chucked it sloppily, and if the dog retrieved it, he recoiled at the ball now slick with drool. Eyeing his dad, he held the ball with the tips of his fingers and pretended to throw it. When the stew was done, I called out to them in my pretty apron: "Lunch is ready!"

That morning, my husband stepped out to collect the morning paper and knew immediately that the dog was gone. There were morsels of meat in front of the kennel, and his leash was discovered outside the gate. After pacing back and forth with the leash in hand, my husband went out into the street and ran into our neighbor, who was calling for her dog.

The thief had taken all the dogs from the neighborhood that lived outside. A police officer arrived. He seemed flustered, surrounded by people who raised their voices at him at the same time. Twelve dogs had been stolen. He recorded the breed and value of each dog in his notepad. With the exception of our dog, all eleven were either Jindos or purebreds recognized by the American Kennel Club. Some were worth over several million won. When it was our turn, we hesitated when we were supposed to write down our dog's breed. Our Yeller wasn't a Pointer or a Collie. He was a common mutt.

"But our Yeller is different!" cried my husband, who was late for work because of the incident.

His voice shook a little. It seemed he wanted to add something more, but the police officer cut him off.

"How much is he worth?"

My husband said that he'd cost fifty thousand won.

"Seeing that the thief nabbed all the dogs in the neighborhood, he's probably planning to sell them to a specialty restaurant for their meat. I bet he used a tranquilizer gun, since he took even the guard dogs."

Since dog soup restaurants typically used mutts for their meat, our Yeller probably played a big part in the officer reaching that conclusion. A woman whose Spaniel had been taken shrieked and sank to the ground. Even after the police left, the neighbors stood around murmuring for a long time. My husband finally left for work around lunch time. Several times he asked that I call him as soon as there were any updates. He started the car and rolled down his window, frowning at me.

"This wouldn't have happened if our fence hadn't been so low. Whose idea was it anyway to have a fence this low?"

"You wanted a house with a yard, too," I snapped. I was also on edge. "And you're the one who brought the dog home, so quit making such a fuss. We're not the only ones who lost a dog."

"But Yeller is different!"

"Of course he's different. He's a cheap mutt."

My husband sped down the street, turned right, and then disappeared. I'd mocked him, but I couldn't concentrate on my work either. Yeller wasn't muscular or wiry, but he had such great focus that he caught the ball easily every time you tossed it. You couldn't help but laugh at the way his eyes sparkled and his tail wagged, as he watched your hand to anticipate the direction of the ball. Though he didn't look elegant or have a smooth coat, he'd never once gotten sick. But more than anything, he filled the emptiness of our home. The instant

I turned into our street from the main road, he recognized my footsteps and started barking. When I stepped into the yard, he dashed toward me as if he'd been waiting all day and rubbed against me. He could even tell my husband's car from the neighbors' cars, just by the sound. My husband had changed because of him.

Our son was still sitting under the parasol where I'd left him. I'd completely forgotten about him while we dealt with the police. I rushed to him and helped him up. His pants were wet. He sucked his finger.

"I couldn't hold it anymore."

I carried him to the bathroom and sat him down on the edge of the bathtub. His wet pants didn't come off easily. After I'd finally yanked them off, I turned on the taps and hosed him off with the showerhead. His shirt ended up getting wet. His upper body was much more developed than other six-year-olds, but from the waist down, he had the body of a three-year-old. As if he were now old enough to be embarrassed, he pressed his thighs together in order to hide his nakedness. It was getting more and more difficult to pick him up and carry him to his room.

The afternoon sunlight flooded into the living room. It was still early, but the yard seemed lifeless with not a blade of grass stirring. When I opened the door, it felt as if the dog would come bounding at any moment and lick my hand. My son's sketchbook was under the parasol. He carried it with him everywhere. While I wiped the lawn chair with a rag, my gaze fell on the sketchbook once more.

In the middle of the page was a large truck. Two men stood in front of it. One was yanking along a dog that looked like Yeller. Another man in a baseball cap stood a little further away. I ran into my son's room. He was peering at a children's book, leaning against the wall. I thrust the sketchbook at him.

"Did you wake up early this morning?"

He nodded without a word. He was a quiet boy.

"So it was this truck? The truck that took our Yeller?"

In response, he pointed at the man, who was dragging the dog away.

"Then who's this?" I asked. "The one with the hat."

"He saw the truck, too. He's the guy who delivers the newspaper."

"Why didn't you wake me?"

After some time, he finally opened his mouth. "I didn't want to bother you. You always get angry when I wake you."

I called the newspaper distribution center. When the phone had rung for a long time, a man's groggy voice came on the line. He said no one was in at the moment, and to call back around one in the morning.

As soon as my husband returned from work, he stepped into the yard and whistled. Yesterday evening, even before he whistled, Yeller had recognized the sound of my husband's car and sat waiting at the gate. My husband was about to open our front door, but turned back and sat in the lawn chair. Cigarette smoke rose above his head.

The paperboy picked up the phone. He talked a little fast, as if he were busy. He recalled the truck from that morning, but unlike what my son had drawn, he'd only seen it pull out of the street. He'd done a double take, because he'd never seen the truck before.

My husband and I called the police officer and before he could finish muttering that there were no updates, we cut him off mid-sentence and relayed very single word the paperboy had said.

The police officer said it would be easy enough to track down the last two digits of the truck's license plate the paperboy hadn't seen, but he didn't call for the next few days.

A small vegetable garden separated our house from our neighbor's. It was thick with weeds, as if it hadn't been tended. The front door opened and a middle-aged woman popped her head out. She asked if there were any updates. The police hadn't contacted her either. Through the half-open door, something like a ball of white yarn scampered out. When she clicked her tongue, the ball of yarn went back inside.

"This time, we decided to get a dog we could raise inside. Let's face it—we're not getting our dog back. You think the police would waste their time, looking for a bunch of dogs, when the world has enough crime as it is? They don't even have time to deal with people, let alone animals."

The woman hesitated for a moment and then opened her mouth again. "Yesterday when we were coming back from our hike, we saw your son. He was singing, sitting right up against the window . . ."

She seemed about to go on, but stopped. When people learned about our son's condition, they all got the same expression. My husband stood waiting by the door.

"She's right. We can't just wait for the police to call. It'll be too late then. You think you can do something? I'd go out there myself, but I can't because of work. I'll leave the car for you."

I gave my son his breakfast. I left his lunch in his room, plus a donut he'd have for a snack, and got in the car. According to the paperboy, the truck had a Gyeonggi plate with the prefix *ba*; the truck had to be somewhere within Gyeonggi. I spread open the map we'd purchased back when we'd been looking for a house. I highlighted the entire Gyeonggi region; it encircled Seoul like a thick band.

I decided to start with the areas around our house. I blindly set out for the main road. When I caught sight of a specialty restaurant, I parked the car and went inside. Three or four of these specialty restaurants stood next to each other on one block.

As soon as I pushed open the door, I was hit with the smell of animal fat. Not yet lunch time, the restaurant was empty. Menu items were plastered on the walls. A woman with bloodshot eyes came out from the kitchen, shuffling along in plastic sandals. I ordered a ginseng chicken soup and sat at a table, facing the kitchen. There was a gigantic refrigerator the size of a wardrobe. As if she had recently rinsed the tile floor, water was pooled in places, but the overpowering smell of meat, together with the fishy odor of water, turned my stomach. Even the wooden table my elbows rested on were sticky with grease.

When the woman brought the chicken soup, I asked her if a truck with a Gyeonggi plate that started with *ba* supplied the meat to her restaurant. She grew suspicious and asked all sorts of questions, finally revealing that she'd been getting her dog meat from the same place for the past ten years. She added that they raised their own dogs and said no more. The chicken soup tasted bad. It seemed she was using the same pot to boil the chicken and dog meat. I took a few bites of chicken, but couldn't stomach it and had to put my spoon down.

I went into the other restaurants on the block, but they all said the same thing. They gave vague answers, busy with getting ready for the lunch rush. At the last restaurant, what looked like fresh meat was piled high in a yellow plastic crate. The instant I saw the hunks of raw meat, bile rose up in my throat. I covered my mouth and ran back to my car. Every commercial refrigerator in a specialty restaurant would be filled with the same kind of meat. All the way home, my head pounded and I felt carsick.

The house reeked of food and human waste; it was coming from his potty. Our son had dozed off while drawing. Hardened grains of rice clung to the edge of the lunch plate. I stepped on something mushy by the foot of the bed. A half-eaten donut. It looked like the Gyeonggi region I'd highlighted on the map that morning. Where could our dog be?

I shook our son awake and heated up some food in the microwave for him. The stench from the restaurants earlier that day hit me again.

There was sauce on his chin, but I didn't have the energy to take him to the bathroom to wash him up.

My husband came home about an hour later than usual. After grumbling about how he'd had to transfer twice on the subway and then take the bus, only to be stuck in traffic because of an accident, he asked if I'd found any leads. I hung up the suit jacket and necktie he handed me, and said that I'd drive out a bit farther the next day.

My husband had trouble falling asleep. He hadn't been able to tell before, but now that he'd walked home, our street just wasn't the same. It felt as if he were walking down a dark alley with no lights. It made sense, since there was not a single dog left to bark, even if a stranger were to enter the street. The silent nights continued.

On the third day, I drove to Yeoncheon. With the Hantan River amusement park nearby, there were many specialty restaurants in the area. Every one of these places reeked with the smell of perilla seeds and meat. It was a smell that wouldn't fade, even if you mopped the floors every day. But no one knew of a truck that had a Gyeonggi plate with the prefix *ba*.

My eyes were tired from driving, and my right calf was sore from stepping on and off the gas and brake pedals all day. As soon as I came home, I pushed open the door to my son's room, calling his name, but his room was dark.

I switched on the light, but he wasn't there. My feet crushed the shrimp crackers he had dropped on the floor. Half-finished drawings, pastel crayons, and crackers were strewn around the room. When I lifted the cloth food cover, I saw his lunch was untouched.

I opened the bathroom door, but he wasn't there either. I looked in the master bedroom and even the storage room, but he was nowhere to be found. I went out to the yard and called his name. Dread gripped my heart. My legs kept buckling. I ran down our street. The street led to the main road where cars whizzed by. Freight trucks carrying lumber and rebar were constantly barreling down the road at frightening speeds. Someone snatched my wrist. It was my husband. He hadn't seen our son on his way home from the bus station, either.

"You can't even look after one kid?" my husband cried, taking in the mess in our son's room. He yanked off his jacket and flung it to the ground. "How does a kid who can't even walk disappear? Did he fly away? Did the ground swallow him up? What the hell have you been doing?"

"What have I been doing?" I screamed. "I've been looking for your precious dog all day!"

At the dead end, where the houses stopped, was a path that led up to a mountain. My husband took a flashlight and went up the mountain. I walked out onto the main road, all the way to town. I kept shouting our son's name, but because of all the traffic, I couldn't even hear my own voice. The town was bustling with students heading home and young people who had come out for drinks. I went into the arcade, but I didn't see any children. I went into a store and described our child, but no one had seen him.

I came back onto the main road. I looked up and found myself standing in front of several love motels, their parking lots filled with cars. I took the side lane up to Goryeo Mountain Cabin Inn. All the way to the inn entrance, pebbles covered the narrow lane, which was just wide enough for a single car to pass. The pebbles glistened in the streetlight. The pine tree was strung with lights and they flashed on and off in sequence. Standing next to the tree, I glanced at the motel windows. Eight years ago, my husband and I had stayed in Room 301. The room was occupied; orange light escaped through the cracks in the curtain.

"Hey, you know that song?" my husband had said back then, proceeding to sing in his tone-deaf voice, "On that green, green grass, I want to build a picture-perfect house—"

I sang along, "—and live forever with the one I love. When spring comes, we sow seeds—"

What we had wanted was a house with a yard, with children both big and small, who would run and play in that yard. But we decided not to have any more children after our son became ill. When we had laughed and sung in Room 301 at Goryeo Mountain Cabin Inn, we'd had no inkling that our future child would not be able to walk.

"What's the name of the song again?" he'd asked.

The name had been on the tip of my tongue. "'On That Green, Green Grass'? No, 'A Picture-Perfect House'? That doesn't sound right either."

On my way home, I hummed the tune, which was now stuck in my head. I started singing louder and louder. Trucks roared past me. A bus carrying just two or three passengers rattled by. Desperately, I kept singing.

Our boy was lying on the sofa. My husband, who had been smoking while pacing the yard, saw me and ground out his cigarette with his shoe. He'd found him in the corn field halfway up the mountain.

His entire body was covered with dirt. It seemed he had crawled out the door, all the way up to the field. I stripped off his clothes and sat him in the tub. He kept dozing off, utterly exhausted. I felt a surge of both relief and anger. As I washed his two bony legs, I had to clench my teeth together. With a soapy washcloth, I scrubbed his skin until it turned red. Even as he twisted in pain, he didn't complain or cry out. His eyes were full of tears.

"If it hurts, tell me it hurts. Why did you crawl all the way there? Did you want to scare me to death? You damn—"

The word *cripple* rose to my throat, but I swallowed it. His knees and elbows were skinned raw, and there were bruises all over his body, as if he'd bashed into rocks. As I was carrying my naked son out from the bathroom, I slipped and banged my knee on the floor. He flew out from between my arms like a bar of soap and landed a few feet ahead. My husband, who had been smoking outside, rushed in. He picked the boy up and carried him to his room. I cleaned his wounds and put ointment on them. He fell asleep crying. By the time I'd bandaged him up and finally stepped into our room, it was past midnight.

I pulled back the covers and crawled into bed. My husband grunted and turned over. "This is exactly why I don't feel like coming home. What was the point of getting a yard and a dog? It was pointless. Completely pointless from the beginning."

"Don't worry. Even if I have to search the ends of the earth, I'm going to find that dog and bring him back."

I bought a three-digit combination lock from the hardware store, as well as a hasp latch for the door. I kept dropping the nail or it kept bending under the hammer. Our boy watched from the living room, trembling each time the nail flew out. I tried again, pinching the nail between my fingers, but I struck my thumb instead. My thumb started to swell immediately, turning blue. Sucking it, I said to my son, who was sitting behind me, "If you had a treasure, something really valuable, what would you do?"

"I'd hide it. So no one can find it."

"That's right. I'd put it in a safe no one can open. A safe only Mommy can open."

He didn't say anything. All he did was watch uneasily as I moved the television and telephone from the living room to his room. I wrote down my husband's and my cell phone number in big numbers on a piece of paper and stuck it on the wall.

"If something happens, just call these numbers, okay? This is only while we look for Yeller. If you'd woken us that morning, none of this would have happened. And if you hadn't crawled up the mountain, I wouldn't have to do this right now. Just hang on. When we find Yeller, everything will be okay."

When I picked him up and tried to carry him to his room, he burst into tears and started to swing his arms and scream. I ended up getting struck in the face and my nose started to bleed. Stunned, he stopped crying. I changed him out of his blood-stained shirt and put his lunch, snack, and potty inside his room.

I closed the door and was scrambling the code on the lock when he called out from inside. His sobs made him difficult to understand.

"So I'm your treasure, Mommy?"

"Of course you are! You're my most valuable treasure!"

I got in the driver's seat. I took out the map from the center console and spread it open. Yeoncheon and Pocheon. I'd circled the places I'd already searched. After I'd wet a tissue with saliva and rubbed the blood off my nose, I started out toward Uijeongbu. I spotted two small specialty restaurants. One wasn't open yet, and the sickening odor of boiling meat wafted from the other one.

The restaurant was small with only a few tables. The woman, who had been trimming green onions, called toward the kitchen. "Mr. Kim—the one who supplies us the meat—doesn't his truck have a Gyeonggi plate that starts with *ba*?"

An old man poked his face out through the hatch and gazed at me. "Hmm, how should I know? He'll be coming soon, so why don't you stick around and ask him yourself?"

While I waited, I helped the woman trim over ten bundles of sesame leaves. When I moved onto the green onions, I happened to look inside the kitchen and caught the man stuffing a dog's leg into a cauldron billowing with steam.

I stepped outside to get some air. I called my son. I had left the phone close to him so that he could crawl to it. After a little while, he picked up. He said he had already eaten lunch. When I asked what he would like for dinner, he said he didn't want anything. He sounded completely different from that morning when he'd been crying. In fact, he sounded as if I'd interrupted his fun.

"Mommy, I have to go. My friend's here outside the window. She just told me something really funny."

I was about to ask him about this "friend," but he hung up. A truck pulled up next to my car. The door opened and a middle-aged man stepped out. He had on a hiking hat and rubber boots that went up to his knees. He took out a box of meat from the refrigerated system in the back, hoisted it onto his shoulder, and went into the restaurant. The woman stuck her face out through the restaurant door and gave me a look.

Hurriedly, I looked at the truck's license plate. It was a Gyeonggi plate, which started with *ba*, but the numbers after were different. Plus, the words ALWAYS QUICK, ALWAYS RIGHT in white letters on the side weren't there. The paperboy had said that there had been a blue plastic tarp covering the back, but this one was a custom-built refrigerated truck.

Yeller had been missing for nearly a week. By now, he may have been boiled and sliced into wedges or served up as a stew. I started heading home. Right then a truck cut in front of me, blocking my vision. A blue plastic tarp covered the back. I careened my neck in order to see the license plate. It was a Gyeonggi plate, and the two digits the paperboy had said that followed *ba* were exactly the same.

I needed to check the side of the truck. But because of all the cars ahead, I couldn't switch lanes. I had no choice but to follow. The driver drove recklessly. Because he tended to brake suddenly, I almost rear-ended him a few times. The truck started to head in the direction of Dongducheon. I did the same. Bars and cafes lined the streets, and I noticed many foreign tourists walking around. Large armored trucks appeared on the road.

The truck with the blue tarp passed downtown Dongducheon and headed down a secluded road. The occasional restaurant or motel popped up. It then started to climb a lane thick with acacias. I waited a bit, and then started up the lane. At the top of the hill was a wide lot with a few makeshift buildings made of plywood and steel frames. The truck was parked in front of one of the buildings, and a young man, whom I assumed had been driving, was urinating into the woods. He turned to look as I drove up the path. The smell of varnish was overpowering. I'd followed the truck to a furniture factory.

The man straightened his pants and grinned at me, displaying yellow teeth. I purposely turned my car around near the truck. The words NU FURNITURE were painted in large, yellow letters on the side. I started down the hill. Through my rearview mirror, I saw two men hop into the back. They pulled off the blue tarp, revealing a wardrobe with missing doors.

When I opened the lock and went into my son's room, I found him asleep. He had fallen asleep while drawing. In his hand was a blue pastel crayon. He had drawn himself sitting by a lake, fishing.

In his drawings, he was always stationary. The lake swarmed with all kinds of creatures. There was a goldfish, octopus, squid, scabbardfish, and eel. The octopus had eight legs and the squid had ten. But the boy with the fishing rod had none. It was always this way; he never drew any legs for himself. Instead, he drew a triangle for his body, a circle on top of the vertex for his head, and attached two long arms like squid tentacles to the triangle. Once, my husband had mistaken this figure for a squid, while flipping through our son's sketchbook. The creatures avoided the fishhook that the boy dangled in the water. He had on a red baseball cap. I had bought him that cap for his third birthday. He was the only person in the drawing.

I turned the page. He'd colored the next page entirely black, and covered it with the symbol for a hot spring, drawings both big and small. The page looked like a sheet of gift wrap. When I looked out of his bedroom window, I saw the same icon strewn across the night sky. All the motels turned on this sign at night. They had started doing this to let people know there was hot water, but from a certain point it had become the symbol for motels.

When Sunday came, my husband just lay in bed. After all, he had no reason to go out to the yard. Dust covered the dog's bowl; the water inside had long dried up.

The paperboy stopped by the house to collect the subscription fee. He was a tall young man, about twenty years old. He was wearing glasses.

"Any news from the police?" he asked, his eyes magnified behind the thick lenses.

I shook my head as I handed him the payment.

"The police called me twice. They asked me the same questions over and over again, it was annoying. Anyway, I really hope they find the dogs. They used to start barking as soon as I stepped into the street, but it's too quiet now."

"Yesterday I saw a similar truck and followed it all the way to Dongducheon," I said. "The license plate even had the same numbers you'd mentioned."

"I should have looked more carefully, but I wasn't quick enough. I wish I could have seen the whole thing. But you saw a similar truck yesterday? With a blue tarp, like that curtain over there?"

I turned my head to look where he pointed. He was pointing at my neighbor's second-story window. It was the room used by their oldest daughter, who was attending college. The curtain was drawn, but it was red, not blue.

"Didn't you say it was a blue tarp?"

He blinked a few times. His face soon grew hard, as if he realized his mistake just then.

"That curtain's not blue, it's red—" I said.

"I'm sorry," he mumbled. "Thing is, I'm a little colorblind. I have trouble telling red and blue apart . . ."

He hurriedly got back on his bicycle and dashed away. His long thin legs moved like scissors. I should have been on the lookout for a truck with a red tarp. But instead, I'd only been looking for one with a blue tarp. And his words about it being a Gyeonggi plate that started with the prefix *ba* couldn't be trusted. His eyes were bad. He could have easily mistaken *ba* for *ma*.

My son, who'd been nibbling at his food, said all of a sudden, "Mommy, my friend said she wants to take me somewhere fun."

He was trying to get my attention. It was natural to start telling a few lies at six. Or maybe she was just an imaginary friend he'd made up because he was so bored and lonely. Long ago, I'd had an imaginary friend, too. Anne, Dorothy, Alice . . .

"So is she coming over today?" I asked.

He grinned instead of answering me.

When I was doing up the padlock, he asked from inside, "Mommy, what's the code for the lock?"

"It's your birthday," I blurted in my rush. After all, there was no way for him to open the door from the inside.

I hurriedly got my car keys and was about to step through the front door when he called out, "Bye, Mommy!"

At the sound of his cheerful voice, I felt better and decided to humor him. "Have fun with your friend!"

I was on the lookout for a truck with a red plastic tarp and a Gyeonggi plate that started with *ba* or *ma*. I drove past Goryeo Mountain Cabin Inn twice. The strange thing about memories is that every time I passed it, I thought automatically of the song I'd sung with my husband. I was so focused on finding the truck that I almost ran a red light several times. When I slammed on the brakes, the car behind me honked and flashed his emergency lights. I saw a truck with a Gyeonggi plate that started with *ba* and followed it for over half an hour, but in the end, I realized it actually started with *ga*.

I skipped lunch and sped along the road. I sometimes saw trucks with a blue tarp, but not a single truck with a red tarp. All of a sudden, a truck with a Gyeonggi plate that started with *ma* squeezed in ahead of me. As it cut in, I saw the words ALWAYS QUICK, ALWAYS

RIGHT painted on its side. It didn't have the red tarp, but it was probably stored away, since there hadn't been any rain for the past few days. I followed the truck. Soon I passed the Come Again sign that let me know I was leaving Gyeonggi Province.

When I was passing Hongcheon of Gangwon, I realized the truck I'd been following didn't even have a Gyeonggi plate, but a Gangwon plate. I stopped by a rest area and washed my face in the bathroom. Someone bumped into me. It was only when I was standing in front of a vending machine to get something to drink that I realized my wallet, which had been in my pocket, was gone.

The car ran out of gas and eventually stopped halfway between Woncheon and Daseongri. My husband, who had to leave work early to get me, put gas in the car and didn't say anything on the entire drive home. It was late when we passed Uijeongbu. We called home, but our son didn't pick up. It seemed he was fast asleep. We passed Goryeo Mountain Cabin Inn. The windows facing the road shone with yellow light, like the cells of honeycomb oozing with honey. All of a sudden, the title of the song that had been stuck in my head came to me. It was called "With You" by the singer Nam Jin, who had performed the song with comical gestures.

I turned the combination on the lock and opened the door. We were hit with a pungent stench. My husband grimaced and turned away. I groped in the dark to find our boy. I found his short, bony legs. He wrapped his arms around me. His breath was cloying. He mumbled as if he were talking in his sleep.

"She couldn't stay long today. There were people working in the vegetable garden all day. She said she doesn't like people."

·

The police called. They had found all the stolen dogs. The neighbors and I carpooled together to where the police had told us to go. It was a deserted farm a little ways from Uiwang. I'd passed it once while following a truck.

There were over forty dogs locked up inside a chicken coop. I saw the truck parked in the lot out front. The thief had targeted houses in the suburbs, but he'd been caught by a dog owner, returning from an early morning exercise. The owner, though, was neither colorblind, nor wearing thick glasses.

We climbed out of our cars and staggered to the coop, calling our dogs' names. Our hellish month was coming to an end. My legs buckled for some strange reason. I approached the coop and called in a cautious voice, "Yeller!"

Yeller had gained a lot of weight. He perked up his ears and drew closer to sniff me. He reared onto his back legs, and his tongue poked out through the fence to lick my hand.

I called my husband on the way home. His voice changed right away. He kept asking about the dog.

"I told you, he's fine. He's the same. He seems to have eaten well, too," I said, gazing at Yeller, who sat in the passenger seat.

In his greed to fatten up the dogs, the thief hadn't slaughtered them right away. There were three from another group of dog owners. The owners were appalled at the sight of the ropes hanging from the zelkova tree out in front. Even a tranquilizer gun was discovered inside the truck. Since all the evidence was discovered, the thief wasn't able to deny a thing. Greed had led to his downfall.

As soon as I opened the car door, Yeller sprung out and loped around the yard. The yard became alive once more. The excited barking of dogs rang through the street. Yeller barked, too, as if in response.

"I guess someone's coming?"

The door to my son's room, which I had padlocked, was open. In my rush, I stepped on the combination lock and tripped, crashing to my knees on the floor. The lock was set to 528, my son's birthday.

A feeling of dread stabbed my heart. I flung the door wide, but the room was empty.

After the police had come and gone, my husband paced the living room uneasily. Yeller, who had been waiting to greet my husband as soon as he came home, sat by the window and kept barking when my husband ran into the house without glancing at him. My husband threw the newspaper at the window. Yeller slowly backed away.

"What the hell have you been doing instead of looking after him?" he yelled.

Sitting in the middle of my son's messy room, I screamed, "You were hoping something like this would happen, weren't you? Have you ever hugged him? Even once? I bet you wished something like this would happen!"

Unlike the dog thief, whoever had taken our boy was careful. Though he'd been taken in broad daylight, no one had seen a thing. It was when the children were in school, and those who normally would have been home had gone to the farm to pick up their dogs. The only one from our block who would have been home at that time would have been our child.

The next day, our son still hadn't come home. The police concluded that he'd been kidnapped. My husband took a leave of absence from work and waited by the phone. We were willing to pay whatever sum the kidnapper demanded. It didn't matter if we had to sell this stupid house.

I hugged our son's pillow to my chest and spent the night in his room. He had left his sketchbook behind. His name was written crookedly on the cover. I turned each page and looked carefully at each picture. I caught a whiff of oil pastels.

I looked again at his drawing from the morning the dog had been stolen. The tarp covering the back of the truck was unmistakably red, like fiery flames. I had never once looked at his drawings carefully. I'd only believed the paperboy that a blue tarp had covered the back of the truck. If I'd looked more carefully at my own child's drawing, maybe I would have doubted the paperboy's words.

Fishing by the lake. In a spaceship flying between the stars. The night sky filled with the hot springs icon. In Room 301 at Goryeo Mountain Cabin Inn, my husband and I had laughed, singing about building a picture-perfect house. Not once had I asked our son why he had been awake so early that morning. He probably still hadn't been used to the new house. He might have woken from a nightmare and not been able to fall back asleep. But he had never said he was scared, because he hadn't wanted to bother us.

I flipped through a few more pages and found a picture he had drawn of me. He'd given me long lashes and painted my lips red, but when I looked closely, I realized it wasn't me after all. Her curly hair came down to her shoulders, and there was a large mole on the left side above her lip. Was this woman the friend he'd been talking about? She wasn't an imaginary friend he'd made up after all. He hadn't been lying to get my attention. I picked up the sketchbook and ran into the living room, where my husband sat waiting by the phone with the detective, who was smoking. They glanced up.

"It's her! This is the woman who took our son!"

The detective ripped out the drawing and called the station.

The drawing, however, proved not enough to crack the case. My gaze fell on the next drawing in the sketchbook, now exposed by the ripped-out page.

Our child and the curly-haired woman sat under a tree in a garden enclosed by a high stone wall. Judging by the musical notes he had drawn, it seemed they were singing. Flowers bigger than human faces were in full bloom, and behind them on a grassy hill stood a white house, overlooking everything.

The wooden door that led to the walled garden was bolted from the inside with a large padlock. Where was he? But the boy in the picture doesn't seem to want to reveal the lock combination. I peered at his round face balanced on the vertex of a triangle. His mouth dangled on his chin. A smile stretched from ear to ear, as if he had found happiness at last.

A Quiet Night

When my banker husband, who seemed guaranteed a bright and secure future, submitted his resignation letter and announced he intended to become a carpenter, I couldn't think of one good reason to talk him out of it. Shyly, like a middle school boy, he revealed that being a carpenter had been his dream since adolescence. It wasn't like he was saying he wanted to become a professional baseball player; being a carpenter was just as practical as being a banker. But he had never touched a hand plane, and I was certain no carpenter shops nearby would hire an amateur like him, whose only experience with a saw was limited to his time in high school tech class. Plus, there was no longer any reason for us to remain in that dreadful city where we had stayed put only because it was close to his job.

He may never become a master carpenter, but until he became at least a joiner, earning a livelihood fell squarely on my shoulders. I had to transfer twice on the subway and take the bus for another twenty minutes to get to the department store where I worked. If I could save at least an hour of commute time, I could perhaps attempt things I hadn't dared until now. I had a dream, too, and selling lingerie at a department store wasn't it.

We were able to get an extra bedroom, since we'd moved from the city to the outskirts. The apartment didn't face south, but we liked the fact that it had an unobstructed view with no high-rise towers in the way that would block daylight. The realtor told us not only would we have peace and quiet because we were far from the main road, but we also wouldn't need a fan during the summer because we could simply open the front and back windows for a cross breeze. There was even a large balcony where my husband could practice his carpentry. But more than anything, the department store where I worked was only half an hour away by bus.

Since we were on the second floor, we saw the tops of trees spread below us when we opened the window. My husband had wanted a quiet, private space where he could take in some sun, away from prying eyes, and there were parks both small and large nearby. Still, I didn't ask whether he'd taken a stroll in any of them while I was gone. All he seemed to be doing was puttering around the apartment, making no real attempt to become a carpenter. A few times I snuck out onto the balcony to check on his progress, but the toolbox, which contained his handsaw and nails, sat tucked away in the corner, and the wood boards were piled in the same spot from the first day he'd brought them home. The balcony, devoid of any sawdust, was spotless.

Though he no longer went to work, my husband seemed to feel that household chores were still my responsibility. The dishes from our rushed breakfast sat untouched in the sink with grains of rice crusted on the plates, and dust piled up in our apartment. The hour of commute time I'd saved went to completing household chores as soon as I got home. It was only when I was doing the dishes at the end of the day that my husband started riffling noisily through the classifieds.

"I couldn't sleep again last night."

In less than a week after our move, we'd realized that there weren't any carpentry shops nearby. No surprise, since these sorts of shops had been on the decline for some time. We'd stopped by a few, but the doors had been padlocked. One had even been converted into a fast-food joint without the old shop sign having been taken down. However, there were two large department stores in the neighborhood, as well as a 200-meter side street lined with furniture stores. Signs announcing furniture sales decorated busy intersections all year round. Perhaps it was a good thing there wasn't a single carpenter shop in the area. In fact, it wouldn't be wrong to say a place like this was an ideal location to open up his own shop.

"You can't be so picky when you're just starting out. We have some savings and I've got my job, so don't worry about making money for now. Of course it would be nice if you could bring in something as an apprentice, but right now, the most important thing is that you find a place that's willing to teach you for free."

Obviously, I didn't feel the pinch yet.

"Must be nice," he said, ignoring what I'd just said. "I can't believe you were able to sleep through the racket last night."

Our apartment was quite a ways from the main road, so the wail of ambulance sirens and screech of cars weren't an issue. As far as I knew, no fight had broken out in any of the apartment suites during the night.

"They were running around until exactly 11:27."

The racket he was referring to was the children from 306, the apartment directly above us.

"Thank goodness that's all they were doing," I said. "Sounded like castanets to my ears."

For the past several nights, we'd heard loud footfalls echoing directly above us, where we lay in bed. But for someone like me who'd grown up in a redevelopment area, it could hardly be called noise. In fact, a bit of noise helped me fall asleep. Plus, I was constantly exhausted. There was always a heap of housework to do when I came home from work. I didn't even have time to plant myself in front of the television and watch a show in peace, so I couldn't join in when my co-workers were talking about what had happened on a show the previous night. It was often past midnight when I finished all the chores, and by nine the next morning, I had to be at work, where I was on my feet the whole day, dealing with customers until I got off at eight in the evening. My calves were swollen by noon. The only thing I could do to rest my legs was to hide the lower half of my body behind a counter and raise one leg at a time like a flamingo.

I suppose it was only natural for my husband to be sensitive to the children's stomping. He was trying to blame his insomnia on our noisy neighbors, but I knew the real cause: he had never found himself in a crisis, not once in the past thirty-three years. Until he'd quit his job at the bank, he'd treaded only life's safest, securest path. He'd never failed an exam, and he was the first of all his classmates to advance in his career. His biggest dilemma until now had been deciding whether to have soup or sushi for lunch. For someone like him, he probably believed he should have been sitting on the balcony floor by now, coaxing a rocking chair's rockers into the proper curve.

I hoped the noise upstairs would also sound like music to his ears, but he had no sense of rhythm, which I believed was why he was so clumsy with the hammer. Rhythm existed everywhere in life; it could be found in any repetitive action. But his hammering contained no such rhythm.

I told him I would stop by the security booth in the morning on my way out and ask the guard to speak with the people upstairs. All household matters, including checking the dates of water service disruption and recycling collection, were my responsibility.

The security booth was empty. I waited, but the guard didn't appear. I noticed only then a Be Back Soon sign on the small door to the left, along with a note that said to inquire at the Tower 236 security booth in case of an emergency. The matter wasn't so urgent that I needed to go all the way there. I ended up running to the bus stop to make up for the five minutes I lost by waiting for the guard.

"Did you even speak to him?" my husband demanded as I was removing my shoes after coming home from work. He read the expression on my face, and said, "I see how it is. You don't even take me seriously anymore."

I registered his sweatpants and the baggy knees. I could tell he hadn't done a single thing all day. I put on my shoes again and hurried downstairs.

The security guard, who had been dozing in his booth, stirred awake. His body, resembling a dairy cow and probably weighing more than a hundred kilograms, was snug inside the narrow booth. As if he had a habit of documenting every trivial incident, he leisurely took down my name and suite number, and said he would speak with the people upstairs, but couldn't guarantee that anything would change. When I apologized for the inconvenience, he laughed and said it was all part of the job. After all, he couldn't expect to relay only good news over the intercom, like letting people know a flower delivery had come for them. His voice, piping out from a thick neck, was high and thin.

"I trust he's going to take care of it?" my husband asked as soon as I got back.

He still tended to act as if there were people reporting to him. But before I could respond, a sharp vibration started on the left part of our ceiling. Footsteps charged from the direction of the front door toward the master bedroom.

"Ha! An electric drill," he said. "Designed specifically for home use."

The noise then started up in a different spot about a foot away.

"So they're going to drill something at nine o'clock at night, are they?"

I made a direct call to 306 over the interphone. After it had rung many times, a woman picked up, out of breath.

"Hello, I'm calling from the apartment downstairs—"

"Security just called me," she snapped, cutting me off. "Un-freak-ing-believable. What do you want me to do? Tie up my kids like a couple of dogs?"

Her voice was shrill. I could picture her: tall, rake-thin, with a weather-tanned face. It seemed the call from security had upset her.

"I hate to break it to you, lady, but kids run. That's what they do. You know, the people who lived there before you never complained. Not once!"

I heard the drill and children laughing in the background.

"It sounds like you're doing some drilling over there."

"So what? We want to hang some pictures, you got a problem with that? Even if I want to turn my house into a beehive, it's still none of your damn business!"

If there's one thing I've learned from selling lingerie for seven years, it's the ability to tell the kind of people I can argue with from those I can't. There are certain women who will come to exchange brassieres they had worn for over a week. After raising their voice for the entire lingerie department to hear, they refuse to leave until they have succeeded in getting their way. The woman upstairs was in the same category. I told her I understood, added that I was sorry, and hung up.

"What do you mean you're sorry? This isn't a department store and she's not your customer! If you don't stand up to her, she'll only be convinced she's right and walk all over you!" My husband gazed at me, as if he found me pathetic.

"Why are you picking a fight with someone who just got home from work?" I snapped, uttering the same tired phrase that husbands sometimes say to their wives when they come home. "Why don't *you* do something for a change? You think you can control those kids when their own mother can't? You try dealing with a woman like that!"

"Oh, you think I can't?" My husband whipped around and glared at me. "Sure, I'll do something about it. I'm not dead yet."

He was definitely wound-up. Perhaps he'd been lying about quitting the bank to become a carpenter. While I grew suspicious about his reason for quitting and my enraged husband smoked a cigarette and paced the living room, the people in 306 drilled in five more nails.

Over the next few weeks, the situation grew worse. The children stomped around the apartment incessantly. They bounced and dribbled balls. My husband urged me again and again to speak to the neighbors when I already had my hands full, getting ready for work.

"Don't stay cooped up all day and why don't you try exercising? How about tennis? Regular exercise might help you sleep at night."

"I guess you're the expert now."

Our conversations usually ended this way. He managed to fall into a light sleep past midnight when everyone in 306 was finally sleeping, and he woke with a curse at six in the morning when the children upstairs started running again. My husband lost a considerable amount of weight. His cheekbones began to jut out and there were dark circles under his eyes. We had only two options, but moving to the fourth floor above the people upstairs seemed unrealistic, so all we could do was call them regularly over the interphone.

Every time the children jumped off the couch and landed on the floor, our balcony window trembled. At night when the children were finally asleep, a pair of plastic sandals paced back and forth on the balcony and water gushed down the drain. A stainless-steel basin was dragged along the tile floor, or it struck something with a loud clang.

Later, they didn't bother to pick up the interphone, though we could clearly hear them. My husband sprang to his feet and ran to the balcony, coming back with a plank of wood. He chased the noise around the room with the plank he'd planned to turn into a wooden chair, and struck the ceiling with it. Wherever the plank hit, the paper tore and the concrete began to show. But the noise stopped only for the second my husband banged on the ceiling, then started up again.

"Just pretend a couple of monkeys live above us. We'll never win against people like that."

But he didn't want to pretend such a thing. Soon, louder footsteps were added to the noise. They sounded like the enraged stomping of a tall, skinny woman, who was trying to add ten more kilograms to her fifty kilograms. Noise is often amplified downstairs. If her heavy stomping wasn't enough to satiate her anger, she dragged a chair or some other furniture across the room and back.

The thermal liner we'd installed on the ceiling when we first moved in was torn in places as if a mouse had chewed through it. The holes were so big you could no longer tell what the pattern had once been. When I lay in bed and gazed up at those spots, all I saw was how my husband had darted crazily around the room with the plank in hand. There was no sign of the professional he had once been. He had zero patience, and was always wry and full of complaints.

I could tell right away that the man sitting on the playground bench was my husband. His head was turned to the left, and the only things in his line of vision were the seesaw and slide.

A little girl stood at the top of the slide with her hands at her hips. My husband's gaze followed her as she slid down. It was a good thing he was out; it wasn't good for him to stay cooped up all day. I walked toward him and placed my hand on his shoulder. He flinched and jumped to his feet, instinctively clenching his fists. His fists relaxed, only after his bloodshot eyes registered it was me. We sat side by side on the bench.

The girl scampered over the sand and then climbed up the stairs again. Her fine hair was bound so tightly on top of her head that her eyes were yanked up by her ears. If it weren't for her two nostrils, it would have been difficult to identify the nose that was buried in her chubby face. The sandals she'd tossed off lay strewn at the edge of the playground, kicked by the other children's feet.

"What are you looking at? The seesaw? The slide? Or maybe your future?"

He slowly raised his arm and pointed at the little girl.

"Why? You know her?"

"Kim Yeseul."

"That's her name?"

"Six years old, goes to Blue Sky Kindergarten. She's in the Elephant Room. Every morning at nine thirty, the kindergarten bus picks her up at the east gate and brings her home between 2:10 and 2:15 in the afternoon. She usually falls asleep on the bus, which really annoys the driver. She hates playing the piano and her favorite thing to do is to run around all day."

"What are you talking about? How do you know all this?"

He laughed soundlessly. "Turns out she's had thorough training in Stranger Danger."

He stood slowly and shook the sand from his feet. I stood up as well, and glanced between him and the girl.

When the girl saw that a boy her age was blocking her way, trying to climb up the slide from the wrong side, her face crumpled. She opened her mouth wide and burst into tears, letting out a sirenlike wail. A woman's shrill voice soon pierced the air.

"What's the matter? Why are you crying? Did I teach you to cry?"

In an effort to stop her sobs, the girl's chest heaved roughly.

The woman who'd stuck her head out of the third-story balcony window yelled non-stop. She looked as if she'd been woken from her nap by the girl's bawling, her permed hair was squashed flat on one side. Her voice was familiar.

"You're driving me crazy! Then go ahead and kick him! Just kick him!"

This time, too, the girl did as her mother said. But she only ended up kicking the air.

"That's her?" I asked.

My husband clapped his hands, dusting off the sand. "Yup. Those monkeys upstairs."

The girl let go of the side and slid down at a fast speed. The boy had no time to move out of the way. They tumbled onto the sand. The boy got up right away and dusted himself off, holding back tears, but the girl, who had smashed her head into the ground, opened her sand-filled mouth and started to howl.

"Nice going, real nice!" the woman screamed once more. Just as I'd guessed, she had a tanned, worn face.

My husband thrust his hands in his pockets and said, "Lee Jeongsuk."

"Who's that?"

"The woman. Born in 1970, the Year of the Dog. Couldn't find out any more than that. She never shows up to the block meetings and she isn't on good terms with her neighbors."

His lips formed a faint smile. Gleaning that kind of information was easy, if you exchanged a few words with the security guard. As for the girl, he'd probably run into her several times on his way home from his walks.

"I guess it's a bit quieter during the day when she goes to kindergarten?"

My husband snorted. "Ah, there's another monkey. Four years old. A kid so hyperactive his own mother doesn't know what to do with him."

"I didn't know you were so interested in the people upstairs."

I looked back to see the girl walking toward the swings. There were children already on the two swings, but the girl shoved off a small boy and took his seat.

"That's nothing," my husband said, without a backward glance. "One time she scratched up a boy's face real good. The boy's mother got in a fight with her mother—it was quite a show."

"Kids fight and get hurt. It's all part of growing up."

He laughed and imitated me. "Of course. They fall, and bruise their knees, and break their legs. It's all part of growing up."

I took his hand. It had been a while since we'd held hands. People needed to get out. Sunlight improved a person's mood. My husband's hand still felt like a banker's. Soon his hands will grow hard and callused.

As if he finally decided to take my advice, my husband seemed to grow a little numb to the noise. The balcony was strewn with ends he'd sawed off the wooden planks. While I was tidying up, I noticed an unfamiliar object in the toolbox. It was a can of wax. When I removed the lid, I saw it was brand-new, untouched. The only use

I knew for it was for waxing wooden floors. To my knowledge, he didn't need wax for his work.

The security guard saw me as I was coming home and recognized me right away. "So what happened? She's a real head case, isn't she? She got in a huge fight with the people who lived there before you."

I laughed.

"But you'll finally get some peace tonight. You probably haven't heard yet, but there was an incident earlier today. Her kid broke his leg and the ambulance came. He received quite a shock it seems, because when he came out on the stretcher, his eyes were rolled back so all I could see were the whites. The lady screamed and cried, caused quite a stir. A big crowd gathered. Good thing the fire lane was clear. If not, I could have lost my job."

The guard was in a talkative mood. As I was climbing the stairs to our apartment, the wax can in my husband's toolbox suddenly came to mind.

"Did you hear? The kid upstairs broke his leg."

My husband didn't have a clue about what had happened.

"I heard even the ambulance came and there was a huge uproar. How is it you don't know?"

"I was sleeping. I didn't hear anything."

It was hard to believe that he could sleep through all that commotion.

"It was just a matter of time before something like that happened. He's always running around, so no surprise there. His mother's probably learned her lesson, too. People should walk, not run. No wonder it's so quiet. Guess we'll finally have some peace."

It was the first quiet night we were having in a long time, but sleep didn't come. From a certain point, the noise had become a part of our daily life. Even my husband kept stirring beside me. I quietly got out of bed and went out onto the balcony. I opened the can of wax. More than half was gone.

The other security guard was discussing the previous day's incident with the women's association of the apartment complex. He said the boy had slipped on the wet floor of the apartment corridor, which had been mopped earlier that day. But what he didn't understand was why the floor had not dried by that point. The women soon started to talk about how things are easier when children are still infants who don't yet know how to walk.

What had my husband used the wax for? He certainly hadn't used it to polish furniture.

When I came home from work, the people upstairs had returned. The boy's leg was probably in a cast. I heard the thump of his crutches.

In just one day, the boy grew quite skilled at using his crutches. There were fewer footsteps, but relentless thumping now filled our apartment. The crutches were even used outside their intended purpose, as toys and weapons. They banged against the furniture, floor, and wall. We had believed that we'd have some quiet until the boy's leg healed, but we couldn't have been more wrong. My husband jumped to his feet, sending his chair crashing behind him.

"Damn it. I guess a broken leg isn't enough. I wish someone would take those kids away. Like the pied piper. You know, all the children in the village follow him and they never come back." It seemed my husband didn't remember the ending of the fairy tale. Not all the children followed the Pied Piper of Hamelin. One child was lame and could not follow quickly enough. Even if the pied piper should come, at least one child would remain and forever torment our sleep with the thump of his crutches.

I'd been getting home later than usual because of all the sales and promotions we were having at the department store. I was about to leave for work when my husband said, "Something fun's going to happen tonight. Get ready."

That night, the sound of glass shattering woke us. The luminous hands of the clock pointed to 3:25 A.M.

"They're awake," my husband said, looking up at the ceiling.

He didn't sound at all groggy. A china plate seemed to have been hurled through the air and at the balcony window, crashing through the glass and shattering into pieces on the balcony's tile floor. A woman screamed. Her two children woke from their sleep and started to cry. I heard the excitable voice of a man, punctuated by a woman's shrill bawls.

My husband laughed out loud, as if he'd been expecting it all. It was only then I recalled what he'd said to me that morning.

"Is this what you meant earlier? When you said something fun was going to happen tonight?

Anyone can figure out the name of a child and the time she goes to and from school. But my husband had predicted the fight between a husband and wife he had never once met, while lying directly below them in his own bed. Several objects hurtled through the air and bounced off the wall and floor. The children wailed. I heard a woman's incoherent babbling, along with her screams and sobs.

"He's a taxi driver. He comes home every night around 2:40 A.M. He got his own cab last year, but he isn't bringing in much more than when he worked for a company. He needs to make payments on his cab, and now he can't receive government assistance for his children's education, no matter how small it might have been. So he's been wondering if he made a mistake, switching over to owning his own cab."

"Anyone could know that!"

"Up to this point, maybe. But it all starts now. I picked up our mail and found an envelope addressed to someone else. Sure, it happens. The postman makes mistakes, too. But that piece of mail turned out to be a credit card statement for number 306. It was addressed to a Mr. Kim Yeongsu. At first I was going to just stick it in their mailbox."

"But you opened it?"

"Most of them were gas purchases. But there was quite a big charge from Lulu Women's Apparel. A brothel, no doubt. You know how those kinds of places will use store names to charge credit cards to avoid paying tax? Well, Kim Yeongsu's wife saw the statement before he did."

All of a sudden, I was wide awake. My husband's face glowed from the streetlights outside. But I still had some questions.

"Then why didn't he try to intercept the card statement before his wife got her hands on it?"

In the dimness, I saw the white of his teeth flash and then disappear. The fight upstairs seemed to be dying down. We heard their murmurs. Even the children had stopped crying.

"Let's go to bed. The show's over and I don't think there's going to be a part two. Still curious? I'll leave the rest to your imagination."

He turned on his side, pulled the blanket up to his chin, and closed his eyes. I lay back down and closed my eyes, too, but I couldn't fall asleep. I shifted carefully, so that the bedsprings wouldn't creak.

Kim Yeongsu must have snuck back into his apartment around the time the postman delivered the mail. Obviously, he would have only checked the mailbox outside and not gone home. To avoid any chance of his wife seeing his cab, he would have parked somewhere else and walked to the apartment. The reason he hadn't been able to intercept his card statement was because a kind neighbor had made sure it would be personally delivered to his wife. The statement, which should have been sitting inside the mailbox, was carried in by his little daughter returning from kindergarten. She would have met my husband on the stairwell on her way up. Since the six-year-old sometimes brought up the mail, her mother would have thought nothing of it as she opened the envelope.

"But things aren't quieter at all! Isn't this the opposite of what you'd hoped?"

"As the saying goes, if you can't go in through the front door, go in through the back door."

"This is an invasion of privacy! You could get charged!"

"You could say the same for them," he muttered. Then as if my protests annoyed him, he pulled the blanket over his head.

Upstairs, someone was sweeping up the broken glass and china.

•

Children get lost all the time, so I didn't pay attention at first. After all, announcements looking for lost children were made every two days on average over the intercom. But when I realized it was the children from 306, I couldn't ignore it.

The younger one was still in a cast. There was no way he could limp out of the apartment complex with a broken leg. A four-year-old with crutches would draw attention. The announcement about the two children, who still hadn't returned, continued until late.

It was the second silent night we were having since our move. After midnight, the security guard and the woman upstairs searched every corner of the building with flashlights in hand. They went down to the underground parking lot to check the vents, but all they saw inside were a piles of cigarette butts, empty snack bags, and popsicle sticks. They climbed to the apartment rooftop and discovered a pair of high school students who were drinking and smoking.

The children had gone to the playground at around four in the afternoon. The woman said she'd glanced down from time to time, while she hung the laundry on the line or tasted the stew she was making for dinner. Each time, the kids had been on the seesaw or slide. At last when she'd opened the balcony window to tell them that dinner was ready, she'd found the playground completely deserted. Less than ten minutes had passed since she'd checked on them last.

The woman looked as far as her gaze would go, but she couldn't spot her children. It was hard to believe that in a mere ten minutes, a six-year-old girl and her younger brother, limping on crutches, could disappear completely from view. Were they hiding in the shade of a tree or under the slide? The woman called their names, but they didn't appear.

Perhaps the boy didn't know any better, but the six-year-old girl was bright and knew her way around the apartment complex. But like most kids, they had never stepped outside the complex on their own.

By the time Mr. Kim Yeongsu dropped off his fare and sped home, the woman was half out of her mind. Howling her children's names in a hoarse voice, she was peering into dumpsters. Dangers lurked everywhere. The deep night. Holes dug in the ground to plant saplings. She raked through the holes, and repeatedly checked the insides of old refrigerators and washing machines that had been left on the curb as people were moving out.

Enraged, Mr. Kim Yeongsu cursed at his wife, and she responded with worse. Two days after they'd filed a report with the Center for Missing Children, they concluded that their children had been abducted.

Many people pitied them. As the incident was relayed over and over again, the girl's plain looks came to indicate her intelligence, and her aggressive nature, which had caused her to harm other children, was translated as healthy confidence.

The parents waited for the kidnapper to call. When she suggested that they alert the police, he rejected the idea. He said a child abduction case required a great deal of sensitivity, and records showed that working with the police only made the situation worse so that things didn't end well. His wife recalled the kidnapping cases from the past year and went into shock. She wailed and fell down in a faint.

On the fourth day, when they still hadn't received a call from the kidnapper, the couple notified the police. The police asked if they were aware of anyone who might be harboring a serious grudge. At first they said no. But the woman opened her mouth soon after. "Actually—" she started to say.

Early in the morning, two strangers rang our doorbell. They asked for my husband, who was still in his pajamas. They claimed he was a prime suspect. Meekly, my husband left with them. A day passed but he still didn't return, and a plain-clothed detective came to the department store to talk to me. On the outside he looked perfectly ordinary. He wasn't tall, and though his leather jacket was zipped up, he didn't look particularly fit.

"I understand your husband didn't get along with the people upstairs? Did you notice any signs of psychological instability after he left his job at the bank?"

"He resigned from his job to become a carpenter. It was his choice to resign, so why would he feel anxious?"

The detective grinned when I mentioned my husband had quit to become a carpenter, but he wiped the smirk off his face immediately and assumed a professional expression once more.

"I guess it would be hard for anyone else to understand," I said. "No one would think it strange if he quit the bank to become a university professor. But you should know, it was always his dream to become a carpenter."

"At this point, all the evidence points to your husband being the kidnapper. He claimed he was home at the time, but there's no way of checking his alibi. I understand he's been threatening the people upstairs by both phone and mail?"

"Is it a threat to tell people to be quiet? And I was the one who called them, not him."

The detective reached into his inner pocket and placed an envelope before me. While I read the letter, he sipped his coffee and glanced about the room.

"At first, they assumed it was a chain letter or something of that sort and didn't bother to open it. After all, letters like that are a real nuisance. But their daughter opened it. That's when they read the letter your husband had sent."

The letter was short and neatly typed. Beginning with "Dear Kim Yeongsu" and a brief greeting, my husband detailed how he was unable to do anything because of the noise coming from their apartment all day, and how repeated pleas for quiet had proved futile, despite numerous calls made to Mr. Kim's wife. A request followed, for Mr. Kim to talk once more to his wife and children about the noise, in spite of his busy schedule. But here, my husband seemed to have gotten carried away, because he went on to say that he found it troubling what these children would grow up to become, considering their clear lack of social etiquette. He finally ended the letter with a surprising line: "If the problem doesn't stop, I might have to play the pipe."

The detective also pointed out this part.

"This here is intriguing. Does anything come to mind when you read this?"

The sentence was underlined in red. He asked me a few more questions and then got to his feet. At the department store entrance, he stopped and said casually as if he'd just remembered, "I noticed you don't have any kids yourself."

As if he didn't need an answer from me, he gave a small smile and turned away. "Play the pipe, play the pipe . . ." he repeated, as if these words were the chorus of a song, and then disappeared out the door.

I was able to meet with my husband on a sofa in the waiting room of the police station. He looked haggard. There were bags under his eyes, and stubble on his chin and under his nose. As soon as he saw me, he glanced at the wall clock.

"You're off work already?"

"A detective came by. He told me you threatened Mr. Kim with a letter?" I lowered my voice so that the police wouldn't hear. "I saw the wax can in your toolbox."

"Hey, that's over and done with—why are you bringing that up now?" he hissed, bringing his face close to mine. "They mopped the apartment halls that day. The kid was running around as usual and slipped on the wet floor." A musty odor came from him, as if he hadn't bathed.

"Y-y-you're really the piper then?" I stammered. I couldn't bring myself to say *kidnapper*.

He laughed out loud. Several officers and the suspects they'd been questioning looked over our way.

"That's just a fairy tale, but I have an idea who it might be. If they keep backing me into a corner, I'll have to tell, but now's not the time."

My husband, who'd been heading back to his cell, turned and whispered into my ear, "By the way, I looked everywhere, but I couldn't find that wax can."

I'd gotten rid of it. I'd slipped it into a shopping bag and tossed it in the trash in the bathroom at work. Over a thousand people swept in and out of the department store each day.

On the way home, I wondered why we still hadn't had any children.

Someone from the apartment complex recalled seeing the little boy with the crutches. She remembered him because he'd been using small crutches that had been customized for him. There had been a girl munching on a cookie and holding a balloon beside him, and they had climbed into the backseat of a small red car. She couldn't remember the car make or model.

My husband returned home the next morning and slept through the entire day. When he finally woke, we received the call from the police that they had caught the kidnapper.

When Mr. Kim Yeongsu had heard that the children had gotten into a small red car, he'd hesitated and then said the car might belong to a woman he knew. The woman Mr. Kim had been having an affair with was arrested at the doors of the café where she worked. The woman confessed that when Mr. Kim had ended their relationship, she'd kidnapped his kids as an act of revenge. She'd only been trying to scare him, she said, and burst into tears.

The two children were found in an orphanage in South Gyeong-sang Province. The woman upstairs was able to spot her kids at once among the numerous children on the playground. Indeed, they would be easy to spot anywhere. And with that, the kidnapping incident was over.

"So that's the woman you were going to expose in the end?"

My husband said nothing. I stopped asking what more he knew of the people upstairs. The children came back and the boy's cast came off. The noise started again. Everything returned to normal once more.

People who came to look at the apartment wondered why we wanted to move before our contract was up. I said my husband had been transferred to another branch at his bank. I added that the apartment was quiet because it was so far from the main road, and that you didn't even need a fan in the middle of summer, because of the cross breeze that blew in through the front and back windows.

We moved to a satellite city in Gyeonggi Province. The paved roads ended at the edge of the apartment complex, and traditional-style homes huddled together, looking as if time had stopped twenty years earlier. The local people referred to our complex as the new city. If you walked out for half an hour, you could see fields, paddies, greenhouses, and pigpens.

My husband found work at a shabby carpenter shop where customers hardly ever came. He didn't make any money, but he didn't have to pay to learn the trade. The carpenter, who was over sixty years old, often left the shop in my husband's hands. Then my husband watched the empty shop, learning to wield a hammer and plane as he practiced on leftover pieces of wood. Sometimes he loaded custom-made desks and cabinets onto the truck and drove into the new city on a delivery.

Gradually, my husband grew more skilled with the hammer. His first piece was a wooden chair, like the kind we'd used in school a long time ago, but because it was off-balance, it creaked every time you sat down or got up. He regained his sense of humor, enough to say that the uneven floor was to blame, not his skills.

Until my husband became a joiner, I had to work at the department store. We still had our savings, but I didn't want to touch that money. In order to get to work on time, I took the first bus out of the terminal, and transferred onto the subway. Because I then had to take a local bus to get to the department store, my commute was two hours each way.

Since I never got enough sleep, I always dozed off on the bus. When summer came and the weather grew hot, I thought about our previous apartment, which the realtor had said stayed so cool in the summer that we wouldn't need a fan. Was that really true? Were the children in 306 still running around? What ever happened to Kim Yeongsu's mistress, who had kidnapped the children? How had my husband known everything? I would think about these things and drift off to sleep.

And what had been my dream, you ask?

I was so tired I didn't even have time to dream.

Pinky Finger

Never get in a taxi alone at night.

It's something I've heard from the time I turned twenty. More than ten years have gone by, and to be honest, not once did I take these words to heart. The blame lies partly with my mother, who would pick the moments I would be busy tying my shoelaces or pinning back my loose bangs to issue this warning. To my ears, it just sounded like nagging to come home early.

For ten years, the men I dated accompanied me home, gladly, without showing a hint of annoyance. There was just one who walked me up to the ticket gate at the subway station, saying it was a waste of time and money to escort me all the way home. Since we had to part by eight in the evening, there wasn't enough time to get to know each other. Eventually, we broke up without even a kiss.

I've recently had to take a taxi alone a lot more, but I got home unscathed each time. I might have paid more attention if someone other than my mother had been giving the advice. Still, during the ten years these words were drilled into my head, nothing happened to me. I never heard of a girl losing her life or coming close to losing it, all because she happened to get into the wrong cab. At the very least, it seems luck has been on our side.

Why does a mother's advice to a daughter sound like nagging, no matter how protective or affectionate? All mothers exaggerate.

•

I didn't know when the rain started. At the late hour, the wet asphalt gave off a bluish sheen as if it had been sprayed with oil. Drunk men swarmed out from every corner of the back street, shrieking. It wasn't raining hard enough to need an umbrella, but it was enough to soak my coat while I stood outside to catch a cab. I wanted to get into one that would take me home before the rest of my clothes got wet.

Taxis sped along the road, but I could tell by their lights, even from a distance, that they were already carrying passengers. For half an hour, I raised and lowered my arm repeatedly, without any success. It was late, it was the end of the year, and it was raining on top of that; of course it would be difficult to catch a cab.

In the end I wasn't the one who caught it. One of the men from work did. He wasn't my boyfriend or husband, and he was past the age to try to wrangle a kiss from a girl by escorting her home. He probably thought catching a cab for his female coworker was the right thing to do.

Someone opened the door and I was jostled into the car.

"See you tomorrow, oh, I guess it's not tomorrow anymore. See you in a few hours. Don't worry, I'll—"

Another coworker slammed the door shut, cutting off his words. At last, I was left alone in peace. But a part of me felt as though I'd been sent packing.

"Jungdong New Town, please," I said, my tone brisk and businesslike.

After enduring the laments of a taxi driver on one particular ride home, I came to believe that a certain distance needed to be maintained between the passenger and driver. The driver, as though in confession, had mumbled he had harmed someone and that he'd been out of prison for nearly a year. While trapped in the backseat, I'd been forced to listen to every detail of his crime, even the exact shape of the red brick, which is what he'd used to strike his victim. But when I'd climbed out of the cab at last, I hadn't even gotten a proper look at his face.

There was a queer, distinct odor inside the taxi. Mixed with the fishy smell of rain on my clothes, it was enough to make bile rise in my throat. The air was dank and musty; the cab seemed to have been shut up for a long time without any circulation. Wipers skimmed the windshield, as though performing a rainy-day duty. They merely smeared the dust around, since there wasn't much rain.

A drunk, middle-aged man ran onto the road toward the taxi. The driver didn't take off, as if he intended to pick up another passenger. I didn't want to share a cab with a stranger who reeked of everything he'd had for dinner. I was just about to say I'd pay extra to go alone when the taxi driver spoke.

"He's copying down the license plate," he said, looking at his rearview mirror.

I turned around to see my coworker, the one who had hailed the cab for me, glancing at the taxi plate while scrawling into a little pocketbook he'd fished out from his pocket. What a nice man. He was jotting down the plate number of the cab that would take me home to make sure I'd be safe.

"Is he your boyfriend?"

"My boyfriend? No, just someone I work with."

I wondered if the driver would find my coworker's action insulting. "I'm sorry if you're offended. I didn't ask him to do that."

He adjusted the rearview mirror and stared blankly at me. He then said slowly, "This is a stolen car."

I didn't catch his meaning.

"So it's no use even if he writes down the plate number," he said.

I was a little shocked. After a short pause, he burst into laughter. "I'm just joking. It's just a joke."

I didn't find it a bit funny. I tried to laugh along, but the muscles around my half-open mouth felt stiff. I was convinced that my coworker had offended him.

"I understand. After all, it's a scary world out there. So, which way would you like to take?"

I wanted to tell him to take the quickest way and floor it at 120 kilometers per hour, but I didn't. I had learned from past experiences that it was best to leave it up to the driver. I hated being terrified, tumbling like beans on a hot pan in a recklessly speeding cab, and I hated cowering in the backseat, listening to the driver swear at other cars. Partly though, I was afraid that what he'd said about the taxi being stolen was not a joke.

"It's up to you . . ."

Instead of responding, he laughed quietly. In the dark, all I could see was the back of his head that showed above the headrest, but I sensed the strain lift at once.

I glanced back before we took off, but my coworkers had already gone. What I saw instead were the stuffed toys that were stuck to the rear window. And not just on the rear window, but on both backseat windows. They dangled everywhere, except from the windshield and a bit of space on the rear window to see out through the rearview mirror. All of them were small enough to fit in your hand, and the suction cups seemed to have been glued on so that they wouldn't fall off. Every time the taxi changed lanes or came to a sudden stop, the toys swung together in the same direction. How wide they swung to the left or right differed, but every one of them moved at exactly the same time. A red rooster's head, crudely stitched and made of cheap material, dangled by my right cheek. The toys looked like they'd been hanging there for quite some time. The fabric was sticky with dust, and grime had collected around the suction cups.

The driver didn't join the traffic heading for the Mapo Bridge. This route—taking the Mapo Bridge, cutting through Yeouido, and then passing Yeongdeungpo-gu—would add about 3,000 won to the meter. Instead he got into the right lane that would lead to Ilsan. He seemed honest and knew his way around the area. The only thing that bothered me was the fact that he was actually following the speed limit at this late hour. A stickler like this would have no doubt been insulted by a stranger copying down his plate number. I wanted to look outside, but it was hard to see between all the stuffed toys.

The sign for Seongsan Bridge came into view. If we crossed the bridge and headed toward Mok-dong, we would be able to merge onto the Seoul-Incheon Expressway. I would arrive home by 1 A.M. at the very latest, wash up, brush my teeth, and go out like a light.

"I see you've had a drink," said the driver, after we'd been on the road for about ten minutes.

I did have a drink. I'd been sitting right in front of a charcoal brazier where the meat grilled, and the heat had made the booze go to my head more quickly than usual. On the way to the bathroom, I'd stepped on the hem of my skirt and landed flat on my backside. When asked to sing, I'd stood up without any hesitation and started to sing. My wool overcoat reeked of charred meat, which the driver probably found nauseating. I tried to roll down my window, but because of all the dolls stuck to the glass, the window only moved down a centimeter. The raindrops that slipped through the crack hit my forehead intermittently. The rain continued to fall lightly, like paratroopers practicing their landing drills.

"It's the year-end after all. These outings are practically a part of work."

Again he smiled with his mouth open. Each time we passed under a streetlight, I caught the faint outline of his face. His hair glistened, as though he had combed it back with pomade. That was probably what I'd smelled when I'd first gotten into the taxi. I didn't know a single man who still used pomade. I suddenly recalled the last person I knew who had used it: my grandfather.

But it was difficult to guess the driver's age just from the fact that he still used pomade. Although it was something older men tended to use, his hair was black and thick. Judging by his voice, he seemed to be in his early forties, but I wasn't sure. I've never tried to guess someone's age by just the voice.

I looked between the front seats. His right hand rested lightly on the steering wheel. He was wearing white cotton gloves. I'd seen plenty of drivers in white gloves so this was nothing out of the ordinary. But each time I gazed at my own hands in my lap, I couldn't help thinking there was something a little odd about his right hand. I soon realized what that was. It was his right pinky finger. It hadn't moved at all since I'd gotten into the cab. It remained straight and rigid each time he turned the steering wheel, not bending with the rest of the fingers. The rest of the gloved fingertips were gray with dust but the tip of the pinky was white. His pinky finger was a useless object.

I didn't have to touch it to know it would be stiff and cold. How had he lost it? I leaned my head against the seat and gazed at the finger. Perhaps he had backed out on a promise he'd made with a best friend. Perhaps that pinky had been the cost of betrayal.

"You've had too much to drink."

Since there wasn't anyone else in the taxi, I had to assume once again that he was speaking to me. I did have a couple of drinks, but I wasn't drunk. I squeezed my knees together and sat up. But it didn't take me long to notice that his attention was focused on his right-side mirror.

A 12-seater van sped along beside us, straddling two lanes. I could tell that the rain made the road just as slippery as if it had been icy. If the van were to skid, all the cars nearby would be in trouble. There was an unusual number of bends in the road. Each time the van went around a curve, it swerved into another lane, yet managed to make its way back once the road straightened out; it did this over and over again.

Other cars kept their distance, leaving a wide gap before and behind the van. The van sometimes veered toward us, as if it intended to crash into us, and then backed away. I watched the van from between the stuffed dolls on the window. I hadn't planned on getting into an accident tonight.

"How much do you think he's had?" I asked.

"Who knows?"

My driver looked tense. His pinky stood upright like an insect's antenna. He changed gears and stepped on the accelerator. I heard the cogs mesh under me. In an instant, we caught up to the van as it raced along in the next lane. As we passed, I saw that the young man at the steering wheel was completely passed out. His face was so pale that it looked purple. The taxi driver honked and tried to alert him, but the man didn't seem to hear at all.

I was so caught up in watching the van that my nose was pressed up against the glass. I could have gotten a better view if the toys hadn't been there. They swung from side to side and kept hitting my head.

"People like that shouldn't be on the road. Someone ought to beat some sense into him," I blurted without thinking. If I had the time, I wanted to follow the van, pull the driver out, and beat him to a pulp. The taxi driver seemed to have read my mind.

"You're absolutely right. He needs to be shown a lesson or two. If you weren't here, I would have followed him. They need to learn never to touch the wheel again after drinking."

In an instant, the taxi driver, a perfect stranger until now, and I were on the same side.

"What kind of people would let him get into a car like that? Could you even call them friends?"

We slowed down. I was hoping that my driver would speed up and leave the van far behind, but there were too many cars on the road. Instead, we were forced to keep it in sight, moving ahead and then falling behind repeatedly.

"How much do you have to drink to get like that?" I mumbled. "A bottle of soju? Maybe two?"

The taxi driver clenched the wheel, glancing around him and then at the van.

"He drank more than two bottles for sure," I said. "Look, he's totally out."

"You want to find out? Should we follow him and ask?"

I took his words as a joke. "There's no reason why we couldn't." I laughed and saw the sign that announced the entrance to the Seong-san Bridge pass over us. The driver seemed to realize only then that something was wrong.

"Shit," he swore as he hit the steering wheel. "I was so busy watching him that I missed the on-ramp."

I decided to believe him. It was partly my own fault, for simply going along with everything. It's okay; we'll take a little detour. I pushed back my schedule by half an hour. Just then, the van swerved out of its lane and careened toward us. It brushed against the taxi and then moved away. I saw orange sparks fly as the vehicles collided. The taxi driver wrenched the steering wheel; we lurched out of our lane, leapt onto the flowerbed in the median of the road, and came to a stop. I saw the van growing distant as it sped away, completely oblivious; on its side was a streak of navy blue paint that had come from the taxi.

The taxi driver put the car in reverse. When he pressed on the accelerator, the two front wheels that had sprung onto the flowerbed clunked back down onto the road. The left headlight had cracked and broken away when we had crashed into the flowerbed. I tasted blood; I had bitten my lip upon impact. We were back on the road, but the van was nowhere in sight.

The driver leaned forward and his gaze swept the surroundings and the road ahead, moving his head slowly from side to side like a lighthouse beacon. "Ordinary people get hurt because of assholes like that. He needs to be taught a lesson."

He suddenly stepped on the accelerator, pitching me to the side. The sign that said Ilsan New Town passed by in a blur. A cluster of apartment towers began to emerge in the distance. I was getting farther and farther away from home. I sat perched on the edge of the seat and was about to point out the quickest detour when the driver squeezed into the next lane without signaling. There was a small off-ramp on the far right of the freeway. He raced toward it. But it wasn't the detour to the bridge.

"Where are you going? This isn't the right way."

"Hold on. It's too late, I don't have a choice."

The P-shaped off-ramp turned into an old narrow road, pitted with small and large potholes.

Every time we passed over the potholes, the undercarriage of the cab scraped against the asphalt. The road was not lit by a single streetlamp; its end disappeared into murky darkness. I grew uneasy. My mother's voice rang in my head: Don't take a taxi alone at night. The taxi pushed its way into the darkness with its one remaining headlight.

"Wait a minute, did you hear what I said?" My tongue felt rigid, as if it had become a block of wood. My salivary glands seemed to have completely dried up; the inside of my mouth was like sandpaper. My throat stung. The driver still leaned forward in his seat, looking for something.

When we reached a fork in the road, he paused for a second and stared into the dark. I couldn't hear the rain anymore. There seemed to be nothing beyond the darkness. In the end, he turned onto the left road.

His pinky finger bothered me. What he'd said about the taxi being stolen might not have been a joke. I tried to guess how much money there was in my purse. Nearly fifty-thousand won in cash and a credit card. How much was I worth? To be honest, I didn't seem very expensive. I started counting to calm down. But I couldn't go past six because I was so scared.

"There's been a mistake . . . I don't have much money. But if it's money you want—"

He didn't say anything. No, he wasn't interested in money. He'd probably been insulted by my coworker taking down his plate number. It was understandable.

"Is this because he took down your license plate? I'm sure that's not the reason why. You don't seem to be that type of person. Even I can tell."

This time too, he didn't answer. In my frustration, I jabbed at the button to lower the window, but a stuffed toy got caught in the crack and the window jammed completely. These damn things. I grabbed the toys to rip them off, but the nylon strings dug into my hand instead. I tried to open the door to jump out of the cab, but the door wouldn't budge. The impact with the van seemed to have jammed that, too. I tried to kick it open with my feet, but the door still didn't budge. My whole body broke into a sweat. I threatened him, speaking to the back of his head.

"You better take me home right now. He took down your plate so if I don't show up at work tomorrow, they're going to call the police."

Only then did the driver glance back. He looked annoyed. "Do you always make this much noise?"

•

There was probably a garbage dump nearby. I recalled passing under a sign that said "Nanjido" a moment ago. I didn't want to scare some janitor who had come to Seoul's official landfill to dump garbage. I'll be brought to a nearby university hospital where they will perform an autopsy to determine my cause of death. Then they'll discover that this poor woman's last meal had consisted of a few pieces of charred meat and some shredded radish, soybean sprouts, greenish yellow vegetables, and several shots of soju.

The coworker who had hailed the taxi for me will suffer from guilt. Perhaps, my body will never be discovered. People at work will whisper among themselves: *She was having a real hard time after her last relationship. What are you talking about? She wasn't going through anything—it was like every other night. No, didn't she seem different to you that night? She kept downing soju; she didn't even hesitate when we asked her to sing—she stood up right away and started singing. She wasn't the type to do something like that. Can't you see? They were all signs. If only we had known, we would have made sure someone took her home.*

"Please, don't kill me." My voice was as frail as a mosquito's whine. I never imagined that I would have to beg for my life.

"I'm not pretty and I don't have a nice figure. I'm not even healthy. I was really sick a few years ago. All I've done is get old."

I'd done nothing but age. I had accomplished nothing.

"At least you're honest," he said. His laughter turned into a dry, hacking cough. Then something flashed in the dark. "There!" he cried.

I understood that to mean he'd finally found a suitable place to carry out his crime. The odometer indicated that he had driven this cab about 100,000 kilometers. He was an experienced driver. He would be familiar with all kinds of side roads unknown to most people. He would also know at least ten quiet, secluded places where he could carry out his work at this hour without being interrupted.

Saliva now driveled from my open mouth. All I could wish for was to die a quick, painless death. And for the women I knew to never get in cabs alone at night.

"I'm not really a taxi driver," he said, shifting into low gear.

That I already knew. We soon came to a stop. He yanked up the emergency break. He opened the door and climbed out. He wasn't very big. I was huddled under the seat. He opened the back door and hauled me out. I flailed, struggling to stay inside. But in less than five minutes, I found myself stumbling in the dark. He forced me to walk ahead.

The factory we'd come to was old and had a zinc roof. The smell of chemicals pierced my nostrils. Dye oozed from the tipped-over drum cans, mixing with the rain and flowed down the drain. The factory seemed to have been shut down for a long time. I noticed the shattered windows once my eyes grew accustomed to the darkness. My knees buckled. I fell a few times. It was then that I first got a good look at the driver's face. I knew then that I would not be allowed to live. He stood close behind and held what I thought was a knife to my back. It was only much later that I realized it wasn't a knife at all—it was his pinky finger.

We went around to the back of the building. There, I saw a

familiar-looking van with a streak of navy blue paint on its side. It occurred to me then that the van and taxi drivers were working together. The van had been waiting for the taxi to bring me here. The rain had now soaked through my coat and was wetting my clothes inside. My teeth chattered from the cold and terror.

The door on the driver's side opened. A man's foot appeared and felt for the ground. His ankle kept buckling. He was so drunk that he could barely walk. He began to urinate against the cement wall with his back to the van. Steam rose up from where the urine hit. The cab driver went and stood behind him.

"Hey, I need to talk to you."

The man turned his head, squinting. The taxi driver's fist flew out, landing a punch right in the middle of the man's face. The van driver fell down to the dirt. Although he was much bigger than the cab driver, he had no chance to swing. I hid behind a drum can and listened to fists thudding against spongy flesh. Maybe they weren't working together after all. Instead, the drunk driver and I had walked straight into the taxi driver's trap. The taxi driver approached me, panting. Now it was my turn.

"Didn't you say we needed to do something about people like him? I only made up my mind after you said that. I'd already missed the exit by that point anyway. Maybe I could have let everything go if my headlight hadn't gotten smashed. Now, you do whatever you want."

He demonstrated. Just as he showed me, I kicked the man, who was still lying on the ground; I stomped his thigh with my heels.

"You mean you followed him all the way here?"

"Why else would I come to a place like this in the middle of the night?"

All my pent-up frustration was transferred to my foot. I should have been home by now, lying in my comfortable bed. The reason I was standing in the rain in this godforsaken place was all because of this man. I kicked and punched him until my anger faded. A large rock that was half embedded in the ground caught my eye. I rushed toward it and tried to dig it up with my bare hands. The cab driver ran up to me and pulled me away.

"Okay, okay, that's enough. Can you help me with something?"

He put his hands under the man's armpits and pulled him up. The foul smell of liquor hit my face every time the man breathed out. The taxi driver stuffed the man in the luggage compartment of the van and shut the door. He then went into the factory and came out, dragging a large tarpaulin behind him. It looked like it had been used as a tent for a picnic. He threw the torn material over the van.

"I'm not a taxi driver."

He grabbed a corner of the tarpaulin and stood on top of the van. He counted, "One, two, three!" and then thrust up the corner. All I saw were the words "Jeongyeon Factory Fall Sports Day" written faintly on the canvas. Rain dripped into my eyes. Right then, the tarpaulin that had been covering the van slid down—more like crumbled—to the ground. The van was gone—along with the man in its luggage compartment. I wiped the rain out of my eyes and stared about me, but the van was nowhere in sight. The taxi driver stood next to me. I ran to where the van had been and stepped on the tarpaulin, which was spread out flat on the ground, but there was nothing underneath; it was just the ground. We had to walk around the factory to get back to the taxi, but the van wasn't anywhere in front either.

"Where did it go? Where is he?" I asked, completely at a loss.

He pulled me along. "Let's go. He won't ever drink and drive again."

It was when we were going up the ramp to get on the freeway: I saw something sparkle in the glare of the streetlamp. There was a group of new apartment towers being built a little distance away. The flash I had seen was coming from the top of the steel framework of

one of the buildings. The sparkling object at the very top appeared
to be the vanished van.

We got on the freeway. Although we were still driver and passenger, our relationship had changed drastically since I'd first gotten
into the cab. In the backseat, I gazed down at my fists, which had
struck a person. The drunk driver would come to his senses on top
of the 25-story apartment building. He will rack his brains, trying to
figure out how he had managed to drive his van to the roof, but he
won't find a single clue.

"I'm sure you know by now, but I'm not a taxi driver."

"And I'm sure you know I'm not just an ordinary office worker."

I kept clenching and unclenching my hands. They didn't seem
like mine.

"Do you see this finger?" He raised his right hand. "When I was
making a zoo disappear for my vanishing act, my pinky disappeared
with it."

•

Forty minutes later, the taxi stopped in front of the playground of
my apartment complex. I rummaged through my purse for the fare.

"Don't worry about it. This cab isn't even mine."

"You mean you actually stole it?"

"To be exact, I've borrowed it for the time being instead of getting
back what I was owed. The man who owns it is a friend of mine,
who collects all those stupid dolls. Whenever he makes any money,
he rushes to the game machines to get more. Even his wife left him
recently because of it."

I knew what kind of machines he was talking about. They were
always placed in shopping areas and on busy streets where they caught
people's attention. But I'd never tried playing it myself.

"He doesn't even smoke or drink. Instead he hands over everything he makes to that machine. All for those few seconds the claw moves to get the toy he wants. You should see his house. It's full of those things."

"Where are you headed now?"

"I'm looking for my finger."

"Do you know where it is?"

The rain had stopped. The puddles were frosting over. I heard ice crack under my feet as I climbed out.

"It's probably where the zoo is."

"Then you know where the zoo's disappeared to?"

The driver rolled down his window and gazed up at me on the curb.

"One day, when you hear that a zoo has suddenly materialized at Gwanghwa-mun intersection, come see me."

"Did you know it's been a while since someone's escorted me all the way home?"

I waved until the taxi grew distant.

He was once a famous magician. Many different circus groups had their eyes on him. His last act was to make a zoo disappear. Cars strapped with giant speakers roamed every street and alley, and clowns wearing sandwich boards advertised that a magic show never seen before in the history of the world would take place. People swarmed to the town's small zoo. Some monkeys, peacocks, as well as several empty cages were all that the zoo had, but it took countless hours to stitch together fabric that would cover the zoo's perimeter fence. Ten seamstresses were put to work for an entire week. His magic act was a great success, but his pinky finger also ended up disappearing with it. Still, the people demanded more. They shouted for him to bring back the zoo that had vanished. And so, in the vacant lot that was no longer a zoo, he kept shouting, "One, two, three!" until it grew dark. However, he could not bring it back. Right now, he is roaming the whole country in search of that zoo. Where in the world could it be?

In the morning I received two phone calls. One was from my

mother, who was staying at my younger sister's house because my sister had recently given birth. Right before she hung up, she reminded me again not to take a taxi alone at night. I will continue to hear these words for the eleventh year. My whole body was sore from last night's sudden bout of exercise. Massaging my arms and legs, I said, "Mom, you're absolutely right."

The other phone call was from my coworker who had hailed the taxi. He'd been worried about me until this morning. I told him that I would not be at work. Then I recalled something right before I hung up.

"Thank you for last night."

He didn't understand what I meant.

"Last night, I saw you copying down the plate number of my cab."

"I did?"

"Yes, in your pocketbook."

I heard him riffle through pages. Shortly after, he laughed. "I couldn't remember because I was so drunk. But it looks like I did write something down. Red Rose Lounge 231-1111 . . . we drank way too much last night."

What he had written down was not the taxi's license plate, but the phone number of the next bar they were heading to. No one had been concerned for me.

I headed to the stores in my flip-flops. I had caught a slight cold from being out in the rain. On my way out of the pharmacy, I saw a claw machine sitting in front of a shop. It was filled with stuffed animals, but they were grimy, as if no one had touched the machine in a while. It seemed these claw machines were now out of fashion.

When I inserted a coin into the slot, the claw began to move. I pressed the buttons to position the claw above an animal. The claw latched onto it and began to move slowly. I suddenly felt nervous. When the toy was almost at the opening, something hit me in the forehead and fell near my feet. I ended up taking my finger off the button and the animal slipped out of the claw. Rubbing my forehead with the palm of my hand, I ducked my head to look for what had struck me. It was a plastic, prosthetic finger. I immediately thought of the driver's finger. Perhaps he had finally discovered where the zoo was. Perhaps this time he had lost his ear instead of a pinky.

I held the prosthetic up to my nose. A faint odor clung to it. It smelled like pomade that no one used anymore.

Daisy Fleabane

The fisherman is trying to drag me to the riverbank.

You just need one look at him to know he's a rookie. Only when the bobber's dancing on the water and he feels the heavy tug on his rod does he lurch awkwardly to his feet, legs wide apart. He's so tense. I guess it's only natural. But anyone who's gone fishing at least once knows; a real pro recognizes the smallest movement of the bobber, well before the fish swallows the hook too deep. Look at this guy, though—he has no idea what he's doing. Now he's even started shouting. All of a sudden, the fishermen nearby who'd been casting their lines into the river gather around. Someone cries, *It's a big one!*

It's catfish season.

The fishhook made a hole in my new jacket. Mom's going to pinch me so hard. If I get the hole mended, maybe no one will notice it? The woman at Myeongseong Cleaners is an expert with the sewing machine. Her shop is right at the end of our street. The same garments are always hanging above her door, but I bet the cherry-pink silk hanbok belongs to her, not a customer. Anyone with a sharp eye would have noticed that hanbok's been hanging in the same spot for 365 days. Many garments meant many customers. *Just look at how busy we are; our customers are always dropping their clothes off to get cleaned.* I'd say at least half of the garments there are for display.

The woman sits by the sunny window and works at her sewing machine all day. When the words on the window, like LAUNDRY and ALTERATIONS & REPAIR, started falling off, you could easily see inside. Like the silk hanbok, the woman looks like she's part of the display, too. Behind her, nails are hammered into the wall, holding spools of thread in every color. The sound of her sewing machine makes me so sleepy. And how about all those tiny stitches? Computer-operated cleaners have started to crop up here and there, but Mom always takes our clothes to Myeongseong Cleaners. The woman there wears reading glasses now. The reason her machine sometimes stops is probably because she has trouble seeing up close. Her vision, which should have lasted her for about seventy years, has been used up in the fifteen years she's run the cleaners.

Oh, I really hope Mom won't notice this hole.

The lights blinking all night along the riverbank—were they the fishermen's hurricane lanterns? It's catfish season. I'm slowly being swept downstream. I think the river is decaying. I can smell it. Everything is murky, too. While I was coming down the river, so many hump-backed fish swam through my legs, limping.

I know this place well. A long time ago, my dad and I used to come here to go fishing. I would place my fishing chair next to his and cast my line lamely, but I only lost my paste bait each time. Mom says I'm too impatient. Says I haven't got one useful bone in my body. I'm always getting in trouble.

I got bored of staring at the water, so I left my dad and went up along the riverbank and saw a whole bunch of flowers in bloom. There were heaps of them. I didn't know their name. How come wildflowers don't have a smell? They give off a whiff of something fishy, that's all. The stems left green stains on the hems of my pants and white socks.

Dad hooked a carp. When I ran back, I saw it being reeled out of the water. I think the carp swallowed the hook deep, because I couldn't see it inside its mouth. Dad tried to take the hook out carefully, but all of a sudden, the innards jerked out, too. He put the carp into the bucket, but it rose to the surface right away.

Would I be able to fix the hole in my jacket? It's new. Mom's going to be so mad.

It's a big one, alright!

All the fishermen have come to catch a glimpse of the big one. Check out how far his rod is bent—it looks like an archery bow. But what did you expect? Of course it would bend like that, trying to pull all of my fifty kilograms out of the water. I can smell the liquor on their stale breaths every time they open their mouths. They've been staring at the water since last night. This place is always crawling with anglers. Even fishing clubs come out here. The road above the riverbank is probably lined with cars. My dad liked night fishing, too. While he fished through the night, I would curl up in a small tent and sleep. I kept waking up because it was uncomfortable, but every time I opened my eyes, I saw his curved back through the mesh screen. Early in the morning, there was dew on the roof of the tent, plus on the yellow waterproof overalls my dad was wearing.

Why are you awake already? Go back inside and sleep some more.

I didn't mind the smell of his breath. The cigarettes on his breath smelled almost sweet.

Fixed on the end of the rod, the fishermen's eyes are glittering. *Why can't I hook a big one like that?* I bet that's what they're thinking. Everyone dreams big when they're casting their lines. Dad's caught lots of big fish before. But he never got his name in the "Biggest Catch of the Week" that the magazine runs. That's because he was never part of any fishing clubs. I've seen my dad catch carp at least forty centimeters long. He used a worm for bait.

Someone please take that rod away from him and show him how it's done! My dad used to say that all the time. He said the more experience a fisherman had, the less damage he'd do to the fish. But just look at this guy—what a rookie. The hole in my jacket is getting bigger.

•

I think those flowers are blooming. The ones I'd seen when I came fishing with my dad. I can smell them—a whiff of something fishy. Like a greedy child, I'd picked so many of those flowers. The stems were covered with tiny hairs. Boy, were those stems tough. Some came out, roots and all, when I pulled, instead of snapping. They look like chrysanthemums. Not the puffy kind you'd take to a funeral, you know, the kind that look like steamed buns, but wild chrysanthemums with small flowers. I picked an armful and ran to Dad, but he told me I shouldn't pick them. *Flowers are prettier when they're in bloom.* Was it because I had run all the way? The flowers were strewn everywhere. What were they called again? Dad told me, but I can't remember. My memory's getting so fuzzy.

I bet Mom is livid right now, because I haven't come home.

How many days do I have left until the vault exam? How long have I been here? I have to practice if I don't want to get in trouble from the gym teacher. Because a kid broke her ankle jumping over the vault, "Hammerhead" is on high alert all the time now. I really hate the vault. My butt keeps hitting it whenever I hop over, and every time, Hammerhead jabs me in the butt with the stick he carries around. I really need to practice. If I don't do well, I'll have to run twenty laps around the field, yelling "Seize the day!" That's his motto in life.

Anyway, I think something's wrong with the river. I can smell it. It's rotting.

In the middle of the night, someone dumped toxic liquid into the water. A truck crept to the riverbank, the back loaded with steel drums. As it drew closer to the edge, it turned off its headlights and slowed down, but I could hear the smallest noise. Everything sounds closer across the water. People who come here to fish know. Dad sometimes talked to the fishermen far away by speaking into the darkness. *Are they biting over there? What are you using for bait? How many have you caught?* They would exchange information this way. Do you know that a man's voice carries farther than a woman's voice? I read that in a magazine, so it's probably true.

I think there were two men. Maybe three, judging from the footsteps. Anyway, one person didn't talk much. I think the steel drums were really full.

It's goddamn heavy. Watch it, man.

Every time they lowered a drum off the truck, the one standing at the bottom protested anxiously. After rolling the containers to the water, they pried off the tops, pouring something gooey into the river.

Seriously, I can't do this shit anymore. I'm freaking out.

I almost pissed my pants at the checkpoint back there.

Hey, lower your voice. You want to go to jail?

If there's free food and shelter, hell, that's my paradise.

They snickered softly together. While the liquid gushed out of the drums, they unzipped their pants and urinated into the river. What had been in those drums? It smelled like gasoline.

This river is the water supply source for Seoul and all of Gyeonggi Province. If you turn on the tap at our house, this water will flow out.

I wish I were water. Then I could travel through the pipes and go home. I'd gush out into the kitchen sink and basin, and if you tossed that water into the yard, I'd water the grass and plants. Would Mom recognize me then?

At this rate, this river will become the Mekong River. You've heard of the Mekong, haven't you? I saw it on television. It was called *Escape on the Mekong* or *Love on the Mekong*, something like that. It was about the love story between an Australian journalist and a Laos woman. In the movie, the Mekong is the river of death. Dead rotting fish and a carcass of a donkey float by. Actually, it was probably called *Escape on the Mekong*, because the couple manage to scuba-dive out of Laos and save their love. *Love, love, love.* My favorite words are *love* and *cookies*. Every time I say those words, my mouth tickles.

But it's not just this truck that dumps things in secret. I'm talking about the lights twinkling along the riverbank. Not the fishermen's lanterns, but the bigger, brighter lights—they're like wildflowers compared to the fishermen's lights, which are like fake plants. I like wildflowers. Anyway, every available spot by the river with somewhat of a view is occupied by hotels. The people from Seoul drive down here to stay at them. The hotels are packed even during the day. Mom won't let me come around here. The neon signs light up the night. It's like Las Vegas. Don't they say you get to Las Vegas by racing through the desert for a long time, until your car is covered in dirt and sand? I'm not a hundred percent sure, but I bet all the drainpipes of these hotels are secretly connected to this river.

But were the flowers called again? It's on the tip of my tongue.

I don't even remember my name now. I think the water's seeped into my memories.

Several people rushed to the rod. If you just pull and strain blindly, your line is bound to snap. People are excited. I can tell what they're thinking. *What could be there at the end of the line?* Just look at the curiosity in their eyes.

Wow, a catfish this big—that's a first! Bro, it's your lucky day!

Maybe it's that Old Fox?

You think it's this easy to hook her? He doesn't look like he's got much experience.

Hey there, Rookie, why don't you settle down?

No one's ever seen the Old Fox. Just a part of her back or her large mouth, that's it. I bet it was the Old Fox that cut your line two years ago and slipped away.

The Old Fox? I've heard of her, too. It's true, no one's actually seen her before. They say when she shows up, she casts a giant shadow in the middle of the river, and if she swings her tail, an eddy forms in the surface. Fishermen are full of lies. They always say they lost a big one the size of their arm after losing a tiny minnow. I think the Old Fox is just a story made up by a bunch of fishermen. Fishermen who dream about catching a big one.

Someone once said her mouth was as big as the width of a boat you climb into at the amusement park. Everyone seems to have an opinion about how big she is. Some say she's as tall as a small child, and some say she's taller than two meters. But can you picture a catfish that's the same size as the basketball player Seo Jang-hoon?

There are so many stories about anglers who managed to hook her, but then lost her in the end. There was one where he was dragged here and there all night, but couldn't reel her in and had to come back empty-handed. A catfish that would pull a boat its size—a boat driven by a robust young man! Now tell me if that isn't a made-up story! In the end, the exhausted fisherman had to cut the line himself. That's why they call her the Old Fox.

But those fishermen think I'm that Old Fox. I'm only 153 centimeters tall. That's far below the average height of high school girls in our country. Maybe I would have grown a little taller by the end of the summer. I know a girl who grew fifteen centimeters in one summer. When we came back to school after the summer break, her blouse had become so short on her that the waistline of her skirt showed. I would have grown a lot, too, after this summer.

While the rookie fisherman wrestled with the line, the hook made a bigger hole in my jacket. I think it's right below the nape of my neck. I don't think I can get it fixed anymore. The tear is in a noticeable spot, and I can't even cover it with my hair, because my hair's too short. Mom will notice the hole for sure. Even the lady at Myeongseong Cleaners won't be able to fix this. Plus, she's too old now. This jacket is practically brand-new. I've worn it only three or four times.

The current here is rough. There were places like this on the way down, where the water looked calm at the surface, but had eddies underneath. Each time, I got caught in a whirlpool, sank to the bottom of the river, and then rose once more.

Mister, you should be careful. The current is pretty rough here. Just a little more, just a little . . .

Oh, no, the line's snapped.

The people shout at the same time. They must have seen the empty line.

Ah, too bad. It was the Old Fox all right.

No one can hook that thing.

They trickle back to their places and soon I hear their rods slash through the air and the lines being cast. A sinker plunges into the water and lands right next to me. I start to sink once more.

I won't have to wash ever again. I've grown as smooth as a pebble. By the time I flow down to the mouth of the river, I will have eroded more and become sand.

•

Granny Gyeongju passed away. She's my grandmother's second youngest sister. She moved to Gyeongju when she got married, so we call her Granny Gyeongju. Before she got married, when she was still a girl, she died, but then came back to life the next day. It's hard to believe that Granny, as wrinkly as a walnut, was a girl once. She loved to suck on candy with her two remaining front teeth. When I asked if it was uncomfortable, sucking on candy without teeth, she rolled it around in her mouth and smiled. *Nope, I don't have to worry about my teeth rotting. And I can have candy every day.*

She dreamed that she crossed a ditch. She said she walked for a long time, but for some strange reason, her legs didn't hurt. An old man was plowing a field. He gazed at Granny and then blurted all of a sudden, *It isn't your time yet. Go back.* It was only then that she looked back the way she had come. The water in the ditch had swelled and was turning into a river. Unconcerned about the fact that she was wearing a skirt, she made a running start and leapt over the water. When she woke from her dream, her family and friends had gathered around her and were wailing by her feet.

It was neither too hot nor cold when Granny passed away. She lived eighty-two years, so everyone said she lived to a ripe old age. Her siblings stayed put in the same spot after she died, in case she should come back to life like before. But I guess she couldn't cross the river this time. She probably didn't have enough energy to make that leap. She didn't wake up, even when I followed my mom into the house.

When she was still a girl, as she leapt over that river, some memories fell in the water. People called her a *dimwit* all her life, saying she wasn't all there in the head. I think I'm crossing that river right now. I can't remember the name of those flowers by the riverbank. I can't even remember my own name.

But the times I went fishing with my dad are so clear.

Dad doesn't go fishing anymore. The machine at the factory took his hands away. The machine had stopped with the power failure, but when the power came back on, it started up all of a sudden and crushed Dad's hands, which had been resting on top. When I came back from school, Dad was sitting at the edge of the living room floor. He was staring off into space with the front gate wide open. Even when I stepped into the yard, he didn't notice me. Before, he would have laughed his booming laugh and given me a hug. I followed his gaze. He was crying, staring blankly at the sky. There was sleep in his bloodshot eyes. I filled a basin with water and washed his face. He kept shaking his head. His shirt became soaked. His eyes were like lightbulbs with broken filaments. I don't like them.

You've heard of phantom limbs, right? When you suddenly lose a limb, you might feel that the missing limb is still attached. Every mealtime, Dad still throws a fit. He twists away when my mother brings the spoon to his lips, and with his severed arm, he tries to hold the spoon himself. Then as if he remembers his missing hand at that moment, he explodes with anger and kicks the low table. Dad still dreams of fishing. He sits up in the middle of the night and rambles for a long time, saying that his palms are vibrating. *It's a big one, a big one!*

You lost your hands. Stop talking nonsense and go back to bed, Mom would snap. Then Dad would sit blankly for a bit and then flop back down and go back to sleep.

My dad is the reason she's always angry. When he still had his hands, she would make things like donuts or sweet potato noodles for me. *It's cold out there. Go put on another layer*, she would say.

That day, too, Mom was on my case all morning. She pinched my breast, because I'd forgotten to put the bar of soap back in the soap dish. Didn't I know it would get bloated and turn to mush, didn't I know how hard it was to make money? Whenever she pinches me, tears spring to my eyes. Maybe she's right. Maybe I'm stupid. Why do I keep forgetting something as small as putting the soap back?

My body is bloated like that bar of soap. I'm fading. What if I keep dissolving and disappear without a trace?

•

Whenever school finishes early, my friends and I go to the train station. We sit on the bench in front of the station and watch the people
come and go. It's the busiest season right now, when the station is
packed with people. College boys swarm off the trains. In the spring,
college students like to come to this town for a little trip. They sometimes gather in the plaza and blast on the radio, dancing or singing along with the music. I love watching them laugh and talk. I
would picture myself as a college student, coming back here on break.
A person holding a banner with the school name and department
would walk by, leading a procession of students. Vendors also appear
around this time, carrying wide wooden boxes filled with chocolate
and gum.

Once when all the groups left, there was a stocky middle-aged
man standing in the center of the plaza. He was wearing a thick, worn
army jacket. He headed toward us, the box hanging from his neck.
The instant he pushed the box toward us, I noticed there was something strange about his sleeves. My friends backed away. Stainless
steel hooks glinted inside his baggy sleeves. We screamed and fled.
He flopped down on the bench we'd just bolted, and lit a cigarette,
pinching it between his split-hook. One day, Dad will probably have
to get hooks, too. Sometimes I think about him becoming Edward
Scissorhands. In the movie, he trims people's hedges into lovely shapes
and styles women's hair in the latest styles with his scissor-blade
hands. But real life isn't as lovely as a movie. I don't know why I took
off like that. I couldn't look at my dad all day long.

It's raining. It looks like the river is bubbling with oil. I'm flowing
down more quickly. I never imagined I'd be in the water like this. I'm
scared of water. I don't even go to the swimming pool. I really hate
going in the water, but I've been in here for too long. But who keeps
knocking on my feet? Who is it?

I can't believe my eyes. I have to tell Dad. I have to tell him that I finally saw the Old Fox. Her whiskers graze my face. They're as stiff as cables. It's the Old Fox for sure. What other catfish is this big? She nudges me with her enormous mouth and turns, her tail fin striking me. I nosedive deeper. She swims away, her large body cutting through the water. The water splits behind her tail fin, just like how the plow would dig furrows into the earth and expose the red dirt below. She's as big as me. I guess the fishermen weren't joking. Just look at that smooth, glossy skin. I don't think anyone would ever hook her. Since it's raining, she's probably heading up to the surface. I think I'm the first person who's ever seen her this close up.

•

In the end, I didn't get the poster of *Romeo and Juliet*. Miseon said it's the scene where Leonardo DiCaprio is screaming, filled with rage, as he holds a gun to his head. Miseon probably got tired of waiting for me and went home.

The Blue Rose stays open until past two in the morning. I've never pushed past the door that's covered with thick foam and red carpet. But I can glimpse the inside whenever Miseon opens the door to come meet me outside. Each time the door opens, loud music comes blasting out. The foam and carpet probably soundproof the door. Miseon said there were plenty of kids who wanted that photo. She said she would give it to someone else if I didn't come quick.

Miseon is my friend from middle school. You know the girl who grew fifteen centimeters in one summer? That's Miseon. As soon as she entered senior high, she quit. No, she was actually suspended. Hammerhead caught her smoking in the bathroom. But she didn't come back to school even when her suspension was over. According to her, there was nothing for her to learn from school. She said she was going to make a lot of money and become rich while I wasted away in class. She works at the Blue Rose. I don't ask her what she does behind that thick door. She looks all grown up now. She's five foot six, and wears a short, sparkly dress and high heels. She wears a lot of makeup, too. Sometimes after the evening review classes, I pass by the Blue Rose on my way home. I've seen her crouching in the dark alley, throwing up. She already seems old. She treats me like a little kid now.

If Mom finds out I'm still friends with her, she'll be so mad.

That's right. I was on my way to see Miseon that night. Mom was sitting in the yard, trimming the greens she needed to take to the market the next day. Housewives these days want convenience, so they prefer to buy greens that have already been trimmed and blanched.

With the bit of insurance money Dad got from the factory, Mom set up a small chicken shop at the market. Not a franchise with a pretty sign. Her shop doesn't even have a sign. All it says at the front are the words EGGS, ENRICHED EGGS, and CHICKEN. Behind the clear glass door is a cooler filled with pink chickens that have been plucked clean. With a money belt strapped around her waist, Mom sits all day before a large cauldron bubbling with hot oil. Her hair gets sticky with the fumes from the cauldron. My mom wasn't like that before my dad lost his hands. She nagged a bit, but her nagging was like the meowing of a cat. Though she didn't read novels, she sometimes flipped through women's magazines, but she's changed 180 degrees. *Take home a fried chicken! Serve it up with his drink—he'll thank you good!* She chats up strangers, and her voice booms. She puts a whole chicken on the cutting board and swings the cleaver, chopping the chicken into pieces. She seems like a stranger to me. I don't think it's the chicken she's chopping. Biting her bottom lip, she looks like she's attacking something else, something invisible.

I think she's always getting angry at me because she's forced to do things she doesn't want to do. A crafts or cosmetics shop would suit her better, but she says it's hard to make a profit from those places.

According to Mom, a food business was the best during a recession like this.

She only recently started selling blanched greens at her shop. My mom's got a real mind for business. She sometimes asks me to come to the store to take home the chicken feet and gizzards that weren't sold. I don't like going there. The other shops beside Mom's have cauldrons out front holding pig heads and intestines. The owners at those places have booming voices, too. They joke around easily with the men who come for a drink. They swear easily, too.

There's a young man who delivers the chicken. I saw him a few times when I went to the shop. I don't like him.

Sis, why don't you fry up a juicy one for me? And with that special sauce I like.

If it's his job to deliver the chicken, he should leave as soon as he's done, but he just sits there. He and Mom are really friendly. She chops up the chicken, tosses the pieces in the cauldron, and they joke around the whole time while the chicken cooks. Then her voice would turn thin and high like before. She even pats his thigh when she hands him a tinfoil pouch with the fried chicken. She's changed.

Miseon always tells me to come visit in the evening. She says she needs to catch up on her sleep during the day. While I was doing the dishes from dinner, I thought only of the movie still. I love Leonardo DiCaprio. I've seen every movie he's in. Each time the plate slipped and made a sound, Mom glared at me. I rushed, stacking the dishes in the rack, and changed into the jacket I'm wearing now. Ah, what am I going to do about this hole? When Mom saw me in my new jacket, she grumbled, *And where are you running off to at this hour? Just like someone else I know.* She meant it for my dad to hear. My dad's crazy about fishing. Before he lost his hands, that is.

Mom, who was putting fresh wood in the outdoor stove to boil some water, called out as I stepped past our gate. *Make sure you come home by nine or you're really gonna get it!* Mom yells all the time at home like she's at her shop.

Mom, my exam is in two days, of course I'll be home early. I'll be home by eight.

I was supposed to meet Miseon in front of the Blue Rose at seven o'clock. That's when she's the least busy.

An occasional streetlight illuminated the narrow highway. Flanked by mountains on one side and the river on the other, the two-lane highway is barely wide enough for two cars. There was a safer route with a sidewalk, but I'd decided to take the shortcut. Cars hurtled past me, their headlights blazing. Dust got tangled in my hair. You couldn't even see the moon. It was so dark. A car appeared around the bend. It took up both lanes and zigzagged wildly toward me. I realized a moment later why it was zigzagging down the road like that. Another car was close behind. I wondered if they would crash. They seemed to be doing at least 150 kilometers per hour. The two cars accelerated, blasting their horns. The car in front was trying to block the car behind from passing. I could tell they were having a race. If a car was heading their way from the opposite lane, they barely managed to get back in their lane, but once that car disappeared, they zigzagged along the road again.

The two cars raced neck and neck with each other. In order to get out of the way, I stood right at the edge of the road. I planned to wait until they had passed. Their high beams pierced my eyes. I couldn't see. In that instant, something struck me in the side. I flew off the road and rolled down the hill. I think the car's side mirror hit me.

I think I dislocated my hip. I tried to get up, but I couldn't. The grass was wet and branches scratched my face. The two cars that had vanished up ahead raced back in reverse and stopped. They got out of their cars and peered down the shadowy slope.

Shit, where the hell did she come from?

One of them spat loudly down the hill.

You lost, so you go down and check.

The young man kept swearing as he came down the hill. Every time he would slip, rocks cascaded down and fell on my back. A hand clutched my shoulder and shook me.

Hey, you okay? Christ.

The one waiting above called out in a small voice, *Is she alive?*

The man picked me up and carried me on his back. My body became bent like a sickle.

Is she dead?

The other man helped lift me up, and gulped loudly. *Um, I think she needs to go to the hospital.*

You moron, are you crazy? Did you forget you don't even have a license? You want to ruin your life? Hurry, put her in the trunk before someone sees us. Shit.

Rough hands stuffed me into the trunk of a car. The trunk was full of tires, car wax, and rags. There was barely any room. *Excuse me, I'm alive. Please let me live.* I don't think they heard me. We stopped at the river. They argued for a long time, as if they'd forgotten all about me. The trunk opened. They dragged me to the river and tossed me in.

When I was in second grade, my desk mate and I always fought. I forget his name. We drew an imaginary line between our desks and if he crossed that line, I got mad at him. When we came back to school after the summer break, there was no longer any reason to fight with him. During the summer he had gone to visit his mother's family in the country, and while swimming in the reservoir, he had drowned. Under our teacher's direction, we observed a ten-minute silence. Some kids cried. But after the ten minutes, we completely forgot about him. As soon as the recess bell rang, we swarmed out onto the field, and laughed and played. We didn't understand death back then. When we asked the grownups to explain death, they told us it meant going to heaven. Drawings and alphabet letters the boy had carved with his stationary knife still remained on his desk, but he was no longer in this world. He had lived just eight years.

Sometimes when I make dinner instead of Mom, I would lay the knife I'd used to chop kimchi or green onion on top of my wrist. There were times I've dunked my face in the basin, holding my breath, while washing my face. I've even looked up at the school rooftop from the field and felt an urge to run up the stairs and throw myself down. But I'm only sixteen. Sweet sixteen. I would have grown taller by the end of summer.

I think Granny Kyeongju knew she was going to die soon. *Dearie, can you fry up some pork for me?* She'd asked her daughter-in-law for some meat all of a sudden. When she never even touched pork all her life. And then she'd enjoyed that pork with her two remaining teeth.

My elementary-school desk mate lived eight years, and Granny Kyeongju lived eighty-two. I'm sixteen. Is sixteen years short or long? I'm slowing down. I think I'm near the mouth of the river.

•

It was a young couple who found me. They were taking a stroll along the secluded riverbank. They stepped into a little nook and kissed. His hand burrowed into the folds of her clothes and stroked her chest. What does it feel like to kiss? Miseon would have laughed out loud. *You've never kissed anyone before?* she'd say and make fun of me. They started breathing heavily. At that very moment, the girl's gaze happened to land on me. Her bloodshot eyes widened and she let out a scream.

There was no longer any current to carry me down the river. This is where the sediment is deposited. There are no pebbles or rocks; everything has been reduced to sand. My head was stuck between two large boulders. Every time the water lapped over me, my jacket billowed to the surface. The frightened girl began to weep, and the man took a cautious step in my direction. When he discovered my half-submerged back, he tripped and fell on his rear-end. He scrambled backward. Ah, I never wanted to scare anyone like this.

I hear the siren. I think the police are here. They pull me out of the water and lay me on the ground. The sun is warm. People start to gather around. The police rummage through my pockets, but they're empty. When I bounced off the car and down the hill, my wallet fell out of my pocket into the weeds. That place is always full of garbage. Because people in passing cars toss empty soda cans and snacks out of the car.

No ID? asks the detective who's standing, lighting a cigarette.

Nothing. Who the hell would do such a—

The one who'd been rummaging through my pockets finds the fishhook stuck in the back of my jacket. He pulls it out. Maybe he's thinking of his youngest sister, who is around my age. I'm still in tenth grade. I'll get my ID card next year, around my birthday.

Ah, it was me giving off that stench. I heard someone say that I'd already started to decompose. This river has polluted my body. It's a good thing I can't see my face.

My student ID would be in my wallet. Maybe I only imagined that it fell out of my pocket into the weeds. Or did I leave it on top of the desk in my room? This jacket's new. As I was changing, I might have forgotten to put my wallet in my jacket pocket. I can't remember. Ah, I think the river took my memories away.

The police detectives load me into the ambulance. These are the only details they know about me: the pleather jacket, which I cherish, my jean shorts, my sneakers, the cross necklace around my neck, and my muddy white T-shirt.

I think those white flowers are blooming along the riverbank. The ambulance picks up speed. They flap like laundry hung out to dry.

Would Mom be at the market? Maybe Miseon ended up calling my house after she got tired of waiting for me. If Mom finds out I'm friends with Miseon . . . I don't even want to think about it. Maybe she thinks I ran away from home. Maybe she thinks Miseon was a bad influence on me. Mom would have closed up her shop and would have started by searching the nearest gas stations. Who will wash my dad's face for him now?

The ambulance is entering the town now. I know, because we're slowing down. I know this place so well. I was born and raised here. I think I see my school in the distance. Right about now, the kids are probably running around the field in single file. Short and sweet, short and sweet. I think I hear them shout.

I finally remember the name of those flowers.

Daisy fleabane, that's what they're called. The ones that had been blooming in heaps when I'd come here with my dad. They're covered in tiny hairs and have small petals. But why are they already in bloom? Isn't it early spring right now? Ah, I'm getting all mixed up. I'm sure they're called daisy fleabane. I can smell a faint whiff of fish.

Ha Seong-nan was born in Seoul in 1967 and made her literary debut in 1996, after her graduation from the Seoul Institute of the Arts. Ha is the author of five short story collections and three novels. Over her career, she's received a number of prestigious awards, such as the Dong-in Literary Award in 1999, Hankook Ilbo Literary Prize in 2000, the Isu Literature Prize in 2004, the Oh Yeong-su Literary Award in 2008, and the Contemporary Literature (Hyundae Munhak) Award in 2009.

Janet Hong is a writer and translator based in Vancouver, Canada. She received the TA First Translation Prize and the 16th LTI Korea Translation Award for her translation of Han Yujoo's *The Impossible Fairy Tale*, which was a finalist for both the PEN Translation Prize and the National Translation Award, and longlisted for the 2019 International Dublin Literary Award. She has translated Ha Seong-nan's *Flowers of Mold*, longlisted for the PEN Translation Prize, Ancco's *Bad Friends*, and Keum Suk Gendry-Kim's *Grass*.

**OPEN
LETTER**

**OPEN
LETTER**

Elsa Morante (Italy)
Aracoeli
Giulio Mozzi (Italy)
This Is the Garden
Andrés Neuman (Spain)
The Things We Don't Do
Jóanes Nielsen (Faroe Islands)
The Brahmadells
Madame Nielsen (Denmark)
The Endless Summer
Henrik Nordbrandt (Denmark)
When We Leave Each Other
Asta Olivia Nordenhof (Denmark)
The Easiness and the Loneliness
Wojciech Nowicki (Poland)
Salki
Bragi Ólafsson (Iceland)
The Ambassador
Narrator
The Pets
Kristín Ómarsdóttir (Iceland)
Children in Reindeer Woods
Sigrún Pálsdóttir (Iceland)
History. A Mess.
Diego Trelles Paz (ed.) (World)
The Future Is Not Ours
Ilja Leonard Pfeijffer (Netherlands)
Rupert: A Confession
Jerzy Pilch (Poland)
The Mighty Angel
My First Suicide
A Thousand Peaceful Cities
Rein Raud (Estonia)
The Brother
João Reis (Portugal)
The Translator's Bride
Rainer Maria Rilke (World)
Sonnets to Orpheus
Mónica Ramón Ríos (Chile)
Cars on Fire
Mercè Rodoreda (Catalonia)
Camellia Street
Death in Spring
Garden by the Sea
The Selected Stories of Mercè Rodoreda
War, So Much War
Milen Ruskov (Bulgaria)
Thrown into Nature
Guillermo Saccomanno (Argentina)
77
Gesell Dome

Juan José Saer (Argentina)
The Clouds
La Grande
The One Before
Scars
The Sixty-Five Years of Washington
Olga Sedakova (Russia)
In Praise of Poetry
Mikhail Shishkin (Russia)
Maidenhair
Sölvi Björn Sigurðsson (Iceland)
The Last Days of My Mother
Maria José Silveira (Brazil)
*Her Mother's Mother's Mother and
Her Daughters*
Andrzej Sosnowski (Poland)
Lodgings
Albena Stambolova (Bulgaria)
Everything Happens as It Does
Benjamin Stein (Germany)
The Canvas
Georgi Tenev (Bulgaria)
Party Headquarters
Dubravka Ugresic (Europe)
American Fictionary
Europe in Sepia
Fox
Karaoke Culture
Nobody's Home
Ludvík Vaculík (Czech Republic)
The Guinea Pigs
Jorge Volpi (Mexico)
Season of Ash
Antoine Volodine (France)
Bardo or Not Bardo
*Post-Exoticism in Ten Lessons,
Lesson Eleven*
Radiant Terminus
Eliot Weinberger (ed.) (World)
Elsewhere
Ingrid Winterbach (South Africa)
The Book of Happenstance
The Elusive Moth
To Hell with Cronjé
Ror Wolf (Germany)
Two or Three Years Later
Words Without Borders (ed.) (World)
The Wall in My Head
Xiao Hong (China)
Ma Bo'le's Second Life
Alejandro Zambra (Chile)
The Private Lives of Trees

WWW.OPENLETTERBOOKS.ORG

Printed in the USA
CPSIA information can be obtained
at www.ICGtesting.com
JSHW082337040624
64186JS00006B/2

9 781948 830171